'It seemed a good idea at the time. I mean, Peter and Bruce were so sexy and persuasive – and Australia is a young, virile country, isn't it? Trouble is that Kate and I never reckoned on all those things getting on top of us – things like Ross Honey, Mick the Greek and the rest of those wild colonial boys. It became so that the Papuan head-hunters were a welcome change from the guys interested in other parts of our bodies. . . .'

If you thought *The Stewardesses* was a gas, wait till you read Penny Sutton's wild, blush-making revelations of her experiences down under.

D1419903

The Stewardesses Down Under

PENNY SUTTON

SPHERE BOOKS LIMITED
30/32 Gray's Inn Road, London WC1X 8JL

First published in Great Britain by Sphere Books Ltd 1973
Copyright © Christopher Wood 1973
Reprinted 1974

TRADE
MARK

Set in Linotype Times

Printed in Great Britain by
Hazell Watson & Viney Ltd
Aylesbury, Bucks

ISBN 0 7221 9333 5

CHAPTER ONE

I don't know what made up Kate's mind that she wanted to visit Australia but I have a shrewd suspicion that it might have been what made up mine: Peter Honey.

Believe me, never did a name more aptly describe a fella. A shade over six feet, shoulders sloping like the roof of a Greek temple, curly blond hair, a face that might have been too pretty if it had not been for the rugged set of the jaw and the piercing blue eyes, a deep tan and wrists so hairy you could hide a penny piece in the foliage – I love men with hairy wrists. And, best of all, his smile. His nose wrinkled up just below the eyebrows and he flashed a set of the most perfect teeth I have ever seen outside a dentifrice advertisement.

"Hi," he said. "Do you girls know the way to a tube around here?"

We – that is my flying buddy, Kate Goodbody, and I – were at a shindig in Kangaroo Valley – or Earl's Court as the locals call that part of London–and I remember thinking what a pity it was that such a dish should be leaving so early.

"Baron's Court," said Kate helpfully, thinking like me that the Aussie hunk was talking about the nearest subway station.

Dreamboat's eyes shot up towards the ceiling. "Baron's Court? Cripes! That's a flaming long way to go for a beer."

For a moment I blinked at him and then I realised what he was talking about. Australians call a can of beer a tube.

"I mean a tube of Foster's," he said helpfully. "That which cheers and inebriates." His voice was rough and manly but not without an underlying hint of warmth. He sounded like a man who did not suffer fools gladly but would be worth having on your side if the fur started flying. I was soon to find out how right this assessment was. We told him that we did not have a drink ourselves and he clicked his tongue in annoyance. "You can tell this is a Pommy party, can't you? The gargle runs out just when you're getting a taste for it.

5

"Probably because there are so many Australians here," said Kate loyally.

"You've got a point there, sweetheart. You'd think some of these jokers had never seen a drink before, wouldn't you?"

In fact the condition of most of the other guests suggested that they were only too well acquainted with liquid refreshment of the most alcoholic kind, but I knew what he meant.

"My name's Peter Honey," said the hunk, sticking out a hand which both Kate and I made a grab for. "Tell you what. I'm prepared to bet I know what you two do. You're stewardesses, aren't you?"

This was a pretty fantastic piece of deduction, for neither Kate nor I were wearing uniform. "How do you know?" we trilled.

"I'm in that line of business myself," said Peter.

Surely you are not a steward, I thought to myself, for those gentlemen are seldom amongst the most rugged of mortals.

"My old man owns an airline back in Oz," said Peter.

"Not Qantas?" Kate's eyes were opening wide and hopeful.

Peter laughed. "No. Nothing like that. A little Outback number. Strictly internal stuff."

"But you have stewardesses?"

"Oh yes. Stewardesses, airfields, planes. It's all very sophisticated."

Kate blushed. "I still don't know how you knew we were stewardesses."

"Grooming, I guess. A good stewardess always looks as if she's just stepped off a catwalk. I could tell one in a poncho and a pair of old jeans." He looked deep into my eyes and switched on that smile. I found myself grinning back inanely.

"Who are you with?"

For the sake of our erstwhile employers I will not reveal my answer to that one. Reaction to my first book* was of a nature that made me realise that the airline was not grateful for the free publicity I gave it.

*The Stewardesses, published by Sphere Books.

6

"One of the big ones," said Peter when we told him. "I was wondering if I could persuade you to come and work for us." You could probably persuade me to do darn near anything, I thought to myself. In fact I did not take his remark too seriously at the time. He went on to tell us that he was in England on a business holiday and said enough to suggest that the airline was just one of daddy's interests. Not that he gave the impression he was trying to shoot a line. With Peter you felt that everything he said was projected straight from the shoulder without any ulterior motive. I find a lot of Australians like that. They may not be the most subtle people on earth but you do know where you are with them.

Kate and I had been invited along to the party by one of our fellow stewardesses who was going out with an Australian. A glance round the room suggested that the call had gone out for more girls, because, fortunately from our point of view, there was a dearth of female competition. Peter had been invited along by an English business acquaintance and most of the beefcake present was clearly Australian – Earl's Court is not called Kangaroo Valley for any other reason than that it houses a host of travellers from 'Down Under'.

"Quit hogging all the talent, Pete. And make with a few intros," said one beautiful, lean reason for emigrating tomorrow. "How do, my name is Bruce Wilson. Don't let old Honeybear soft talk you into anything."

"Why don't you shove off and come back when you've found something to drink," said Peter good-naturedly. "I'm more parched than an Abo's armpit."

"Did he say 'soft talk'?" murmured Kate by my side. "It's not exactly the stuff of which romantic novels are made, is it?"

Kate is definitely more Latin-orientated and has a photograph of Marcello Mastroianni pinned above the end of the bath. He is beginning to curl a bit at the edges which may be due to embarrassment or, more likely, steam. I go for all the hot-blooded chat (what girl wouldn't?), but I never believe a word of it. My basic Anglo Saxon nature says 'Yes, that's all very nice, but I know what he's after. He's

7

trying to get me back to his apartment to show me the Michelangelo on his bedroom ceiling. And we all know the best position from which to view that!' It is all a bit silly because – perhaps unfortunately – I am far from being a prude. It is just that I respond more to the blunt unaffected approach. I think too that my attitude is conditioned by an unhappy experience I had with a married man – my unhappiness being caused by the fact that I did not know he was married. Since then I have been even more wary of showing too much of my emotions. I can remember all the things Mike and I said to each other and still feel the pain. With someone like Peter I know exactly where I am.

Eventually, Peter and Bruce decide that the only way to save the party is to nip round to the nearest pub and invest in "a few tubes of Foster's". A levy is made amongst the uncomplaining guests and we are left with our host who seems thunderstruck by the amount of liquid refreshment that has been consumed.

"I got twice as much as I thought we'd need, just to be on the safe side," he said. "I don't know what they do with it all."

The sight of one bilious-looking guy being helped towards the bathroom by two of his mates gave me a shrewd idea. Boy! Those Australians really know how to put it away. Luckily, being an air stewardess automatically entitles one to become an authority on drunks and there is no sight connected with the consumption of hard liquor that can now surprise me. A twinge of disgust sometimes, but that is about all.

Although there is some very danceable music playing no one has taken to the floor – unless you count the fellow whose feet are sticking out from underneath the food table. He is wriggling a toe rhythmically but I don't think he is dancing with anybody. Distant recollections of this kind of party suggest that no one will start dancing unless it seems that there is no other way of obtaining a woman. Most male Australians regard dancing as an activity only indulged in by fellows in stretch tights or creatures of dubious hormone balance – often the same thing.

"Are you from Sydney?" says one of the less lovely Aussies present. "Stone the crows, but don't these Pommy thrashes make you want to throw up?"

I am considering a number of alternative ways of handling this question, when I become aware of a commotion near the entrance to the flat. A number of bodies are milling around and out of the huddle shoots our host who must have wished he had forgotten about the party and curled up in front of the television. He has been struck in the face as becomes evident when one sees him sitting on the floor clutching his bleeding nose. The donator of the blow is an ugly leather-jacketed individual with less hair on his head than a moulting gooseberry. He is not alone. Several more 'B' movie heavies are pushing in behind him. They all look like skinhead refugees from a feature on Hell's Angels. Decidedly not nice.

"Let's have a drink then," says one of them truculently. I feel like suggesting that this may be more difficult than he imagines, when Peter and Bruce reappear. They are not empty-handed. Both of them are clutching two crates of bottled beer.

"You want a beer, mate?" says Peter good-naturedly. "Here, cop this lot." And he drops the crate on the gate-crasher's foot! Luckily the guy is wearing thick boots or his tootsie would be part of the carpet pattern. No sooner has he let out a yell and started hopping on one foot than Bruce kicks it away and he comes down like a falling chimney stack. That does it! Before you can say 'boomerang!' the whole room is in uproar. The Aussie contingent are no slouches when it comes to fisticuffs and bodies are bouncing off all four walls. Kate and I take shelter in one of the window alcoves but we soon change our position when a flower pot sails past us into the street, nearly followed by the fellow who threw it. We find the bathroom locked, which does not come as a complete surprise to us, and then take shelter in one of the bedrooms. This move solves the mystery of where the girl who invited us to the party has been since shortly after we entered the flat.

"Oh, well. They are going to get married soon", says Kate, as we retire blushing.

When we peer into the living room it is to find that the battle is over. A few shouts can be heard echoing up the

9

stair-well but the intruders have clearly been put to flight. Our host is sitting on the floor where we last saw him but he now has a black eye to go with his bleeding nose. One of the exultant Aussies pats him on the shoulder. "Great party, Sport," he says sincerely. "For a moment there I thought I was back in Oz." He helps himself to a bottle of beer and starts looking round for an opener. I am looking round for Peter who seems to have disappeared.

"Goodness, what a mess!" exclaims Kate and it is impossible to disagree with her. Only the legs of the man lying under the table appear to be where they were before the brawl started, and even he seems to be wearing different socks. I distinctly remember that they were red. Now they are green. Hey, wait a minute! I get down on my hands and knees and – yes – there is Mrs. Honey's pride and joy stretched out with an ugly bump on his beautiful head. He is making gentle groaning noises and these do not get any softer as Kate and I start dabbing away with moist tissues.

"One of those yobboes must have tried to wrap an iron bar round my head." He winces. "Where's Bruce?"

"Just saying goodbye to the guests," observes a slightly dishevelled Mr Wilson re-entering the room and polishing his knuckles. "What happened to you, mate? You tuckered out or something?"

Peter's reply to that does not really suit a book that might find its way into children's hands, and will not be quoted. "Those jokers say they're going to be back," continues Bruce. "Do you have a lot of trouble like this, Adrian?" Bruce pronounces the word Adrian as if it causes him physical pain to do so.

Adrian groans. "Not until tonight."

"Hard dos," says Bruce sympathetically. "Well, we'll be ready for them this time, won't we? Now, let's get outside some of this limey nectar."

"I'm sorry," yelps Adrian, "but the party is over. My flat is ruined and I'm going to report the whole thing to the Police. It's going to take me all night to clear up the damage as it is."

"I'm very sorry," says Bruce. "I took particular care not to knock anyone down on anything breakable."

"Spoken like a true Australian gentleman," grins Peter shaking his head and beginning to perk up. "Come on. I can understand Adrian's point of view. Let's help him clean up and then we can push off round to my place." He singles me out with his eyes when he says that and I am practically breaking into a trot to find a dustpan and brush. In fact, things appear a lot worse than they are and by the time we thank Adrian for a lovely party and leave the flat is looking almost normal.

"Listen," says Peter as we stand at the top of the stairs and, sure enough, we hear the sound of a key turning and a chain slotting in to place behind us: The others are amused but I feel slightly frightened. Some of the skinheads had looked really mean and I can sympathise with Adrian.

"Do we want to go round to Peter's place?" whispers Kate. "They seem awfully wild. Do you think they do anything else but drink?"

"They must do," I tell her. "Which reminds me. Pattie must still be in there." Pattie Smith was the girl we had arrived with.

"Poor Adrian. I wonder if he'll ever get to bed tonight." We come out of the front entrance of the block of flats and a bottle whistles past my nose and shatters against the wall. A garishly painted old banger is drawn up on the other side of the street and around it is parked a phalanx of motor bikes. My first reaction is to bolt back into the flats but the front door has locked automatically behind us and with missiles showering round our heads there is no time to elicit sympathy through the intercom. There is a park opposite the flats and we are being attacked from behind the railings. They, no doubt, having been selected because they afford protection should the police show up. I would very much like to see one of London's famed policemen at this moment but, as always when you really want one, there is not a sign of that familiar helmet.

"Get in the car!" shouts Peter who has risked another bump to race over to a nifty Italian model parked mercifully near to the flats. We pile inside and a clatter of footsteps coincides with the door slamming behind Bruce. A leather-coated hand snatches at the door handle and a gobbet of spittle slides down the window as our attacker is denied entrance. Peter slams the car into gear and we roar away from the curb.

"Look out!" Motor bikes buzz round us like jumbo-sized midges and it is clear that reinforcements are arriving at every minute. Something bangs against the side of the car. We weave crazily, and then speed towards the river.

"Are we all right?" says Kate. Nobody answers her.

"They're coming after us," says Bruce grimly. "Where the hell are you going?"

"Wait and see. I am sitting next to Peter and his jaw is jutting out to meet the windscreen as his hands balance lightly on the wheel. There is a thoughtful determined look in his eyes and I feel confident that he has something up his sleeve beside a generous helping of brawny Australian arm.

"That banger's gaining on us."

"Good." Peter is almost smiling.

We skip through some traffic lights, just as they start to turn red, and turn off to the left with a squeal of tyres. Peter seems to be heading towards the Thames and I cannot understand why he should be choosing to plunge into these mean, dark streets when he would surely be safer from attack in a built-up area. The same thought is obviously troubling Bruce.

"If you're trying to lose them you're wasting your time."

"Don't get your knickers in a twist. Sorry, ladies!" I don't know whether he is apologising for his language or his driving because he swings the wheel over again and we go sailing round a corner practically on our hub-caps. We are now in dockland and I can see the cranes and warehouses looming above us. Not a glimpse of people, though. Behind us there are now half a dozen independent yellow lights pursuing us and they remind me of wolves' eyes closing in for the kill.

"Where the hell are you going?"

"Here."

The wheel spins again and we are now bumping over cobbles that challenge even the Italian beauty's suspension. Ahead of me I can see what looks like the funnels of a liner.

"Hang on to your hats!"

"They're right behind us."

I try and catch Kate's eye but she has both of them

12

closed. I recall that she wanted to stay at home and wash her hair, and feel rather guilty. Why did we have to get mixed up with these mad Australians? Peter is now accelerating and, unless my sense of direction has gone completely to pot, we are heading straight for the water!

"Peter! – " On my left towers the hefty bulk of an ocean liner and for a moment I wonder if the bump on Peter's head has persuaded him that he can drive aboard. Then I see that there is a wire fence between us and the boat. Thank God! My relief is short-lived. A narrow jetty lies before us and beyond it I can clearly see water shimmering in the hazy moonlight. If I was more dynamic I would make a grab for the wheel but I can only cower in my seat and try to remember if you open the door before or after the car fills with water.

"Wheeeee!" At the last minute Peter jams on the brakes and wrenches the wheel over so that we dart off at right angles, the tyres whacking against the planks of the jetty. I am practically smeared across the windscreen and I can hear Kate's sharp intake of breath from the back seat. But if I think we have problems they are nothing compared to those of our pursuers. The driver of the banger sees the danger too late, nearly stands his vehicle on its nose, veers to the right and slowly topples off a corner of the jetty into the water.

"He should get his brakes tested," says Peter dryly.

Two of the motor cyclists are more ambitious. They shoot off the end of the jetty like it is some kind of ramp and they are trying to jump the river.

"Are they going to be all right?" says Kate's worried voice.

"Provided they don't try and ride back to the bank."

Three more riders have to lay down their bikes in a shower of sparks and one of them only just separates from his machine before it skids into the water. Shouts of rage, pain and fear fill the air.

"You led them down here on purpose, didn't you?" I asked Peter. He nods his head slowly. "Some of them looked as if they could do with a bath. Come on. Let's get out of here."

But this is easier said than done. Peter tries to drive along

13

the quayside but finds his way barred by a stack of packing cases. We have to turn back. This is not easy on a narrow wharf and the task is made more difficult by some of the Hell's Angels who have abandoned their bikes and are trying to push obstacles in our way. As Peter reverses, his back wheels are nearly over the edge of the quay. A heavy packing case crashes down and narrowly misses the front of the car. We are completely hemmed in! Now it is Bruce's turn. He leaps out of the car, swings a mighty fist at a leather-jacket who tries to bar his way and starts man-handling the packing case aside. Peter is revving his engine as if we are on the starting grid of a Grand Prix and the second he has a gap to nose through he darts forward pausing only to allow Bruce to scramble aboard.

"Better than the movies, isn't it, girls?" He grins as another packing case comes crashing down.

"Give me 'The Sound of Music' every time," grits Kate as we charge into the night.

Dashing back the way we have come we run the gauntlet of a shower of missiles and I look back to see the familiar sight of headlights following us.

"They're still after us," I pant, as Peter narrowly avoids a motor bike that seems bent on emulating a kamikaze pilot.

"Yeah. I think we need reinforcements." Peter steps on the gas and we rocket away with our motor cycle escort – like royalty a couple of hours late for their own coronation.

"Where are we going now?" I ask. "Chelsea Barracks?"

"Not a bad idea. I wish I'd thought of it myself. Hang on!" I don't need any second bidding as we screech round a corner and I find myself in one of London's most swinging streets, the King's Road, Chelsea. Normally I like to saunter up and down trying to take in all the beautiful and weird people who are flitting about, but this evening just is not one of those times. I would need eyes like a high-speed camera to stand a chance of recognising my own mother. We are driving at a speed that would give a New York taxi driver the heeby-jeebies and the only pedestrians I see are those throwing themselves out of our way. I could swear we went under a petrol tanker but Kate assures me that I had my eyes closed and we went round it.

"Nearly there," says Peter, answering my unspoken question. He still seems as cool as ever and I find myself admiring his light hand on the wheel as we weave in and out of the traffic. I always find the act of a man driving a car very sexy. The sinews tightening on the back of the wrist, the feet dabbing at the gears. A sharp left turn and we rocket over a multiple intersection. Right, right again and, to my amazement, we are pulling in to the curb. I gaze out of the window and discover that we have stopped outside Chelsea Police Station! Three motor bikes that have been following us falter momentarily and then accelerate when they see where we are.

"O.K." says Peter. "We'd better go and tell someone about those poor fellows who piled in to the drink."

Half an hour later I am curled up on one of the sofas in Peter's flat with an enormous brandy balloon in my hand. To complete my pleasure the brandy balloon has a generous measure of brandy in it. The flat is really something with wall to wall carpeting, three bedrooms, a well-stocked bar and soft music at the touch of a button. Peter tells us that the flat belongs to his father and is used by the family when they are in Britain. It certainly confirms my opinion that the Honeys are loaded. I do not want to sound too money conscious but if I am honest – and I usually am – I must confess that a lot of the appeal of being an air stewardess has to do not only with meeting men, but meeting rich men. The kind who might one day ask you to wear a ring on your finger and share their wealth with them. Mercenary, maybe, but true. Of course, we want love as well, and that is probably why so few of us get the dream quite right. I can count all the stewardesses I knew who married rich passengers they met when flying on the fingers of one hand – one envious little hand turning slightly green at the finger tips.

The police were very nice but they could hardly be anything else the way Peter handled his account of the evening's happenings. By the time he had finished I quite believed that we had strayed in to the docks in a desperate effort to escape from pursuers who would stop at nothing to catch us. Peter, ably supported by Bruce, managed to sound like a slightly bewildered visitor to our shores who was utterly amazed that such goings-on could occur at all, let

15

alone to him. Although everything they said was true there was no doubt that Peter had acted with calculated ruthlessness in leading the tearaways to what might have been a watery grave. His action made me slightly wary of him but at the time I had to confess I was fascinated. I respond to a streak of hardness in a man and in Peter I knew I had met someone I could not take liberties with. You may spend all your time trying to persuade a man to do something, but if you succeed you often wish you had been unsuccessful. No woman wants a man she can boss around.

"What are you thinking about?" Peter is sitting with his arm along the back of a curved sofa and a glass of whisky in his hand. He pats the cushion beside him. "Come and tell me."

Maybe I should not get up so quickly but I do not think of that until I am half-way to Peter's side.

"I'd better not tell you," I say.

Peter laughs and I notice again how his nose wrinkles up. "I couldn't tell you my thoughts either. They're far too flattering. They might turn your head."

"I'm impervious to compliments."

"You get so many I suppose. All those smooth-talking international boyfriends you must have."

"Acquaintances, not boyfriends."

Peter shakes his head. "I don't believe that."

"I came to the party by myself, didn't I?" I say defensively.

"Thanks a lot," says Kate who has just come into the room. "Now you see me, now you don't."

"You know what I mean. You're not a man."

"It's no good trying to flatter me. No amount of sweet-talking can make up for the fact that I don't exist."

"Hold it, you two," laughs Peter. "O.K. I'm prepared to believe that neither of you has any boyfriends."

"What do you mean?" squawks Kate. "I have thousands of boyfriends. In come circles I'm considered very desirable. Not around here, of course. I can see that."

"Oh, my gosh!" says Peter. "How did I get into this?"

Luckily Bruce comes to the rescue. "I think you're beaut beyond description," he says. "Despite that I'm prepared to try and describe you. Come with me and I'll show you that

16

a duplex isn't a new kind of foundation garment."

He spirits Kate away and I am left with Peter who wanders over to a sumptuous drinks-tray and pours himself another Scotch. "What do you like doing when you're not flying or going to parties alone with your friend?" he says.

"Everything a normal red-blooded girl enjoys. Theatre, cinema. I read good books and not such good books. I like swimming when I can find some water that is warm enough."

"It's warm enough in Australia. You live in a bathing suit over there." While he is talking his eyes are checking me over as if assessing my vital statistics. I take a deep breath and lean back crossing my legs. Peter comes back to the sofa and stands looking down at me. He has got a pretty good body himself, slim hips that do not look as if they have spent their formative years bent double in a rugger scrum. I like broad-shouldered muscular guys but not when they have back-sides like a fat old lady. Any man who has a bigger bottom than me is on the way to Forgetitsville. I can see that Peter is screwing himself up to deliver a pass and I wish I could help him. It is often as bad being on the receiving end as having to make with words and gestures. Sometimes I wish that Womens' Lib was enough of a reality for a girl to start chatting up a fellow but I know the result would be disastrous. Go up to a chap you fancied and ask him if he would like to go to the movies with you and he would run a mile. Not that I would blame him too much. As I have intimated earlier, I am basically in favour of men being men, and women being women. It is easier to know where you stand that way. I cannot understand all the female rights malarkey. Any woman worth her salt should be capable of establishing herself amongst men – or anyone else for that matter – by employing the female armaments with which nature has equipped her. I do not want to be treated like a man, thank you very much. I think most of them get very badly treated.

"What are you thinking now?" I say, helpfully. Really, it is funny isn't it? He can rout a gang of thugs virtually single-handed but now he is shuffling from one foot to the other like a nervous schoolboy.

17

"I was wondering how I can get down there to kiss you," he says.

"Try bending your knees," I advise him. "They should have a hinge in the middle." I stretch out a hand and almost instantly Peter's firm mouth is against mine. He kisses me with surprising tenderness and then draws away. "Come back to Australia," he says.

"With you?"

"More or less. Come and work for the airline. Bring your mate with you."

He leans forward and gently strokes the back of my neck.

"You expect me to throw in my job, just like that, and come to Australia?" Peter kisses me again.

"I don't expect you to. I hope you will. We can offer some pretty good inducements."

These are not bad, I think to myself as our lips collide again. "I'll think about it," I say as I place a restraining hand on top of his – "Seriously."

CHAPTER TWO

"So what happened to you?" asks Kate.

"Really, Kate. I'm surprised at you. You know I'm not one to kiss and tell," I say primly. "I'm surprised that you should wish to pursue the subject."

"Just kissing, was it? It didn't look like that when I came to see if you wanted to share a taxi."

"I don't remember that!"

"Well you wouldn't, would you? It was so torrid it was almost horrid. I could have started beating a gong and you wouldn't have heard anything."

"Oh, well. You know what it's like. Sometimes you meet someone and – Kerplung!! That's it. You can't help yourself. It may last for ever, or twenty-five minutes, but while its there you've got to have it, drink its heady waters to the fill – snatch each precious moment –"

"Heady on – I mean, steady on! I'm getting hot flushes. You sound just like me."

"Well I *am* just like you. That's the trouble. That's why

we both ended up spending the night with two men we'd never seen before in our lives."

"I tried to get you to come home," squeaks Kate.

"Why didn't you get a taxi by yourself?"

"I didn't have any money."

"Couldn't Bruce lend you any?"

"I didn't ask him."

"Why not?"

"I don't like to borrow money from people I hardly know."

"Kate! You're incorrigible."

"Careful. I might look that up and sue you."

I defy anyone to remain serious with Kate for long and soon we are having a girlish heart to heart about the events of the previous night. And not so girlish either. Some of the confidences we exchange might surprise any man listening. The net result of our conversation is that we both agree that, on a sample of two, Australian men have a lot to offer and are worthy of closer inspection.

"Did Bruce say anything about joining up with Outback Airlines?" I ask.

"Outback Airlines? Are you joking?"

"No. Peter's father owns it. They fly around inside Australia. It's rather like an airborne bus service."

"Sounds incredibly glamorous. Do they actually have stewardesses?"

"They have some. Peter was telling me they want to expand the airline to fly inter-city all over Australia and that they need to engage some foreign stewardesses to add a little excitement and help groom the locals."

"Marvellous! I've always fancied myself instructing some eager recruit in the art of balancing fifteen trays on top of each other while the florid gentleman in row 14C is running his hand up the inside of her leg."

"Are you interested?"

"In the florid gentleman in row 14C? Not usually. It depends if – "

"No, you fool! I mean are you interested in coming to Australia?"

"Oh, that! You should have said. Well, I don't know. I don't want to emigrate."

"You wouldn't have to. Peter could fix us up with work permits. It would only be for a few months, initially."

"Are you serious about this?"

"Yes I am. I think it would be ideal. You know how when this Mike business blew up I nearly threw the job in? Well, I still feel like a change and this could be the ideal compromise. A job I love but in a totally new setting. More responsibility too."

Kate looks thoughtful. "How settled is this?"

"As far as I can make out, the jobs are there if we want them."

"How about money?"

"I haven't worked it out exactly in Australian dollars, but it's more than we're getting now."

"I suppose we could get our jobs back?"

"I've checked on that. They won't promise anything but they're pretty confident we shouldn't have any trouble."

"When would we start?"

"Peter's father is in the States at the moment and the two boys are touring Europe. If we handed in our notice and took a boat we would arrive at the same time as the family reassemble."

"A boat. Of course, that's the only way for stewardesses to travel, isn't it? Why don't we take advantage of our cheap flight entitlement?"

"Because I've never been on a cruise and this could be the only chance I'll get."

"I don't know. What do you do in Australia? There aren't a lot of theatres and cinemas, are there?"

"When did you last go to the theatre, Kate?"

"I saw 'Charley's Aunt' – ooh, it must have been – yes, I see what you mean."

"The airline is only a few miles from Sydney."

"A few hundred miles, I expect."

"Maybe, Kate. It's a big country. You could lose Europe in it."

"That's the trouble. I don't want to lose Europe."

"It's only for a few months. And think of all those groovy, bronzed coast guards you'll be bumping into."

Kate's eyes light up. "Yes! What took you so long to get around to them?"

20

"And then there's all the wild life. Kangaroos and duck-billed platypuses."

"And those cola bears!" says Kate enthusiastically.

"You mean koala bears," I say. Sometimes with Kate it is difficult to know if she is being funny or not.

By the time we both rush off to catch our flights Kate is really beginning to warm to the idea and I am hoping I have not over-sold it. If Peter never gets in touch with me again I am going to look pretty stupid. Two days pass and neither Kate nor I receive a telephone call. "We'll never be able to call those two guys 'boomerang'," says Kate. "They didn't come back."

I wish I could joke about it but Peter Honey had really turned me on and the thought of never seeing him again hurts. I had given myself to him completely for no other reason than that I could not stop myself. I had believed that he felt something too. Maybe I was wrong.

And then, on the third day, the telephone rings. I pick it up and immediately experience a tingle of anticipation even before I hear the operator's voice at the other end. "Miss Sutton? Go ahead caller."

"Hi there," says a voice I am grateful to recognise. "Thank God I've caught up with you."

"I haven't been hiding anywhere," I say, slightly hurt.

"No, it's not that. I got your telephone number down wrong. Or rather, my skinny friend did. You remember Bruce and his fat little pencil?"

"Bruce is not skinny," says an indignant Kate who is craning forward to catch every word. "And there's nothing wrong with his pencil either."

"Sssh!" I tell her, because Peter sounds as if he is speaking from an old 78 record.

"His fives are very like his threes, as well," continues Peter. "I kept ringing up this number and getting some old girl who rambled on in Greek and then put the phone down. I'd nearly given you up when it occurred to me to try a few alternatives. How are you?"

Fantastic, now that I have heard from you, I feel like saying.

"Fine," I say coolly. "Life has been pretty hectic lately."

In fact I have not done a thing except fly to Dublin and wash my hair.

"Wild parties with all those 'acquaintances' of yours, huh?" says Peter, cheerfully. He does not seem at all worried about it. Damn!

"Where are you speaking from?" I ask, seeking to imply my involvement in all kinds of wild goings-on by my sudden change of subject.

"Amsterdam. It is a diabolical line, isn't it? Are you flying today?"

"Yes. Paris."

"Well, why don't we meet up? Can you stay the night?"

"Er – yes, I suppose so."

"Which do you prefer, Paris or Amsterdam? I know. Let's say Amsterdam. I expect you've been round Paris more times than a metro train. I'll leave a ticket at the bureau for you. What time does your flight get in?"

If I understand Peter correctly he is going to fly me from Paris to Amsterdam for the evening. That does seem a little like the lush treatment that could turn an impressionable girl's head.

"Are you still there?" says Peter.

"If you can't say anything, tell him *I'll* go," bleats Kate.

"If your friend with the big knockers is around why don't you get her to come?" continues Peter.

"Charming!" exclaims Kate. "He can't even remember my name."

"A rose by any other – " I soothe her.

"You mean a pear, don't you?"

Something tells me that Kate is trying to be funny but I don't dwell on it.

"I'd love to come," I say, "but I'm afraid that Kate is flying to Athens."

"Try and keep the satisfaction out of your voice," hisses Kate.

"But I'm certain she'd love to hear from Bruce," I trill. "Is he with you?"

"Somewhere," says Peter. "I haven't seen him since the early hours of this morning."

"Obviously pining away for you," I observe to Kate who

sticks her tongue out at me. "My flight gets in at Orly at four thirty," I tell Peter.

"O.K. Excellent. I'll have some tickets waiting for you and meet you at the airport. Glad you can make it. I must go now as I've got a meeting to get back to."

"Boy. He's quite a mover, isn't he?" breathes Kate. "Lucky Penny."

The same thought is occurring to me as I board my flight to Paris, and I have to confess that I am a trifle preoccupied, not to say downright excited. I start pouring coffee instead of tea and give the Captain so much sugar in his coffee that you could stand a spoon up in it. "You're not in love again, are you, Sutton?" he says, suspiciously.

"Oh, no. It was just that I couldn't remember whether I'd put any sugar in so I thought I'd better be on the safe side."

"What were you using? A shovel?"

I smile apologetically and go on my way, but it is a bad day for those unfortunate enough to be flying with Stewardess Sutton. One passenger gets served a sherry and tonic instead of a whisky and soda and another gets a wet nappy on his lap during an 'emergency' with one of our tiny charges. Not surprisingly, I get a few old-fashioned glances when it is time to say goodbye.

In this case there is no excuse, but – in general – I would like to plead for a little more charity towards stewardesses. We are only human and, just like you, we have our off-days: things persist in getting fouled up, it is the wrong time of the month, our lover has run off with our best friend. Sometimes a girl just has to groan and bare it, rather than grin and bear it. My plea for tolerance and understanding is especially directed at those passengers who go berserk every time a flight is delayed. O.K. We know it is infuriating, but please don't vent your wrath on us. Listening to some of you, one would think that we were personally responsible for that leak in the hydraulic system or the fog round the airport. In fact, we are usually just as keen as you to get to our destination on time, if not keener. We do a lot of our living outside the fuselage, believe you me.

I am still not completely convinced that Peter will have a ticket waiting for me, and I find out my check-in time for the return flight and go to the airline information desk in some trepidation.

"Mademoiselle Sutton? Certainement." The tickets are slapped down on the desk before me. Impressive. Peter is such an unshowy guy that I find it difficult to think of him as a tycoon. This kind of international wheeler-dealing needs to be wrapped up in an Old Etonian accent before I can really believe that it is going to happen. I must be pretty well indoctrinated with the British class system, I guess.

It is fun flying as a passenger for a change. Especially as Peter has booked me first class! I am travelling on a French plane and I have to confess that they really do things well. The girls are very chic and charming and the choice of snacks we are offered is a definite threat to my waist line. And champagne, as well.

Small wonder that I am slightly squiffy when I trip, literally, down the gangway. Of course, stewardesses are not allowed to drink when on duty so the temptation to weigh in to all that free booze is too much to resist.

I get through customs and look around for Peter. At first, I do not recognise him. When I last saw him he was wearing a faded denim shirt and trousers to match. Now he has on a smart lightweight suit and is carrying a brief-case. Quite the international executive.

"You're looking marvellous," he says treating me to a kiss on the cheek. "I never thought I was going to get here. I've been in meetings all day. Anyway, that's over now, thank the Lord. Let's go and have a drink while we decide what to do. Do you fancy some champagne?"

"Er – super," I gulp.

Peter summons a taxi and sweeps me away to a delightful bar by one of the many waterways that intersect the city. Amsterdam has a deliciously unspoilt flavour and the cobble-strewn streets and tree-lined canals make an ideal backdrop against which to while away a few happy hours.

"I expect you'd like to freshen up," he says when we have agreed that dinner and some more sight-seeing would be the perfect way to spend the evening.

"Yes," I say. "Er – I suppose you've booked me into a hotel?"

24

"I thought you might like to stay at the family place" says Peter almost apologetically.

"You have a flat here as well?"

"My old man has some business interests here and he uses the place for conferences and things like that."

Peter Honey's father sounds like Mr Australia and I look forward to meeting him. I have always had a soft spot for the older millionaire.

"Are you holding a conference there at the moment?" I ask.

"No. It will just be us. Disappointed?"

"Relieved." I brush my lips against his cheek and he slips his arm round my waist.

"Let's go and change," he says.

I was impressed by the London apartment but the one in Amsterdam is even more stunning. The top two floors of a terraced house by a canal. From the enormous studio-like living room one can look down through the trees to see the lock gates opening to let the barges through. There is a great copper stove in the middle of the room and the furniture is mainly composed of a variety of giant cushions made in all kinds of fabrics and colours.

"Do you like it?" says Peter, as he piles some logs in through the open mouth of the stove.

"It's fantastic. But it doesn't seem exactly right for business conferences."

"There's a boardroom on the floor below. Entertaining is a big part of business life, you know. What can I get you? Some more champagne?"

I am going to have champagne coming out of my ears soon but I nod agreeably. That is one of the worst things about me, I have very low reserves of self-control. I also feel sexy at inconvenient moments. Peter misinterprets my shiver.

"Do you find it cold in here?"

"No. Will you show me the rest of the place?"

"Natch. We'll pick up some champagne on the way."

"Do they pack it in tubes for the Australian market?"

"They haven't quite got the demand yet. When are you coming over to help build it up?"

"Oh, you remember our conversation, do you?" I say casually.

"Cripes, of course I do. I was dead serious about it. You and your mate with – "

" – 'the big knockers.' Don't keep going on about them. You'll give me a complex."

"You've got nothing to worry about. You've got a beautiful figure. I talked to you about it. Remember?" Peter stands on tiptoe to reach into the back of an enormous fridge and I watch the way his muscles swell under the beautifully-cut suit. He removes a bottle of champagne, unwinds the wire and with professional skill holds the cork steady while he rotates the bottle.

"I prefer you in casual clothes," I say as he fills my glass.

"Then you shall have me in casual clothes," he says with a flourish. "Anything else your ladyship requires?"

I raise my glass to my lips and hold his glance over the rim.

"I'll leave you to do whatever you think is necessary."

Peter smiles a slow, comprehending smile and narrows his eyes.

"I think we'd better continue with the conducted tour," he says. I had hoped that the subject of our trip 'Down Under' would be enlarged upon but mention of Kate seems to have jarred it from Peter's mind. Curse Kate! She can interrupt a conversation even when she is a hundred and fifty miles from it. Maybe my 'conducted tour' will give me an opportunity to reintroduce the topic.

"Boardroom," says Peter briskly as he swings open a door.

"Hey! Let me have a look," I squeak, because the door is closing swiftly before I have even glanced inside. Peter steps to one side obediently and takes my glass as I go in. The room is not a large one and is dominated by a table that seems to cover most of the floor space. Around it ten chairs hug the walls. The table is remarkable in that it is covered in some kind of soft leathery material.

"Can you press on this?" I say innocently. Peter smiles. "I mean with a pen," I say hurriedly.

"What else could you mean?" grins Peter. He puts down the glasses and comes towards me so that I find myself

26

pushed back against the edge of the table.

"What about the rest of the rooms?" I murmur.

"Later," says Peter. His fingers are gently stroking the sides of my thighs and his mouth probes for mine. Maybe the champagne is making me reckless or maybe I am just built like that. My fingers pull his mouth down on to mine and I enjoy what he is doing to me. Firmly but gently he pushes me back on to the table and I tingle with a delicious expectancy. What happens now is very important because the mood of impromptu naughtiness can be so easily shattered and something exciting and slightly wicked becomes merely clumsy and grotesque. He peels me with professional ease and gently pulls me forward to the edge of the table. His fingers are tenderly stroking the very fount of my sensations and I suddenly feel him boring into me with a hot firm warmth that makes me stretch out my arms to hold him and draw him even closer to me. I hear myself cry out and his own half-muffled bay of pleasure as he probes me.

We say few words after that until our love-making is finished and I have bathed and changed. I come into the studio and there is Peter, with his broad back shielding the fire. He is gazing into the embers and so absorbed in his thoughts that he does not immediately register my presence.

"Have you forgotten me already?" I tease him.

"Quite the reverse," he says, taking me in his arms. "I was thinking how I can keep you here."

"Don't start mussing my make-up," I scold him. "You haven't got a chance. I've got to be on the first plane to Paris tomorrow morning. You make me a firm offer about that Australian job and I'll guarantee you the services of two first-rate stewardesses as soon as Kate and I can give in our notices. I suppose the trouble is that your father will have to ratify our appointments."

Peter reacts in exactly the way that I had hoped he would.

"My old man doesn't have to ratify anything. I'm a director of the Company and if I say you're hired, that's it. You give me your address and I'll put an offer in the post to you tomorrow."

"Both of us?"

"Both of you."

"Well. I promise I'll give it full consideration," I say primly.

" 'Full consideration'? You said a moment ago that you would guarantee me your services."

"I was probably being a bit hasty. A girl is allowed to change her mind, you know."

Peter shakes his head. "Don't tell me I've met another one of those," he says bitterly.

"What do you mean?"

"Oh, it's a long story. I was engaged before I left Australia. I'm not any more. Get the picture?"

"She broke it off?"

Peter nods. "Wanted to think about it. Thought she might be a bit young to settle down. Needed to see more of the world. It's her mother. I'd send that old baggage off to New Guinea, tomorrow."

What an idiot, I think. Fancy letting a hunk like this slip through your fingers. Just how many eligible guys do they have in Australia, anyway? I thought the place had a population smaller than London.

"I'm sorry," I say, trying to sound sincere. I make a lousy job of it.

"Oh, it doesn't matter. I'm well out of it."

I wish I could believe him but I have a feeling that Peter still hankers after the lady. Maybe it was her he was thinking about when he was looking into the fire. This is bad news for Honey-hungry Sutton and I am brooding about it when Peter spirits me off through the mist-draped streets to a delicious fish restaurant. Our love-making has given me quite an appetite and by the time I have chewed my way through a large plate of prawns and half a lobster I am feeling more like my old self again.

"More champagne?" says Peter, filling my glass.

"I couldn't. I feel as if I'm ninety-nine per cent composed of bubbles as it is. You'd better watch me when we go for that walk, otherwise I might float away."

"Don't worry," grins Peter, leaning across to kiss me. "You haven't got a chance of getting away from me now."

He pays the bill, leaving an enormous tip – I hate men who are mean tippers – and we go out into the street. We are both a little bit drunk, and in that happy state when anything we do or say seems wildly amusing. Even when I suddenly sit down in a puddle for no apparent reason we split our sides whilst passers-by gape and give us a wide berth.

I am soaked to the skin and there is nothing for it but to return to the apartment and put on some dry clothes. At least, I want to put on some dry clothes. Peter seems more interested in taking off wet ones. Eventually I persuade him that the night is young and that I would like to see some more of Amsterdam before we sample the sleeping accommodation. The problem is that I only have my stewardess uniform to wear.

"You don't mind me giving the airline some free publicity, do you?" I ask Peter.

"If you insist on going out, I don't mind if you wrap yourself up in a Union Jack," he says.

Half an hour later we are at the end of a narrow street which contains a great many brightly lit shop windows. There are also a considerable number of people milling about. Mainly men.

"Gosh, they're not still at it, are they?" I ask. "They must be incredibly industrious. You wouldn't find shops open in England at this hour."

Peter laughs. "I don't think you have any shops like these in England."

We start to walk down the street and I see what he means. In each shop window sits a girl, sometimes quite a beautiful girl. They are knitting, reading books or just smiling out into the street. Their dresses are alluring without being too provocative. They look not totally unlike girls sitting out a dance. The men hurry or dawdle along the street according to inclination and occasionally enter one of the shops. After a few words the man either comes out again or a bargain is struck and the protagonists leave the stage. Sometimes there is actually a bed or divan in the window and the blind is lowered when madam is 'engaged'. It all seems rather decorous and relaxed. Not like all those raddled old bags standing on street corners that I associate with prostitution.

"Thanks for bringing me here," I say. "Are you thinking

29

of setting me up? Wait a minute! This must be how your father made his millions. Why didn't I think of that before?"

"I wish you were right," grins Peter. "Unfortunately, that's one business he isn't in."

"Oh dear. I had this lovely thought that you might be employed to seduce innocent young girls into a life of vice."

"Where would I find any innocent ones? Hey! Watch it."

I swing a playful fist and it is Peter's turn to step back hurriedly and take a seat on the cobbles. I find this very funny and it is left to a thin-faced man with a pencil moustache to help him up and dust him down.

"That will teach you to cast aspersions on my virtue," I chortle.

Peter pats his breast pocket and the smile fades from his face.

"I think that joker stole my wallet," he says. "Which way did he go?"

"What? Are you certain?"

Peter dives his hands into all his pockets. "It's gone. It must have been him. Come on!"

He dashes off and I pant along behind. It is not easy because the street is full of men and I bet that some of them think I am a tart chasing a welshing client! I lose Peter in no time and stop to get my breath back. It is at this moment that I turn round and catch a glimpse of a man I am convinced is the one who helped Peter up. He is sidling into one of the doorways. He sees me and disappears.

"Peter!" I squeal, but of course he is not there. I run across the street and try and remember which doorway the man disappeared into. There is a door open beside a darkened shop window and I go through it and up a narrow flight of stairs. I wonder what I am going to do if I come face to face with the man. At the top of the stairs there is a door with a padlock on it and another which has a chink of light under it. I try and peer through the keyhole but there is a key in the way and I can see nothing. I listen carefully. Not a sound. Holding my breath, I gently close my fingers round the knob and turn. The door gives and I push forward an inch so that I can peep inside. Oh dear!

30

I have occasionally wondered what it must be like to watch other people making love and now I know. I close the door quietly and decide that the gentleman I have seen performing would have to be a world championship class quick-change artist if he could have stripped off and boarded in the time it took me to get up the stairs. No. He must be a customer. Which explains why madam is not sitting in her window. Wait a minute! Maybe the villain slipped in to the darkened window. He has probably escaped by now but I had better check. I go downstairs and stealthily open the door at the bottom. There does not seem to be anything behind the darkened window but there is a curtain on the far side which may conceal something. I walk towards it, aware of the movement of people in the street outside.

Immediately, the door clicks shut behind me and the light goes on! A brilliant fluorescent light that dazzles me so much I trip over something and find myself stretched out on a chaise longue. Help! I must get out of here. I leap to my feet and streak across the room. In a panic I snatch at the door knob and – disaster! – it comes away in my hand.

What am I going to do? Already I can sense that my presence is causing quite a stir outside. Probably not used to seeing tarts in air stewardesses' uniforms, I guess. Air stewardesses' uniforms? Oh, no! If this got in the papers – the mind boggles. I rush to the window and start miming that I want to be released. Few of the fast-swelling crowd seem to realise what I am getting at. Where is Peter? The crush of bodies outside is threatening to break through the window. To my relief there is the sound of someone forcing open the door. My relief is short-lived.

Standing in the doorway is a short thick-set man wearing a leather trench-coat and a pork-pie hat with a cockade stuck in the side of it. He could be Dutch or German – or anything. Get me out of here! He winks at me lasciviously and produces a bundle of greasy notes.

"Nein, danker," I squeak pathetically, but this only makes him count out more notes. Another figure appears behind him. And another. They start arguing and pushing. The whole thing is some kind of nightmare. Where is

Peter?! I am becoming desperate. As if I did not have enough problems, madam reappears and seems understandably furious that someone is muscling in on her territory.

With madam seizing me by one wrist and Leathercoat by the other I am well on the way to being torn down the middle. My eyes probe the sea of faces that are now beginning to jam the entrance for a sign of Peter.

But I do not see Peter. I see a small, worried man with a face permanently prepared to greet the disaster that lurks round every corner. It is a face I know well. It belongs to Mr Sebastian Redmond, Staff Recruitment Officer of the airline I fly for. From the set of Mr Redmond's features I can tell that he recognises me too.

CHAPTER THREE

" – And wearing her uniform, as well," sobs Redmond. "That was the last straw. And the gestures she was making to the crowd – urgh! It was disgusting."

"I've told you a thousand times," I shriek. "I was trying to make them understand that I wanted someone to fit the door handle on to the sprocket."

"Don't do it again!" yelps Redmond. "Do you see what I mean?" He is addressing Miss Sybilla 'Binkie' – known in some circles as 'Kinky' – Fanshawe who is the shrivelled old hag held together by Helena Rubenstein beauty preparations who is responsible for the spiritual welfare and unwanted pregnancies of the airline's female staff. When I say 'responsible' I do not wish to imply in the latter case that Miss Fanshawe, despite her rather masculine appearance, is working in an other than curative capacity.

These two august personages are gathered together to sit in judgement upon me, my exploits in Amsterdam having been celebrated in legend and national newspaper ever since my return. As Redmond has been swift to point out, my association with the airline could be nearly at an end. The same thought has occurred to me but for different reasons.

"Do you really believe that I was seeking to offer my

body for hire like a common strumpet?" I say, drawing myself up to my full five foot four and a half inches. "And is it conceivable that I would attempt to inflame the base lusts of prospective clients by decking myself out in the habiliments of my chosen calling or profession?" – It is not difficult to see who has been reading back numbers of *The Times* law reports prior to preparing their own defence, is it?

"You've already said that," sniffs Redmond. "It seems no more unlikely than your story of what you actually were doing. Chasing pickpockets, indeed."

Something inside me snaps. "And what were you doing there, then?" I accuse. "That doesn't bear too much thinking about either, does it?" Redmond turns an interesting shade of scarlet. "I'm surprised you can still blush," I continue triumphantly. "Your funny little ways are no secret to us, you know. We all know why Liz Braithwaite had to leave." In fact Liz Braithwaite left quite innocently to marry a man who ran a garage in Ongar but I am not one who easily surrenders an advantage.

"Really!" sniffs Miss Fanshawe.

"Yes. And you have no cause to look smug," I say, rounding on her. "Your little tryst at the staff party did not go unnoticed."

"I don't know what you're talking about," snorts the old bag, slipping on her haughty expression.

"You and the last of the red hot lovers here. That's what I'm talking about. Sitting at the same table. Pawing each other. Your exhibition on the dance floor was disgusting. Talk about 'Last Tango in Paris'. The last one at the Connaught Rooms would take some beating."

"Silence!" shrieks Redmond. "How dare you talk to us like that. Shameless hussy, besmirching the proud name of the airline."

"You still haven't told us what you were doing in Amsterdam," I accuse. "You always had an eye for the fillies, didn't you?"

"I don't have to explain my movements to you," shouts Redmond.

"I don't want to know about your 'movements'," I say, trying to get the right balance of contempt and revulsion into my voice. "I can imagine what they're like." I shudder expressively.

"Miss Sutton," says Redmond icily. "I am but seconds away from terminating your employment."

"Save your breath," I say. "I'm resigning."

"You're fired!" shrieks Redmond.

"I've resigned."

"Fired."

"Resigned!"

Both the stupid old fools are obviously determined to have the pleasure of sacking me and I think this makes things better for me from the tax point of view, so what the hell. Now that I am at it I might as well make Kate a free agent at well.

"All right," I snarl. "Have it your way. But you don't know the half of it. A pity you never flew on any of our flights." Their eyes widen in horror. "The Flying Mattress. That's what our plane was called. Why do you think the airline carried so many more passengers last year?" I nod into their horrified eyes. "That's right, Kate Goodbody and me." Without taking his eyes off me Redmond writes something on his pad. "We used to have them queuing up in the aisles. Boy, how we fleeced those suckers," I cackle fiendishly. "I was really looking forward to the jumbo jets, too."

Miss Fanshawe's head drops forward on to the table and Sebastian Redmond closes his eyes. Something tells me that Kate and I are now free to join Outback Airlines – or anything.

"You said, WHAT!!??" screeches Kate, when I tell her of my meeting with the airline's personnel officer. "When did I ever tell you I worked in a brothel?"

"So, I exaggerated a bit. You did say that things used to get a bit out of hand at that riding school you worked in. What does it matter? You're sacked. That's the main thing."

"What do you mean, 'the main thing'. I'm not certain I want to be sacked."

"You're not having second thoughts, now? I thought you'd already bought your surf board."

"I don't like being rushed, that's all. You have no right

34

going around telling people that I've been misbehaving with the passengers."

"But you have been misbehaving with the passengers."

"Not on the plane, I haven't! And very few of them. Not as many as you!"

"Don't worry. I've been sacked too."

"That's not the point. Oh, dear. I hope we're doing the right thing. If we don't get that letter from Peter, we're really in the cart."

But we do get a letter from Peter, this time with a Turin postmark, and, most influential in making up Kate's mind that she is mad keen to go to Australia, a visit from Bruce. He spirits Kate away for a weekend in the country and when she comes back she is clutching a steamship catalogue and is planning her wardrobe.

As usual it falls to me to make all the arrangements and the only chore I bequeath to Kate is organising our farewell party. We have made a fantastic number of good friends whilst working for the airline and we could not leave the country without saying goodbye to them in style. Kate is usually very good in this department but she is so preoccupied with plans for the trip that a week before we are due to embark nothing has been fixed up. She scolds me for not reminding her and we have quite a set to before we both agree that some urgent action is required. Money is not in good supply at the moment which is no surprise considering all the outgoings connected with our trip. Peter has offered to pay half our fares and once the offer has been made in the name of Outback Airlines we accept with swift dignity. Nevertheless, there is not as much cash as we would like for the party. Kate goes out and buys some jars of white wine and I look for a recipe I remember cutting out of a magazine. Of course I cannot find it and have to make up the rest of the ingredients from memory and Kate's wildly improbable recollection of brews she has sampled at past rave-ups. The result is, to put it mildly, a disaster. I have tasted some sickly, insipid cups in my time but this is the worst of the lot. "This stuff tastes more like tap than punch," says Kate and she is right. What are we going to do?

"Let's hope some of the people coming bring some stuff

35

we can add to it," she says. I do not take much notice of her words then, but later it occurs to me that it would be wiser not to rely on the generosity of the guests. I take the last few pounds I can spare and buy a bottle of brandy. Feeling as if I am pouring the precious liquid down the drain I add it to our brew and take a sip. It still tastes pretty terrible but I comfort myself that it now has an acceptable alcohol content.

Comes the night of the party and our guests start to pour through the door. We have invited everyone – even Fanshawe and Redmond, though I do not think they are going to show up – and there are hugs and presents from everyone. I am determined to be on my very best behaviour so I do not have anything to drink.

"I hope the booze is going to be all right," I say to Kate.

Kate winks at me. "It should be O.K. I laced it with a bottle of brandy."

"That's funny – Hey! Wait a minute." I pause as a glassy-eyed man slides down the wall.

"What's the matter?" asks Kate.

"I do wish you'd tell me when you do things."

"Why? What's happened?"

"I put a bottle of brandy in as well!"

"Oh, no!"

"Oh, yes!"

We look around us in horror and there is no doubt that our brew is having an effect. One or two people are beginning to sit down already and Mr Richards from Traffic Control is mopping his brow with a large spotted handkerchief.

"Shall we tell them?" says Kate.

"I don't think we need to," I say, watching an empty glass slip from the faltering fingers of one of my friends.

"Fantashstick drink, Darlingsh," she burbles, and grinds the glass under foot as if it is a cigarette end.

"They all seem to like it," hisses Kate: "Do you think we've got enough?"

Kate need not worry. To the best of my recollection nobody has had more than two glasses of our brew. Nobody *can* have more than two glasses of our brew. I suspect that Kate put something else in the mixture and refuses to admit it, or maybe I got the bottles mixed up. Whatever it is we have discovered a really knock-out drink. And I mean knock out! Half an hour after the start of what was supposed to be a wild rave-up the guests are strewn round the room like it is a sit-in at an old peoples' home. Some of them are actually asleep! Kate turns the stereo on full blast and they hardly bat an eyelid.

"What are we going to do?" says Kate desperately.

"There's only one thing we can do." I pick up a scoop and fill a glass from the punch bowl. "If you can't lick them, join them. Cheers!"

"Cheers!" says Kate, following suit.

The interesting thing about our party is the reaction we get from people after it. Everybody who rings up to say thank you seems incapable of remembering what happened and automatically suspicious of the part they played in the proceedings. You can sense them trying to probe you for an account of what they got up to, yet not really wanting to know because they suspect that it was something rather wicked. In general, people have a pretty low opinion of themselves.

In fact, I seem to remember that we found a copy of 'Hymns Ancient and Modern' and sang from that until there was only Kate and I left awake. Boy! If only I could remember the recipe for that drink. I can think of a lot of parties I would like to use it at.

On the day of our departure our spirits are really down in the dumps. Right 'down under' in fact. We are both wondering if we have done the right thing and suddenly England and all our friends seem terribly important to us. "If only you hadn't been so rude to Mr Redmond," says Kate for the hundredth time. "I wouldn't mind if I thought I could get my job back."

"You've heard of burning your boats?" I tell her. "Well, I've burnt our aeroplanes. Nobody could have done anything else in the circumstances. I wasn't going to sit there and be called a whore."

"I always thought it was boots," says Kate, thoughtfully. "You know. 'Burn your boots': to experience danger."

"How interesting," I say, sarcastically. "I can see we're going to have a very stimulating voyage with you in that

37

form. Now, maybe you can use the lower half of your brain and sit on this suitcase so I can get the lid closed."

We take a taxi to the station and both of us sit silently as we watch our beloved London slipping past the window. Of course, the sun has to be shining and I see five really good looking guys who remind me of what I am leaving behind. Unlike Kate, who is dotty about foreign talent, I usually prefer our home-spun boys. Though they do not sweep you off your feet with honeyed words, I usually believe what does come out of their mouths.

Both Kate and I would be in better heart if Peter and Bruce were around to remind us of the goodies to come. When last heard from they were in Buenos Aires which seems an awful long way away. I often think of my night in Amsterdam and get a warm feeling when I recall the tricks Peter and I got up to. Peter said that he would never again be able to concentrate when sitting in that boardroom and I know what he means. Some of our activities in front of the big stove were pretty distracting, too!

We arrive at the station, find a porter and head for the boat train. And then – surprise! A veritable wedding reception is waiting at the barrier! A bevy of flying chums plus confetti, streamers, tinsel – the lot. Even a banner saying 'Goodbye Penny and Kate. Australia's loss is our gain'. It occurs to me, later, that somebody got that a bit wrong. Or did they?

We have to run a gauntlet of back-slapping well-wishers and the train pulls out of the station with us waving until our arms nearly fall off. After that we collapse into each others' arms, have a good cry and spend the rest of the journey getting our faces straight again.

The train goes into the docks and we suddenly see the funnels of our liner rising above the transit sheds,

"It's big, isn't it?" says Kate.

"It needs to be with all the luggage you've brought," I say maliciously.

When we get to our cabin another surprise awaits us. Flowers. I have never seen so many apart from at funerals. The same thought occurs to Kate.

"They're beautiful, but they'll have to go. They use more oxygen than I do. If I had them here I'd feel I was lying in state."

"The whole cabin is like a padded coffin, isn't it?"

"Exactly. And I don't think I'll ever be able to find it again. We went down so many corridors I'm certain we must be on the outskirts of Southampton."

"I hope they're water-tight. What's this?" My bunk is six inches from the ceiling and there is a tube directly above where my head will lie.

"That's for shouting instructions to the Captain: left hand down a bit – that kind of thing."

"No it isn't. It's a fresh air supply."

"It would have to be, wouldn't it? I wish we had a porthole. I was looking forward to leaning out and feeding the flying fish."

"It is claustrophobic, isn't it? I was expecting palatial staterooms and all that kind of stuff. When you look at the boat from outside you would think we would each have our own swimming bath, wouldn't you? There's almost as much room on a plane."

"I think they've given us a cupboard by mistake. When the maid comes in and collects twenty-five pillow cases you'll see I'm right."

We chatter on like this, trying to keep our spirits up and become acclimatised to our unfamiliar surroundings. Our cabin really is tiny and we feel no inclination to stay in it any longer than we have to. Being cooped up in a stuffy broom cupboard for weeks on end is not my idea of a glamorous ocean cruise.

Another drawback to our cabin is brought home to us by a sound like that of a giant ghost checking its chains prior to setting out on a night's haunting.

"What on earth is that?" I yelp.

"Sounds like the under-carriage retracting," says Kate. In fact, she is not far from the truth. It is the anchor coming up.

"At least they won't be doing that every five minutes," says Kate.

We go up on deck and the miseries descend again. How can everyone around us be so cheerful? The tugs ease us away from the wharf and I feel as if the dressing is being pulled from an unhealed wound. Past the Isle of Wight we go and when I see The Needles, the rocks that mark the western tip of the island, and the land begins to fall away behind us, I am nearly in tears.

"Your first trip?" enquires a soft, well-spoken, male voice beside me. I look up to see a darkly attractive man in his late twenties looking down at me through considerate eyes. He is wearing the uniform of a ship's officer and has some gold rings on his sleeve. His face is weather-beaten and the dark hairs at his temples have been turned gold by the sun.

I nod. "I've been across the Channel a few times. This is my first ocean voyage."

"Are you emigrating?" He looks out to sea and eases his hat lower over his eyes. He does not seem completely relaxed and I get the feeling that he is really quite shy and only talking to me because I look miserable. I like him for this.

"Not completely," I answer him. "I'm going to work for an Australian airline for a few months and see how I like it."

"Sounds interesting." He smiles a trifle nervously and suddenly I feel responsible for keeping the conversation going.

"You know Australia well, do you?" I ask.

"I've been to Sydney and Perth. But I've never been in to the interior."

"You make it sound like darkest Africa."

"Don't let it put you off. I've liked what I've seen of it. If you like the outdoor life it's a great country."

This is stirring stuff for the Australian Tourist Board but not calculated to win any auditions for a TV chat show. Kate arrives to help things along.

"Oh," she says, fluttering her eyelashes at my matelot. "Complaining about our cabin, were you? It really is terrible. One of us has to wait outside while the other one gets undressed. It's so small, you see."

Captain Hornblower looks uneasy. "I'm afraid that's not my province. Anything to do with accommodation should be referred to the purser."

"You just drive the ship, do you?" says Kate knowledgeably.

"Er – yes. That sort of thing. In fact if you'll excuse me

40

I think I'm probably needed on the bridge."

"Brilliant!" I snap as my prize strides away. "You soon put the fear of God into him, didn't you?"

"What do you mean? I was just being chatty."

"Scatty. More like. You can be so tactless, can't you?"

"You mean I should have left you alone? Heavens, you don't waste any time, do you? You've only been on the boat an hour. Love at first sight, was it?"

"Don't be ridiculous. I was referring to your lack of subtlety. Didn't you realise that he was obviously a bit shy?"

"I didn't think sailors could be shy. Anyway, you've got this big thing going with Peter. What are you getting worked up about?"

"I'm not getting worked up. I'm merely making an observation that you could profitably take cognizance of."

" 'Cognizance'. Oo-er. Look who's been doing her 'It Pays To Increase Your Word Power' quiz. William Funk would be proud of you."

I am furious. Mainly because I did get the word from 'It Pays To Increase Your Word Power'. Kate is not a total idiot.

In the days that follow Kate and I cheer up a lot. We sail down the coast of Spain and by the time we can see the African coast we are beginning to turn a satisfying shade of brown. One thing we are determined to do is arrive in Australia with a really good sun tan. We learn that the ship's officer we talked to off The Needles is called Richard Gentleman and no name ever suited a man better. He is both gentle and a complete gentleman. Too complete, maybe. Anybody that dishy has an obligation to make himself more available. Kate and I, being the kind of hussies that we are, start a competition to see who can make him deviate from the straight and narrow first, although I do not fancy either of our chances overmuch.

When it comes to showing restraint, Richard Gentleman is very much the exception to the rule. The rest of the crew, or the ones we come into contact with, are amiable rogues with a twinkle in their eye for any pretty girl, and the male passengers are also a friendly lot. The passengers seem equally divided between emigrants, people going on a

41

cruise and those visiting relations in Australia or en route.

One thing that does surprise me is the rapacious familiarity of the lady passengers. Kate and I are no slouches when it comes to moving in on the male talent but – phew! Some of these females leave us standing. Kate has a theory that it has something to do with the sea air but I think it stems from all the free time there is to fill in, and the holiday atmosphere. 'The Devil finds work for idle hands' is never truer than when applied to matters sexual. One lady in particular catches our eye. Though no longer in the first flush of youth she is always there to greet the duty barman in the morning and last to leave the dance floor at night – though seldom with the same man. Mrs Pickering is her name and she is soon known at 'The Merry Widow'. It is rumoured that her husband is but recently dead, and that his sad demise has furnished the wherewithal for her current trip.

"I reckon I know what killed the poor bastard," I overhear one of the crew telling his mate.

"Yeah. But what a way to go," is the envious reply.

For some reason Mrs Pickering makes Kate and I her confidantes and is swift to fill us in with the latest news of her sexual derring-do.

"Don't waste your time with the doctor, dears," she warns us. "Very apathetic performance."

"You've been to–er–bed with Doctor Woods?" we gape, thinking of that very respectable and antique gentleman.

"Oh, yes. I always start with the doctor on a ship." She makes it sound as if she might start with the second officer on an aeroplane and the guard on an inter-city express train.

"It's habit more than anything," she continues. "Very silly because drink usually gets to them first. That and apathy. They get so much, you see. One's much better off with the younger members of the crew. Preferably those who have just put to sea, or whatever they do."

"Richard Gentleman," we chant.

"Is he the dark one who blushes every time he says anything to you? Yes. Isn't he a lamb? I have a very soft spot for him."

"You haven't – er?"

42

"No. Not yet. He's on my list, though."

"You have a list?!"

"I believe in being professional about it. The first couple of days I wander about, keeping my eyes open and seeing what the form is. Then I pick my fancies, work out timings and I'm off. I find I have to do that; otherwise I can get snarled up in one relationship and find that half the trip has gone before I've really got anywhere. I'm all at sea, if you know what I mean." She nudges Kate. "Did you get my little joke, dear?"

Kate nods. "You're very frank, Mrs Pickering."

"Call me Rachel, dear. Why shouldn't I be frank? It's the hypocritical ones who infuriate me. The 'butter wouldn't melt in my mouth' baggages who look at you all hoity-toity and come down after breakfast to lay the cabin stewards. I don't mind what anyone gets up to. It's hypocrisy I can't stand."

Just at that moment a man of quite devastating loveliness comes into the saloon and we turn to Rachel expectantly. He is wearing a diaphanous silk blouse that flounces up round his waist and is held in place by a belt of large golden links. His expensive woollen trousers are slightly flared and his shoes white and buckled. He brushes a well-kept mane of hair from his eyes and orders a gimlet. He does not look like a man with a passion for carpentry so I assume he is referring to the drink. Both Kate and I have lusted after the creature but assumed that his studied lack of interest marked him down as a fag. Well, what is any self-respecting girl going to think?

"I never have truck with the hired hands," says Rachel, following our eyes.

"What do you mean? He's queer, isn't he?"

"No, my dears. He's a gigolo."

"A gigolo?!" Our eyes open wide. Suddenly he seems even more attractive.

"Who's he with?"

"No one."

"He must be very well off if he can afford to travel on liners."

"He's probably very good at his job," says Kate, hopefully.

43

"He doesn't pay anything," says Rachel.

"But you said he didn't have anyone keeping him."

"My goodness me, you are green, aren't you? The shipping line supports him. Don't you understand?"

"He's related to the chairman?"

"No!"

"He's having an affair with the chairman's wife."

"No! You are dumb. Why do women go on cruises?"

"Their health, I suppose."

"Don't be naive. They go to find a lover. Or in my case, lots of lovers. If you were selecting a cruise wouldn't you choose one that could guarantee you a high standard of available playmates? There's big money in these cruises. You know how much you're paying for your rabbit hutch. People like Alfonso, there, don't even need a cabin. They're boarding out every night."

"Do they get paid?"

"Not by the shipping line. They live on their tips. The pieces of information they can pick up and put to good use. I knew a fellow once who played the stock market on the basis of the tips this woman used to give him. He made a small fortune."

"And to think we thought he was queer," sighs Kate.

"Well you would, dear. I'm afraid that you're not really what our friend is looking for. I don't wish to appear rude, but you're clearly not heiresses, are you?"

"Not unless something incredible has happened since I left home," says Kate. "Tell me, do they have tarts as well?"

"They don't need to," says Rachel cheerfully. "Not with girls like me around."

"Uuum," says Kate, and I know what she is thinking. The Merry Widow could probably close down every brothel in Europe.

One member of the crew who is a complete bore and a pest is Rodney Cole, the Entertainments Officer and self-styled shipboard Romeo. He seems to have more hands than a brace of octopuses and is always wheedling, chivvying and coaxing one to take part in some monstrously unamusing team event. Kate and I are very happy lying on the deck working at our tans and keeping a weather-eye open for any attractive males. We do not want to dress up in grass skirts and perform in a tug-of-war team against the girls from the next deck above ours – one of many.

"This place is like a floating holiday camp," moans Kate. "Why don't they leave us alone?"

"It's the same principle as serving people food every five minutes on an aeroplane. It keeps the passengers occupied and stops them from getting bored and restless."

"I'm not getting bored. I just want to get a sun tan. Uh, uh, here he comes. God's gift to women strikes again." Closing with us fast is Rodney wearing white flannels and a blazer which sports a badge depicting two crossed rifles and the message 'Purley Small Bore Association'. Kate says that Rodney is being too modest. He is now ready for the large bore association.

"Well," he says, surveying us. "It's all over bar the shouting, isn't it?" He is waiting for us to ask him 'what is?' But we know that and don't say anything. "Just a question of which one of you is going to be first," he continues, lamely. If he means first to punch him on the nose, he has a point.

"What are you talking about?" says Kate wearily, pulling a towel over her exposed thighs in case the sun reflected from Rodney's piercing eyes scorches a hole in them. Rodney regretfully transfers his gaze to her face.

"The Beauty Contest. Two beautiful girls like you can't fail to walk away with it."

"I bet you say that to all the girls," says Kate scornfully.

"Of course I do, but with you I really mean it."

"I'm sorry," I say with all the dignity I can muster. "My Women's Lib principles would not allow me to demean myself for the gratification of a pack of drooling male chauvinist pigs."

"You can't have a pack of pigs, can you?" says Kate who gets on my nerves sometimes.

"I can have whatever I like," I say coldly.

"I understand your feelings girls," pipes Rodney. "I can't bear to see women exploited, myself. But this isn't a serious beauty contest. It's just a bit of fun. Come on. Be a couple of sports. I've only got three entrants at the moment. You've got to be the winners."

So, of course, we end up with the rest of the contestants, nervously preening ourselves in a hastily improvised changing room behind the swimming pool. Rodney keeps popping in to see if he can catch anyone with her knickers down and the atmosphere is electric.

"Relax girls, relax," he keeps saying. "There's nothing to worry about. Uncle Rodney will see you're all right. Remember, I'll call you out in numerical order, you walk up to me, turn round to give the audience a chance to get an eye-full of your vitals, stop while I ask you a few questions about yourself, and then round and back to the dressing room. Don't get changed because you might be one of the lucky winners and we don't want the audience to see you in the altogether, do we?"

"No!" we chant.

The rest of the entrants do not make me feel I have wandered hopelessly out of my class and I reckon, being the modest, unassuming little English rose that I am, that the contest lies between Kate and myself with the odds in her favour because she is more typical beauty queen material – tall and generously proportioned, 'big knockers' as Bruce Wilson would put it. There is another girl who is particularly well-favoured in that department and I reckon that her bra must have needed planning permission. If the contest was judged on bosoms alone, the rest of us could pack up and go home.

Big Boobs is the first to go and the rest of us huddle together and make stupid jokes to drown our nerves. We cannot see what is going on but are surprised by the gales of laughter that blow back to us. "I expect her bra exploded," says Kate. We laugh nervously and check our support.

When the first contestant returns in tears with both knees lacerated we learn the reason for the mirth.

"It was horrible," she sobs. "He made the most terrible remarks about my breasts. He asked if they were balloons and threatened to pop them. I was so embarrassed I tripped over."

"Poor pet!" says Kate indignantly. "If that's the way he's going to behave we should refuse to go through with it."

46

"That man needs to be taught a lesson," says another girl. "He put his hand up my skirt when I was leaning over the rail the other day. I nearly dived into the sea."

The second contestant returns saying that Cole mimicked her accent to get a cheap laugh and the girls are near mutiny.

"Right," I say. "Let me go next. I'll fix him."

"What are you going to do?" says Kate.

"Wait and see." I get something out of my bag and wait for girl number three to return.

"Hang on a minute," says Rodney Jerk as he sees me approaching. "We've got a bit of a mix-up here. Can't you count, dearie? With that lot, you look as if you should be very good at figures."

He winks at the audience in case they miss the joke and makes a playful grab for my boobs. I sway away so that he has to stand with his back to the swimming pool if he wants to be in front of me.

"Hello, hello. We've got a shy one here, ladies and gentlemen. I wonder if she's got anything to hide? Maybe she's another candidate for the falsie test?" He produces a pin and waves it in front of the audience. What a creep! "Come on, darling. It's only a little prick. I'm certain it's not the – aaaRGH!!"

I know that Rodney Cole wants to make a splash and that is exactly what he does do. I, too, have a pin. A very large one of the kind sometimes stuck through ladies hats. It make contact with the lower part of Mr Cole's anatomy and that gentleman does a spectacular backwards leap into the pool. It is very impressive, especially coming from someone who cannot swim.

"Help, help!" screams the poor sap, while the audience kills itself. Talking of killing people, maybe I should do something to fish him out.

This manoeuvre proves to be even more of a gas because the first implement that comes to hand is the slippery pole used in pillow jousting and other jolly water japes. Cole grabs hold of this and starts to pull himself up, only to slowly slide down its whole length and topple back into the water. He does this three times until the audience are having to hold each other up. It is pretty cruel, but really,

Cole deserves it. Eventually, he gets close enough to the side to be hauled ashore like a drowned rat and promptly tries to pretend that the whole thing was planned. He waves to the audience and then hands over to Richard Gentleman before staggering away.

Richard is absolutely hopeless as a compère but a vast improvement on Cole. The voting takes place and the well-stacked girl who went on first is an easy winner with Kate second and me third.

"I can't see what you're surprised about," says Rachel, when we are discussing the contest afterwards. "She cried, didn't she? And she was so ugly that the audience could identify with her. You two are far too pretty. You look like professionals. Of course, you can't be ignored, but you can't enlist their sympathy like the girl-next-door type. It's all to do with supporting the underdog. Pushing that fellow in the pool, too. That was a bit flash, wasn't it? That must have alienated all the male voters."

"I don't know why I bothered to go in for the blooming contest," says Kate.

"You never had a chance of winning. Not at this level. You've got to gain their sympathy. It's like Richard and me, I suppose."

Kate and I exchange glances. "Richard who?"

"Gentleman, of course. You know. The one we were talking about. He stepped in –"

"Yes, yes. We know who you mean. Are you saying that – er, you – er – "

"Yes, dear. Of course I am. Very nice it was, too. I was quite surprised. Once you get through the inhibitions he's a very eager lad."

"But how do you get through the inhibitions?" we inquire urgently.

"Well, dear. You know he's shy?" Our expression shows Mrs Pickering that we do know that. "He's frightened of young girls so he responds to a bit of mothering. You know the relationship boys have with their mothers?"

"I thought I did," I say.

"They like to feel looked after, yet at the same time fill the role of the protector. They've trying to push their father out the whole time. Richard started off by being

48

relaxed in my presence because I am a mature woman. I then asked him for help on a number of occasions – where to post letters, that kind of thing – until he began to enjoy supplying my needs. Eventually I asked him to have a look at my air conditioning and – voilà!"

"He referred us to the purser, didn't he?" says Kate sadly.

"The Purser's not bad. But he does snore," says Rachel reflectively.

"I wonder he got the chance," says Kate when we are alone. "What on earth are we going to do? There's Rachel Pickering devouring every eligible man on the boat and we can't even win a beauty contest against a bunch of girls who would be pushed to get a job shoving soap coupons through letter boxes."

"No bitterness," I scold her. "It is serious I grant you, but we must be able to find a way. How are we going to get at Richard if he only likes mother figures?"

"Don't look at me," says Kate. "I've got a coil. It's that lovely gigolo I'm fretting about. I've always wanted to know what they're like. I mean, you must be good if you make your living out of it, mustn't you?"

The same thought has occurred to me and I would not be at all averse to a spot of market research, given the opportunity. It is hell being poor, isn't it?

The weeks pass and out situation becomes desperate. Everybody else on the boat seems to be indulging in mad passionate love-making from morn till night whilst Kate and I have difficulty in finding someone to lean over the ship's rail with us – except when we hit some rough weather off Colombo.

It would be easier to bear if Alfonso was remaining faithful to one lady but he does the shipping line proud and is seen with a string of consorts, some so hideous that you have to admit he is earning every penny he gets. The one thing they have in common – two if you include the fact that they are all women – is that they are stinking rich.

"That's the one criterion, dear," says Rachel who is making us sick with envy as she ploughs remorselessly through the complement of passengers and crew. "If only one of you could suddenly come in to a fortune." We nod glumly. "Wait a minute! I've got an idea. I'll spread it around that you are both heiresses travelling second class to avoid fortune hunters. That should do the trick. I don't know why I didn't think of it before."

"I don't know why I didn't think of it before," says Kate. "Make sure we both have the same amount of loot. We don't want anybody having an unfair advantage."

"Brazen baggage," I tell her. "Have you no pride?"

"Very little," says Kate. "And what I do have will evaporate completely, unless I get my hands on a man before we reach Australia."

I hate to admit it, but she is right. Thank goodness that another great Cole-organised extravaganza is arriving to provide the right back-drop for romance. The Masked Ball is the social highlight of the voyage out and the one occasion on which the crew are officially allowed to socialise with the passengers. I say 'officially' because most of them are at it like knives the whole time, regardless of any sanctions from the bridge.

I can see that Rachel has started passing the word around because the members of her bridge set – yes, she does have time for a game of bridge occasionally – begin nudging each other and making 'that's them' type gestures to each other. There is no immediate reaction from Alfonso but on the morning of the ball I suddenly feel a couple of eyes boring into me as I lie on a deck chair, and look up to see him smiling down at me.

"It eez a very beautiful morning, eez not it?" he says. "You minda if I sitta down besida you?"

His eyelashes are so long he must have difficulty seeing through them and when he smiles there are dimples on both sides of his chin and a cleft in the middle.

"That's quite all right," I whimper. "Yes, it is lovely, isn't it?"

Without looking round Alfonso raises one finger and a steward standing forty paces away breaks into a gallop. "You lika something to drink?"

"No, well – er yes, perhaps I would. That would be very nice." Why am I behaving like such a tongue-tied ninny?

Mainly because Alfonso is so Twentieth Century Fox it is not true. More like twentieth century wolf in fact.

"What is your pleasure?" he purrs.

I restrain myself and order a Bloody Mary. I'm sophisticated, see?

"It is strange that I have taken so longa to speak with you," he says, sounding as if the words are being extracted from him on the rack, "but I find myself on the horns of a Dalai Lama."

"How uncomfortable for you," I say sympathetically.

"It is, very." He nods. "You see, I have two problems. Firstly, you are so beautiful that I finda my tongue tied." Of course! I knew there must be a reason.

"And secondly?" I say.

"Your sister. She, too, is so beautiful. I fear that, maybe, I fall in love with you both at first sight. You thinka such a thing is possible?"

"I've never heard of it before," I say.

"No. Neither have I. That is what puzzles me so much. I am frightened by my feelings. Helpa me." He puts one of his hands on top of mine and suddenly drops his head on to it. "Please."

"What can I do?" I say, eagerly.

"Let me be your friend until the mist of uncertainty blows away and my heart can see where to go."

How could anyone refuse such a request?

"You can rely on me," I say in my best "Rah, 'Rah, St Trinians!' manner.

"Blessa you." Alfonso's divine lips immortalise the back of my hand. "Oh, my little Tuppence. If you knewa the effort it has cost me to plucka upa courage to talk with you." He shakes his head and closes his eyes as if trying to shut out some horrible memory. "I have done so many evil things. Cheated, betrayed, lied." He shudders pitiably. "Made love to thousands of women and deserted them. You know why?" I shake my head. "I was looking for something." That figures. "Something I dida not believa existed until I saw the two of you. Mental love. Love of the mind. Not mere passion that is gone as soon as it is come. Not the wild physical rutting of animals that I used to indulge in night after night. That is passed. Finished!"

51

"Oh," I say. "You don't think – no, well I suppose you know best."

"You mean, you believed all that drivel?" says Kate when I tell her of my conversation with Alfonso. "Really. You are so gullible where men are concerned."

Half an hour later I see Alfonso and Kate wandering along the foredeck with Alfonso gesticulating into the sky and Kate gazing up at him spellbound. "It's an amazing coincidence isn't it?" she says when I see her later. "Falling for the two of us like that."

"Oh. So you believe him now, do you? I thought you said he was talking drivel?"

"Well, I was a bit septical – I mean sceptical – before I spoke to him, but he's so honest isn't he? I mean about all those women."

"Yes," I enthuse, "and he didn't mention money once."

We look at each other. "You don't think, by some incredible, one in a million chance, that he might just be on the level?"

"I don't know," I say. "I really don't know."

By the time evening comes we are both in a complete tizzy and have decided that as far as Alfonso is concerned it is a case of may the best woman win! In our cramped cabin, or 'The Shoe Box' as Kate calls it, there is no room to swing a cat and even less for two very determined ladies to prepare themselves for mortal combat. When we enter the ball-room we are hardly on speaking terms.

"You look lovely, my dears," says Rachel. "Why don't you both have him?"

Kate's expression suggests that she finds the idea both vulgar and repellent. "Please!" she says.

"What's the matter with her?" enquires Mrs P.

"It would take too long to explain" I say.

"What's he been saying to you?" says Rachel suspiciously. "You don't want to believe a word, you know."

"She's jealous, poor old thing," says Kate, as we move away.

"Obviously," I agree with her.

But, by the end of the evening I am very grateful to

Rachel Pickering. To my despair and consternation Alfonso proceeds to pay Kate far far more attention than me. Sure, he dances with me a couple of times, and there are tears in his eyes, but it is Kate he seems to be pouring his heart out to. When I see them on the dance floor he is holding her tight in his arms and whispering into her ear in a way that just does not happen with me. I have a number of dances which I enjoy, but nothing that can rid my mind of a passionate desire to be made love to by Alfonso. It is the first time that I can ever remember being actively jealous of Kate.

Rachel is not slow to see what is happening. "Looks as if Kate has got her talons into Alfonso or vice versa," she says. "What are your plans?"

"I think I'll go for a swim."

"In the pool?"

"No. In the sea."

"Don't be like that, dear." Mrs P. takes me by the arm and guides me to a chair. "Do you still fancy young Gentleman?"

"That's no good. I had a dance with him and he could hardly string five words into a sentence."

"He's still so shy, that's why."

"If you say that again I'll scream."

"I'm sorry. Now, listen." Mrs P. darts a glance about her and lowers her voice – something she is not in the habit of doing. "I have a problem you might enjoy helping me with. Young Gentleman is on watch at the moment. When he comes off in half an hour he'll be going to my cabin."

"Congratulations," I say through gritted teeth.

"The thing is that I've just made some alternative plans. I don't want to disappoint Richard and it occurred to me that you might like to stand in for me?"

"But I terrify him."

"There's no reason why he should know it's you. We always do it with the light off – my figure isn't what it was – and he's not a great talker as you know. You just have to lie there and snaffle him."

Of course it is absolutely ridiculous but – I look across the room and see Alfonso and Kate leaving the dance floor hand in hand.

"O.K." I say. "What have I got to lose that I haven't lost already?"

Mrs. P. tells me the number of her cabin, hopes that I have 'a nice time' and returns to the arms of her next prospective lover. He looks like the man responsible for driving the ship so I hope he has a reliable deputy.

Rachel's cabin is far more sumptuous than 'The Shoe Box' and I begin to get cold feet the minute I am through the door. What a stupid idea the whole thing was! What on earth made me agree to it? I am on the point of going back to my own cabin when it occurs to me that I may well find it occupied. Kate and Alfonso looked as if they were going off to find a quiet spot and Alfonso has nowhere to lie his head. Kate will hardly thank me for interrupting her idyll. What am I going to do? I do not fancy sleeping in a lifeboat. Better take advantage of Mrs P.'s bed. She will not be using it – lucky old thing! I slip off my dress, tights, bra and panties and peel back the sheets. Richard probably won't show up anyway. Still – I go into the bathroom and rub some toothpaste round my teeth. One might as well prepare for any eventuality. My toilet completed, I slip into bed and pull up the sheets. How delicious to feel some space above my head and not the mass of pipes that press down above my bunk. In the distance I can hear music which means that the ball is still going on. I wonder what Alfonso and Kate are doing. No! don't think of that. The minutes go by and I turn on the light and look at my watch. Richard should be off duty in fifteen minutes. Wait a minute! The lights! I had better do something about those. Using my panties to protect my fingers against the heat, I unscrew both the bulbs in the room. I am now safe from being recognised unless Richard carries a flashlight. Not that he will turn up, of course. I turn my back on the door and try to sleep. Not a chance. I hear every sound, every footstep on the deck outside. It is as if I am waiting for a bomb to go off. How long I lie like this it is impossible to say but, suddenly, I hear a click and a splinter of light bisects the wall in front of me. I hold my breath and feel absolutely horrified. There is the sound of clothing being discarded and the sheets are drawn back as a body slips in beside me. I smell after-shave lotion and hear a long drawn out sigh, as cold hands steal round my tummy. Richard might have warmed himself up a bit after coming off watch but I expect he is eager to avail himself of Mrs P.'s charms. I make a mumbling noise suggestive, I hope, of someone being awoken from deep sleep and turn on to my back. There is a reciprocal moan and a mouth finds its way to mine and kisses it deep and long. Evil wanton that I am, I can feel myself responding and return the kiss with interest, letting my hands slide down the slim, firm buttocks of my unseen lover. He presses himself against me and I feel him long and strong, eager to show that he is ready to take me. His hands stroke my breasts and then travel down my body as they give way to his mouth. He nibbles the cherries at my breasts while his gentle fingers stroke me to melting readiness.

Mrs. Pickering was right. Richard Gentleman is revealing signs of unsuspected skill. 'Still waters run deep' and all that kind of thing. You have to hand it to her as a talent spotter. Him as well.

Unable to restrain myself any longer I send down my fingers as messengers of my desire and draw him into me. He fills well and I groan in happy pleasure as we bend to each other's rhythm. I would like to speak to him but there is in our silence a mysterious excitement that stimulates my already ravenous appetites. It is as well that my lover has stamina as well as style for I am in need of more than ordinary satisfaction. How often, in my wilder moments, have I lain in my lonely bed and wished that I could press a magic button and be transported into the arms of a lusty lad in a similar state of deprivation to myself. In a way this fantasy has now come true.

At last, Richard kisses me tenderly and withdraws from the bed. He pulls on his clothes and I ache to hear his voice. Surely now, after what we have done together, we will be able to speak to each other. The tongue-tied fumblings will be swept aside. We will be two grown-up people, frank in the knowledge of the precious possession we have shared. I stretch out my hand and Richard takes it and bends to brush my lips with his. It is farewell. The words build up in my throat but find no release before my lover has gone. I feel elated yet at the same time saddened.

Exhausted and physically satisfied I curl up and prepare for sleep. Whatever else it has done my experience has cured my jealousy of Kate. Good luck to both of them. I close my eyes and release a long, contented sigh.

At that moment the door opens again. My first reaction is that it must be Rachel returning earlier than expected. Thank goodness she did not come back even earlier. I am about to speak when I hear Richard Gentleman's voice.

"I'm sorry I'm late," he says, sounding very breathless. "I had to report to the bridge. Are you asleep? Oh, Rachel. I have missed you so much."

At first I cannot think what he is talking about. And then it hits me! The other fellow was not Richard. A whiff of after-shave lotion that wafts into my nostrils proves the point. What am I going to do? I can hear the real Richard's clothes hitting the floor and his heavy breathing matching my thumping heart. Should I confess? Before I have made up my mind the sheets are torn off the bed and a heavy body plumps down beside me.

"God, I feel sexy!" gasps my new visitor in a most un-Richard-like manner. He draws me to him and proceeds to lick my neck and plunder the area between my legs. Ah well, I think. If I say anything it will be very embarrassing for everyone and put Rachel in a spot. Also, I am beginning to enjoy myself again. I pull the sheets up over the two of us and prepare to put a brave face on it.

It is seven o'clock the next morning when I stagger back to my cabin and there has been no sign of Rachel. I do not know how she manages to keep it up night after night. I have had about two hours sleep and I am exhausted. Not that I am complaining, mind you.

With that natural sense of delicacy for which the Suttons are renowned I gently open the cabin door and peep inside. Kate is curled up in her bunk and there is no sign of Alfonso. I examine Kate's face for the symptoms of lingering ecstasy but there is nothing. Her clothes are strewn all over the floor, but then they always are.

Eager to tell her my news I shake her awake and ask her the inevitable question. "What was it like?"

"Go away," says Kate.

56

"Didn't he make love to you?"

Kate looks as if she is going to burst into tears. "I don't want to talk about it."

"Kate. What happened? Couldn't he do it?"

Kate turns her head so that one eye is staring reproachfully from the pillow. "It wasn't like that at all. We spent one of the most marvellous evenings of my life, and then we came back here." She pauses and I crane forward eagerly. "Filthy little hole!"

"What happened?"

"We took off our clothes."

"Yes!"

"And then I lay down on one of the bunks."

"Yes!!"

"And then he tried to get in and slipped a disc. It was awful. He couldn't move without experiencing the most excruciating agony. In the end he had to crawl away down the corridor with a bath towel draped over him." She looks at me. "That's right. That's typical. That's just what I'd expect from you."

I know it is very unkind but I am laughing until the tears run down my cheeks.

CHAPTER FOUR

I never do find out who my mystery lover was. I thought that perhaps Mrs P. would be able to throw some light on the matter, but she never mentions it and I am not anxious to confide in her that I had two lovers that night.

I am just an old-fashioned girl at heart, you see.

Poor Alfonso has to be put in plaster and is a pitiable sight as he lies in a Bath chair on the foredeck.

"What did you do to him, dear?" asks Rachel admiringly. "Have you been reading some of those Eastern sex manuals?"

Kate's reply is not printable. I feel very sorry for Alfonso because his whole livelihood must be in jeopardy. You cannot afford to take chances with yourself if you are a gigolo. At least, I am relieved to find he does have a cabin of his own. I had a sad picture of him crawling round the companion-ways on his hands and knees until the ship berthed.

Richard Gentleman continues to be ultra-polite and slightly tongue-tied whenever I see him and several times I am on the point of spilling the beans and seeing what he says. Some strange almost imperceptible streak of decency buried deep within me makes me hold my tongue.

Not entirely to my surprise, the romance between Kate and Alfonso fades faster than bottled sun tan once Dream-fodder is confined to his Bath chair. Rachel confides that she has cancelled the heiress rumour and certainly Alfonso's indifference dates from that moment.

"Heiress today and gone tomorrow" I say, while Kate winces.

Neither of us is too disturbed, because the Australian continent is now visible and we are within a day's sail of Sydney. All our shipboard activities seem very unimportant and our thoughts are firmly directed towards the future.

Of course, my account of our life on board has not covered any of our trips ashore and I could write a book about those alone. (Please do! Ed.) However, this tome is supposed to be about our adventures in Australia and it occurs to me that we had better hurry up and get there before someone asks for their money back!

I do not know what the eight wonders of the world are supposed to be but I'm prepared to bet that Sydney Harbour must be one of them. And that bridge! Looming out of an early morning mist borrowed from London, it takes the breath away.

Kate and I huddle together on the rail and feel our excitement cutting through the early morning chill. It is the size and modernity of the place that so impresses. I think that both Kate and I had formed a picture of the country as it might have been when the first convict set eyes on it. Three gum trees, two Koala bears, a few wooden houses and millions of acres of bush. We are not prepared for a sight that more than stands comparison with any city in the world. As we watch the shore getting closer so the sky begins to flood with light and we see Australia's most precious asset – the sun.

"I don't think they're going to be there," says Kate, who has a habit of bathing every occasion in melodrama.

"They're going to lose their investment if they're not," I say. "What makes you so pessimistic?"

"I don't know. It's just a feeling." In fact, I know that Kate is only saying that to make sure that they are there. She believes that the fates will take a delight in proving her wrong and lean over backwards to have Peter and Bruce lining up on the quayside.

"Good-bye 'Shoe Box'," says Kate as we close the door of our cabin, "and good luck to all who sail in you. Because they're going to need it!"

We go up on deck and take a last look at the swimming pool, scene of my greatest triumph. Rodney Cole walks past and pretends that he does not see us.

"I don't know why they bother with a swimming pool," says Kate. "If they had a hole going straight through the middle of the ship you could swim in the sea. Think of the money it would save."

"Supposing you couldn't swim? You'd fall out of the bottom and be chopped up by the propellers."

Kate thinks for a moment. "You could put a net in it."

"Of course. Well, there you are. Why don't you talk to the Captain about it?"

"Do you think he's the right person? I mean, he's just responsible for the ship when it's finished. He doesn't have anything to do with designing it. I think I'd better get in touch with the steamship company."

"You do that," I humour her. "And make sure you talk to the top man. You don't want anyone stealing your idea."

"You're right," says Kate. "You can't be too careful these days."

The ship berths after lengthy manoeuvres and our eyes comb the quayside for a sight of Peter or Bruce. It suddenly occurs to me that we are going to have problems if neither of them turns up because the only address I have is that of Peter's family home outside Sydney. The quayside

59

is thronged with people and it is not easy to pick out anyone.

"They all look healthy," says Kate. "Nice tans." She is right. The Aussie muscle lined up to greet us is impressive. "I knew they wouldn't turn up though."

"Shut up!" I snap. "Look! There they are!"

Peter is wearing a plaid shirt and gazing up at the side of the liner. Bruce is drinking from a can. Surely not at eight o'clock in the morning? Oh well, I guess they do things differently in Australia.

"Yoo Hoo!" sings out Kate. "Here we are!" She starts hollering and waving, but it is a waste of time because nobody on the quayside can hear her.

Eventually Peter does recognise us and waves enthusiastically, but it is another half hour before we are embracing.

"Hello, you beaut sheila," he says, flinging his arms wide. "Have you been a good girl, or just been having a good time?"

I hope he does not expect an answer to that, and gratefully dive into his arms. Immediately he hugs me I experience that special feeling of security that makes me forget the thousands of miles that now separate me from the life I have left behind. I burrow into his embrace and am not surprised to find tears stinging my cheeks. It is the smell of him that I respond to most. Rough, male and with an outdoor tang that seems to belong far beyond the boundaries of the city. A very individual and very Australian smell.

"Have you lost your voice?" he says.

"It's been such a long time," I say. "I've thought about this moment so many times that now it's here I'm speechless."

"Don't worry," he says. "We'll go and have some coffee. That will lubricate your larynx. Have you got your baggage under control?"

If we did not have the boys with us I do not think Kate and I would ever see our hold luggage again. Mind you, I think that says more about Kate and me than it does about the Baggage Master. When we have eventually got everything together Peter whisks us away in an enormous car

60

called a Holden. I am now getting used to the fact that the streets of Sydney are not lined with gold prospectors wearing long beards and slouch hats, so it is no surprise when we pull up outside a very modern hotel and Peter tosses the ignition keys to a parking attendant. We go through to the terrace and there, with a fabulous view of the ocean stretched out below us, I confide some of my preconceptions to an amused Peter and Bruce.

"Don't shed your illusions too quickly," says Bruce. "It isn't all like this. We can promise you a basinful of Old Aussie that will be just as you imagined it. Right, Pete?"

"Right, sport. Some of the places you girls will be flying out to haven't changed since Ned Kelly's day."

"He played the trumpet, didn't he?" says Kate, innocently.

"No!" I say, eager to show how knowledgeable I am. "He was a famous bushwagger."

"Whacker," says Peter with a grin.

"I must have been thinking of Wagga Wagga," I say.

"Or even Wogga Wogga," says Bruce drily. "Aren't we lucky to have found two girls who already know so much about the country?"

"Very," says Peter. "I only hope we'll be able to use them."

"What do you mean?" we squeal. "We travel twelve thousand miles and you say you may not be able to use us?"

"Relax, relax." Peter holds up his hands. "It's just that all the money isn't through yet and one of my father's partners wants to see you before he puts in his share. It's only a formality. He's a very thorough operator, this joker. He likes to check over every piece of a deal before he chucks in his ante."

"Your letter didn't say anything about that."

"No. I'm probably a fool to mention it now. It's so unimportant. Just a formality. The old guy is giving a party tonight and we're all invited along. It's a beach barbecue. Enjoy it for itself."

"And keep your hands off the spoons or you may be on the next boat back," says Kate.

Bruce shakes his head. "We should never have raised

61

the subject. Even if the guy does back out it's not the end of the project."

"Not that he will back out, of course" says Peter firmly.

Kate looks at me quizzically. "Do you believe these two silver-tongued antipodean charlatans?" she asks.

"Nobody has even called me an antipodean charlatan before," says Bruce admiringly." Did you go to Roedean or something?"

" 'Or something','' I say, unkindly, wondering where on earth Kate dredged the phrase up from.

"You're probably tuckered out after your trip" says Peter hurriedly. "I expect you'd like to see where you'll be slee – I mean, staying? We thought of booking you into one of the large hotels and then it struck us that you'd probably prefer something more homely after so long at sea."

"How thoughtful," says Kate. "After the last few weeks, anything larger than a rabbit hutch would be spectacular."

"My parents have got a place along the coast a bit," says Bruce. "You can spend a few days there getting acclimatised before we move up country."

"How long is it going to be before we actually start doing some work?" I ask.

"Very soon," says Peter. "The airline is a going concern. We're only after more cash to expand. Get some more airplanes and that sort of thing. That's where Renfrew comes in. He's the guy you'll be meeting tonight. If you two girls can turn on the charm we'll be in like Flynn."

"How old is he?" asks Kate.

"Mature."

"Married?"

"Three times. And divorced three times."

"Will we like him?"

"He'll like you," says Bruce evasively.

Bruce's parents live in a ranch-style bungalow and could not be nicer. They make us feel at home from the minute we cross the threshold. "The boys were all for putting you up in a fancy hotel," says Mrs Wilson, "but we wouldn't hear of it. We said 'Those poor girls will have had quite enough of tinned vegetables and noisy air conditioning. You bring them home'. What's the matter Brucey?"

Bruce has been vainly signalling at his mother to shut up and is now thoroughly embarrassed. "Nothing, Ma," he says, while Kate and I exchange smiles.

After we have been shown to our rooms and unpacked, the boys suggest a swim and we jump at the idea. It is half past eleven and the sun is really giving us a taste of what life in Australia is all about. On the way to the beach we cannot resist teasing them about the hotel manoeuvre. "I don't think those naughty boys wanted us to stay at Bruce's home," says Kate. "I think they wanted to install us in some anonymous hotel where we would be a prey to their deprived appetites."

"You mean 'depraved', don't you?" I say.

"It comes to the same thing" says Peter. "It's been a long time since we last saw you both."

"I can't believe that you've existed all that while without female company?" I say.

"Virtually," says Bruce. "We had tea with Peter's aunt one afternoon but that was about it."

"Very funny," says Kate. "That seems highly likely, I must say."

"What about you?" asks Peter. "Didn't you meet anyone on the boat? I bet you've got a score of telephone numbers tucked away."

"Not a score," says Kate, so it sounds like the real number is nearer eighteen. In fact the only passenger who pressed an invitation on us was Jack Truman, an eighty-five year old cabinet maker from Leeds, going out to visit his daughter who had married a Greek who ran an Italian restaurant in a part of Sydney known as King's Cross.

"How's your fiancée?" I ask Peter who frowns.

"My *ex*-fiancée?" he says firmly. "I haven't seen her since I've been back."

"Of course. You haven't been back long enough to renew all your old acquaintances, have you?"

"I won't be renewing that one," says Peter grimly and I think it wise to change the subject.

When we get to the beach I do not feel like getting out of the car. The surf would cover a small house and the waves are coming in with a force that suggests they have a personal grievance against the shore.

"I'm not going to swim in that," says Kate. "I'll drown in it but I won't swim in it."

"There's a bit of surf running –"

"That makes two of us," I interrupt. "I'm running as well. Kate's right. I wouldn't ask Rodney Cole to swim in that."

"For Chrissakes! Who the hell is Rodney Cole? Is that some kind of limey slang?"

"It would take too long to explain," says Kate. "You must understand, fellas. I only have to look at all that water to get goose pimples. It is very rough. R-U-F-F. Rough."

"Once you swim through the surf it's O.K.," says Bruce cheerfully.

"I would rather try and swim through a mincing machine," says Kate.

"You've got to get used to it," says Peter. "Around here little kids would go out in a sea like that."

"How many of them would come back?" I ask.

"Don't be ridiculous!" says Bruce. "We'll be with you."

"Just the two of you? I want a team of life savers before I venture in to that. Where are they?"

"They're down the beach a few miles where someone might need them."

"Typical. You can't get us into a hotel and your airline will never get off the ground, so you're going to do us in."

"Do you in what?"

"Drown us!"

"Drown you! How ridiculous can you get?"

"I don't know. I've never tested myself. Look – " Kate points a shaking finger towards the sea – "even if we do get through the surf, what about the sharks?"

Peter shakes his head. "We very rarely get sharks inshore around here."

" 'Very rarely' is a lot too often for me," I say.

Bruce points to a hut on stilts. "That guy is employed to keep a lookout for sharks and people in difficulties."

"I don't care if a shark is in difficulty," says Kate. "He should concentrate on the people."

'God help us," says Peter, slapping the flat of his hand against his forehead.

"Anyway, I don't see what he can do up there except report on the action: 'It's unbelievable, folks. The little lady has beaten off the man-eaters and is dragging herself ashore now. Give her a big hand'. And a foot, and an arm, and – "

"Stop it, Kate!" I squeak.

"O.K. girls. you stay here and swelter," says Peter. "Don't say we didn't try and tempt you."

" 'Tempt'!" sniffs Kate. "You must be joking."

We settle down on the beach and pretend that we are not watching like hawks as the boys disrobe. If you males thought that you were the only ones casing the joints on a crowded beach, then I have news for you. Everything – and more – we have seen before but it looks a lot better with a coating of sun-tan, and these two Aussie fellas are a couple of beauts, to use their own parlance. Lean and hungry with a suggestion of muscle where you need it, rather than mini Michelin tyre-men. For over-developed men I have no yen.

Kate and I thought that we had worked up a good tan but when we look around us we feel like a couple of slugs. If some of these people left Australia they would have trouble getting in again. Talk about brown! They make Cassius Clay look pallid.

"See you later, girls."

The boys bound down to the sea and plunge into the surf with a disdain that makes me feel very chicken-hearted. Half a dozen lusty strokes and they have breasted the waves and can be seen bobbing up and down on the swell.

"He's gorgeous, isn't he?" says Kate, dreamily.

"They both are," I say.

"I'm sorry they didn't book us into that hotel," says Kate.

"Shameless baggage!" I scold her. "But, seriously. We've got to be careful how we conduct ourselves. We're very much in the position of the secretary who sleeps with her boss. It could prejudice things in the long term."

"How wise," says Kate. "How I admire your ability to step outside a situation and take a cool objective look at it before returning to carry on exactly as you would have done if you had never bothered to move in the first place."

"Thank you," I say. "You may scoff but, if you think about it, you'll realise that I'm right."

"Maybe. But I didn't have quite such a passionate trip as you. Remember?"

I have not got an answer to that one which would not involve me in a heated argument so I return my attention to surrounding hunks. Even in a bikini I am soon beginning to feel very hot and this prompts my sense of adventure.

"Come on, Kate," I say. "Let's give it a try."

"Swimming!? You must be mad. Wild sea-horses wouldn't drag me into that lot."

Kate will not be budged so eventually, feeling very brave, I set off down the beach by myself. Now that I have been watching the sea for a while it does not seem quite so menacing. As Peter said, even small children brave the breakers without showing fear, so it cannot be too bad. I had hoped that Peter would see me and come inshore to give moral and physical support but he is a long way out now and would not hear me even if I shouted. I feel the surf whip against my ankles and immediately all my old fears return. Frankly, even the most placid sea fills me with foreboding. It is so vast and implacable, hiding so much from the eye. Here, the feeling of inadequacy is magnified a hundredfold. Looking to right and left the breakers stretch for as far as the eye can see without any manmade bulwarks to restrain them. To the limit of the horizon the waves have a whetted curl. Now that I have come so near I cannot turn back and run the gauntlet of all those sun-bronzed Aussies. I must go in. Swallowing my fear, I step forward and immediately feel the pull of the undertow. My fear is regurgitated swiftly. Supposing I cannot get back? I reject the thought. I must be able to get back. The surf breaks across my thighs and knocks me back a couple of paces. I feel that everyone on the beach is watching and laughing. I must not look back. Pull yourself together, Sutton. There is only one way for you to go. Forward! I must judge the waves carefully because if I got underneath one if would be like a house falling on me.

The water is up to my waist now and ahead of me I can see a wave beginning to curl. Don't panic! DON'T PANIC!!

It is no good. I know that wave has my name written on it. I turn round and desperately start wading to the shore, feeling the water holding me back like the grip of restraining arms. Behind me I can sense the monster wave girding itself to strike me down. Rearing up, trembling, curling at the edges – WHOOSH!! I am swatted like a fly and feel myself turning over and over in the water. It is almost a pleasant situation. I feel relieved. And then – wham! I hit the beach with a force that half stuns me. I try and struggle to my feet and am bowled over again. Another wave breaks over me and I cartwheel through the surf and flounder towards safety. The undertow still plucks at my ankles but my panic is stronger and I break free and stagger to firm sand.

For a few moments I can only stand with my eyes closed, drawing in great mouthfuls of air. Nearly drowned on my first day! What a beginning.

Eventually, feeling calmer, I pat my hair into place and start to walk back up the beach. The first few people I pass hardly look up so I do not feel that my escapade was seen by everybody. Thank goodness! I take a few more paces and then observe that I am getting a lot of glances. Flattering ones. Even two girls nudge each other as I walk by. The ultimate compliment. I have been feeling quite pretty lately. The rest and the sea trip must have done me good. I cast myself down gracefully beside Kate who is sitting with her head resting on the back of her hands.

"What's the matter?" I say. "Are you all right?"

Kate does not move and speaks out of the corner of her mouth.

"Your bikini top has slipped down to your waist," she says.

CHAPTER FIVE

"Call yourself a friend!" I say to Kate, later. "How could you let me walk up the beach like that?"

"What do you expect me to do? Shout 'Your boobs are hanging out!' at the top of my voice? Anyway I didn't notice till you were nearly on top of me."

"Well, there was no need to mention the incident to Peter and Bruce. I was humiliated enough as it was."

"It didn't make any difference. Everybody on the beach was talking about it. They would soon have found out. I thought it was very funny. I can't see what you've being so uptight about."

"You would if it had happened to you," I say, thinking that Kate can be incredibly thoughtless for someone who is supposed to be my best friend.

"Do you think Peter was serious when he started talking about topless stewardesses?"

"What do you think? Can you imagine what it would be like balancing a pot of hot coffee against your naked boobs. And think of the effect on the passengers. Most of them go ape when you've got all your clothes on."

"Yes. And I don't expect the International Air Transport Authority would allow it either."

"Of course not. If you allow one airline to have topless stewardesses somebody else will have their girls in black suspender belts, and so on till we're all parading down the aisle starkers and it's compulsory to make every first-class passenger a member of the Mile High Club."

"Don't. I'd rather put on a nun's habit."

"Now there's an idea for you. 'The Flying Nuns'. It would be very distinctive, wouldn't it? Inspire confidence too. 'Fly with the Flying Nuns. Whatever happens you'll be in heaven.'"

"Cloud number 707. I like it. It would get stuffy, though, wouldn't it? They would have to build some air conditioning into the habits."

" 'Fill in a complaints form if you find any of our girls

have dirty habits.' You know, I think we've got a great idea here."

I do not think I have ever been able to remain angry with Kate for longer than two hours. She can be exasperating but she is more fun to be with than any other three girls I know. Not that I know a lot of girls. I have been too busy chasing men to meet many.

When we get back to the Wilson's house we have lunch on the terrace and I have a chance to see how the whole place can be opened up to take full advantage of the weather. Walls slide back or are lifted like hatches and it is possible to stand outside and see right through to the vegetation on the other side of the house without the eye being hindered by even a pane of glass. At first this openness seems rather strange after the constriction of so many western rooms but we very soon get used to it.

"You have a beautiful house, Mr Wilson," I say to our host.

"Thank you, my dear. We're quite proud of it."

"That's the understatement of the year, Dad. And you know it. There isn't a house to touch this one anywhere along the coast," says Bruce.

"I don't know. The Renfrew place isn't bad," says Mr Wilson as if he could be given an argument on the subject.

"What's Mr Renfrew like?" I ask.

"Anything in a skirt," says Mr Wilson.

"Tom!" Mrs W. looks put out.

"Well, it's true. Everybody knows it. The girls will find out soon enough. You're going there tonight, aren't you?"

Bruce nods hurriedly as if caught off balance by the question. "Yeah. We're looking in for a couple of tubes. The house isn't a patch on this one, though, dad. I don't fancy the position much either. It's too near the sea. The noise gets a bit much if you have it on top of you all the time." Bruce rambles on like this and it becomes obvious to me that he does not want to talk about his reason for going to the Renfrew house that evening. This is very surprising because one would have thought that Mr Wilson would have known all about the airline enterprise if not actually being a stakeholder in it. I decide to discuss the subject with Kate.

"Maybe Renfrew and Mr Wilson had an argument. Mr Wilson didn't seem to like him much".

"Maybe. But I think there was more to it than that. This airline deal is more complicated than we thought."

The boys disappear 'on business' after coffee so we do not have the opportunity to tax them on the subject.

The Wilsons have a swimming pool and Kate and I agree that this is far more our scene than the wild ocean. Lying beside it I am able to observe how the house has been sculpted into its surroundings so as to be almost united with them. The open plan nature of its construction means that plants and vines grow 'through' the walls and create the feeling of a joyous harmony with nature. It is no surprise to learn that Mr Wilson is an architect of some standing in Australia.

Mrs Wilson continues to be kindness itself and even insists that we book a phone call home to tell our parents that we have arrived safely. I feel so guilty when she does this because I have not thought of my mother and father since we landed. The call comes through an hour later and I learn that there is snow at home. It seems so funny hearing that while I sit in gorgeous sunshine. Also, to think that it is dark in England. Mum and dad's voices come and go and it is difficult to conduct a conversation apart from the awkwardness of trying to find something to say. I had always thought that people on inter-continental radio hook-ups sounded incredibly tongue-tied but now I find myself in exactly the same position. It is like visiting someone in hospital. The confrontation with the familiar in unusual surroundings seems to reduce one to talking about trivia. I am not helped by the knowledge that the Wilsons are paying for the call. Every second must be costing a fortune. Thankfully, my canny parents are well aware of this and they soon wish me God's blessing and ring off. It is strange but it is only when I am holding the dead receiver that I really feel aware of how far away I am from them and burst into tears. Kate responds in exactly the same fashion so once again we are left blubbing in each other's arms.

At about four o'clock we partake of a cup of tea and Mrs Wilson asks what time we will be going out. We do not know so it is agreed that we will all meet up again for a 'sundowner' at six and go to our rooms in the meantime. Oh, the ecstasy of having a room to myself again. Much as I love Kate I do like a little privacy sometimes. I would never share a flat unless I had my own bedroom. I settle down and decide that I will wash my hair, cut my nails and catch up on my correspondence. And what happens? The next think I know is that Kate is tapping on my door and telling me that it is six o'clock! I have drifted off to sleep and accomplished nothing. I am furious with myself because I had intended to look my very best when I emerged from the bedroom. I drag a comb through my hair and apply some make-up, knowing that Kate will be at her radiant best, and make my way to the terrace, feeling like Cinderella going to the ball after the fairy godmother had failed to show up. As anticipated Kate is looking like a million dollars and I notice her critical eye giving me the once over. Although it was nothing to do with her I find myself trying to find some reason why she should have come round earlier.

"They look all right, don't they?" says Peter.

"They'll do," says Bruce.

If you thrive on honeyed compliments I cannot recommend a trip to Australia. An Aussie male will seldom remark favourably on anything you are wearing unless you drag it out of him. And if he has his cobbers with him – that is it. He would as soon utter a compliment as slip on a ballet skirt. By Australian standards Peter and Bruce have just enacted a love scene from Romeo and Juliet.

"They look lovely! What's the matter with you?" says confidence-boosting Mrs Wilson. "Don't just stand there. Give the girls a drink."

Mr Wilson is wearing a white tuxedo but the boys are both in shirts and slacks. Nobody seems to dress up too much except for very formal parties. I have a whisky sour and Mrs Wilson, or Joan as she tells us to call her, asks if we are eating in.

"I don't think so, Ma. There should be some grub where we're going."

We have another drink and then Peter looks at his watch and suggests that we should be on our way. There is now a fabulous new, gunmetal Jensen-Healey outside which he waves us into.

"I brought the Holden to the ship because I thought it would have more room for your baggage," he says matter of factly.

"I was surprised that your father didn't seem to know about the airline deal," I say to Bruce.

It is Peter who replies. "Bruce's old man is only interested in architecture. He doesn't fill his mind with a lot of other things. Right, Brucey?"

"That's right, Pete. He's all wrapped up in his work."

"I'm looking forward to meeting your father," says Kate to Peter.

"He'll be there tonight, won't he?"

"There's a chance he may have to miss it," says Peter. "He's got something important on in Newcastle and he may not be back in time."

"Newcastle? He won't be back for days," says Kate.

"Not the Newcastle in England, sweetheart. We have our own poor colonial substitute up the coast."

"Oh," I say, thinking it all sounds pretty strange. "Who else will be there tonight?"

"I don't know exactly," says Peter. "Mostly Renfrew's friends, I guess. Like we said. It's all very informal. Just a chance for the old basket to meet you."

"He's a business associate of your father's, is he?" I say suspiciously.

"They've done business in the past. Cripes! You girls certainly ask a lot of questions, don't you?"

"I find it's the only way I can get any answers," I say. "And even then it's not always easy."

"I thought we were hiring you girls as stewardesses, not management consultants."

"We throw in the service as a free bonus – oops!"

"Sorry," says Bruce innocently. "Was that your leg?"

I suppose the boys are right about it being none of our business but, having come twelve thousand miles for a job, I am keen to see that it does not evaporate. Peter and Bruce are obviously both loaded and I have no worries that they are suddenly going to welsh on us. It is just that I feel we are being told less than the whole truth and this rankles. I suppose that if I was not sleeping with Peter I might feel differently, and this is an example of what I was saying to Kate. If you are having an affair with someone you expect them to be on the level with you about everything. You cannot separate their business life from their private life if you are playing a part in both.

Bruce is right about the Renfrew pad. It is impressive but not up to the Wilson standard. Grander, but fighting against its surroundings rather than blending with them. Standing nearly on the beach it looks like a tanker that has been washed ashore. Long and oblong. One incongruous feature is the pair of stone heraldic beasts mounted at the end of the driveway. They do not seem to belong in Australia. I point them out to Kate and Peter smiles grimly. "Renfrew is what we call a new Australian. There's a lot like him still in the old country."

"Some people would like to see even more," says Bruce and both men laugh.

No sooner has the car drawn up than two enormous alsatians appear with saliva dripping from their jaws. "Don't leave your arms hanging over the side of the car or they'll have them for breadsticks," warns Bruce. I need no second warning and cower apprehensively whilst my least favourite dogs throw back their heads and start to bark loudly.

"Dasher! Dancer!" The voice sounds like that of a well-bred, supercilious Englishman. Not the flat, honest Australian vowels I am becoming used to. The dogs respond to what is, presumably, their master and slink round behind the heels of the man who presents himself to our gaze.

He is tall but heavily built to the point of fatness. About fifty I would say, with receding hair and a florid complexion that looks as if it has suffered from too much good living. It is not a face I take to, combining as it does elements of licentiousness and cruelty. This impression may be accentuated by the ridiculously frilly shirt which falls like a gutted candle over the spreading paunch, and the downwards set of the mouth. I try to remember where I have last seen anything quite like that mouth, and then it comes to me: on a fishmonger's slab. The cold eyes are a good match for it. They gaze at Kate and I much as I imagine a trout must look at a tasty morsel drifting past its lair.

"Evening, Hugh," says Peter with less than his usual confidence. "I hope we're not too early."

"Never too early, Peter, especially with such charming companions."

Kate and I smile politely and step out of the car, keeping a wary eye on the alsatians. Hugh Renfrew is swift to offer a hand that grips with unneeded vigour.

'My name is Hugh Renfrew," explains our host. "You'll realise from the fact that you can understand what I am saying that I am a comparative newcomer to this land."

"Penny Sutton," I say. "I find that I can understand everybody I've met so far. I only hope they can understand me."

Renfrew throws up his hands. "What a diplomat! If only I wasn't so honest. How much easier life would be."

I am speedily deciding that H.R. could end up on my list of all-time hates but he is hardly into his stride.

"Another toy!" he exclaims, looking at the Jensen-Healey. "I don't understand what you want my money for. Won't Daddy play ball?"

Peter does not have to answer that question because Renfrew attaches himself to Kate like a spider and scuttles into the house.

"What an awful man!" I hiss at Peter. "Do you really have to do business with him?"

"I'll talk to you about it later," mutters Peter as we cross the threshold.

The inside of the house seems very dark and gloomy but maybe this is because I am comparing it with Bruce's house, or because I have taken an instant dislike to the owner.

"I must say that your choice of stewardesses appeals to me tremendously" says Renfrew as we go into a room almost as large as one of the staterooms on the liner. "If they can recruit up to their own standard I will be very happy. Now, let me make a few introductions."

Huddled together by a giant stone fireplace are a group of people who look as if the conversation has been flowing like fish glue before we arrived. They look up hopefully as fresh blood is tipped into the circle and I find myself talking to a middle-aged man who says he is a banker. Inevitably, he asks me what I am doing in Sydney but when I tell him there is no glint of recognition. I had imagined that everybody present would be connected with the airline venture but this is clearly not the case. As I move round I find that those present are merely neighbours of Renfrew's. Mostly well-to-do but seeming to have no knowledge of, let alone interest in, the quaintly named Outback Airlines.

"More like Out Of Print Airlines" says Kate when we have a word together. "Nobody has heard of them."

"And for a local outfit in a place with so few people that's really saying something," I add. "What do you make of our host?"

"Gruesome. He keeps giving me sexy glances and trying to fill my glass up. I think he's getting ideas."

"I think he had them before we got here. Some of the people I talked to were intimating that he was a bit odd."

"Three divorces. He would have to be, wouldn't he? They can't all have been scheming minxes."

"More like screaming minxes if they were married to him for long. I can't make out what he's doing in the country."

"Apparently he had an uncle who had a sheep farm that was worth millions. The old boy left it to him because he was the only remaining male heir. He's only been here two years and one marriage. His last wife went back to England."

"Sensible girl. Look out. Here he comes. Buckle your chastity belts."

Renfrew sways towards us and it is difficult to know whether his exaggerated gait is an attempt to look seductive or the result of too many drinks. "Divine creatures," he gushes. "You have no idea how marvellous it is to find someone who can speak English in this God-forsaken hole."

"Don't you think you'd better lower your voice? Everybody in the room can hear you," says Kate.

"I don't give a bugger, darling. Excuse my French. I've only got to sort out a few legal complications, find a buyer

75

and I'll be out of this place before you can say 'thank God'."

"Which is what everybody else will say," says a quiet Australian voice behind me.

"But what about your involvement in Outback Airlines?" I ask.

"Ah, yes." Renfrew sounds as if he is thinking about the question for the first time. "That's up to you, isn't it?"

"What do you mean?"

"Well, if I feel that the proposition is right I might be tempted to invest." Renfrew rolls his eyes at us and something tells me I have been here before.

'I still don't understand," says Kate doggedly. "What has the business side of it got to do with us?"

"It depends what kind of business you're in," says Renfrew with a leer.

"If you mean what I think you mean – " I am winding myself up for the kind of brush off that needs a horse and cart to pick up the pieces, when a guest arrives to make his farewell and we take the opportunity to escape.

"Did you mean to ask him if he meant what I was meaning to ask you if you thought he meant?" says Kate.

"I'm not certain, but I think the answer is probably yes. Would you settle for a positive maybe?"

"I think that creep was definitely angling for services far beyond the call of duty."

"So do I. And a further unpleasant thought has struck me."

"Even the same that is at this moment circling inside mine own noddle, I mean." We nod at each other and make a grab for Peter and Bruce.

"Did you two creeps make a deal with Renfrew that depended on us sleeping with him?" says Kate. "I use the word 'sleeping' without any conviction that any such blissful release would ever present itself."

"What do you mean?" says Peter, looking stupified.

"Don't let's go through that again," says Kate. "You know what we mean: services rendered for services rendered."

"What has that joker been saying to you?" asks Peter.

We tell him the gist of Renfrew's remarks and Peter nods grimly. "I'm sorry girls. I hoped nothing like this would happen if we just dropped by for a drink. Let's get the hell out of the place. Renfrew can frig himself. We don't need his money."

I wish I could believe him. Something tells me that a man like Peter would never have come to Renfrew in the first place had there been any alternative. Unless he was trying to use us as bait, and I do not consider that a serious possibility. If the deal means so much to him maybe we should not be so hasty.

"Hold on a minute," I say. "We've been insulted by experts. This fellow can't eat us. I don't mind playing along with him as long as you two blokes realise that our contract doesn't include sleeping with the customers."

"Of course it doesn't," says Peter. "But you don't have to stay here another minute. I'll tell Renfrew where his shooting stick can spend Christmas."

"Penny is right," says Kate. "We have to handle fellows like that every day of our lives. Often with the liquor falling out of their mouths. He won't trouble us."

Peter looks at Bruce who looks relieved. "Well, if you're certain you can handle it. Don't stand any nonsense. I'm not running an aerial call girl service. Renfrew knows that."

No sooner have we struck off on our own again than Renfrew heaves into view. "Ah. There you are. The only bit of class in the whole place. How glad I am that you could come."

I manage a winsome smile, but from the way Renfrew looks at Kate I can see it is going to be her evening. Lucky girl!

"I wonder if you'd care to take a turn round the house," he says. "It has one or two interesting features." Nothing in his tone suggests he means wall irons, and he sounds as if he has made a big effort to pull himself together.

"Er – yes," says Kate. "That would be nice. Wouldn't it?"

She is looking straight into my eyes as she says it so there is no chance of Sutton missing out on the invitation.

"Very interesting. I expect Peter and Bruce would like to see it."

77

"They've seen it," snaps Renfrew.

"Maybe they'd – "

"This way." Renfrew is opening a door beside the fireplace. We go through it and the boys waggle their fingers at us.

"Abandon hope all ye who enter here," mutters Penny.

"What was that?" inquires Renfrew civilly.

"Nothing, nothing," breezes Kate. "I was just saying what a band of dopes some of the immigrants are over here."

"Yes. But don't you find the locals a coarse breed?"

"I like coarse men," says Kate loyally.

An ugly flicker of excitement illuminates Renfrew's eyes. "Really?" he breathes. "How very interesting."

"What a silver-tongued little creature you are," I whisper to Kate. "When you were a kid I bet you went out with a bag of candy looking for dirty old men."

"What wicked secrets are you whispering about?" leers our host. "Nothing too indelicate, I hope?"

"I was wondering where the little girls' room is," says Kate.

"Of course. How inconsiderate of me."

Renfrew leads us down a passageway and up a flight of stairs. I am on the point of mentioning that we have just passed what seems like a perfectly acceptable loo when I think better of it. After all, it is his house so he can have us powder our noses wherever he wants us to.

"Here you are. You can use the one in the master bedroom – just next to the mistressbed room." Renfrew kills himself at his little joke and Kate raises her eyebrows at me.

"What a laugh riot," she says when we are inside a loo that looks like it escaped from Grand Central Station. "Thank goodness you're with me. That guy gives my creeps the creeps."

"Sssh. He's probably listening outside the door. He's all right. Keep humouring him and then we can get out of here."

Kate hops on to the throne and I check my make-up. I am repairing my mouth when there is a loud crash from the room next door simultaneous with a yelp of pain and the wall-shelf opposite the loo falling to the floor.

"My God! What was that?" gasps Kate.

"Sounded like someone falling over," I say.

"It must be Renfrew. What on earth is he up to?"

It is when I start picking up the male cosmetic bottles that have fallen with the shelf that I begin to get an idea.

"He must have come down with a crash if he collapsed the shelf on this side," says Kate.

"Look!" I say. I have picked up the shelf to see how it fitted on to the wall and find myself looking at a small hole that does not match up with any of those that have held screws. It is bored immediately behind where the bottles were arranged.

"A spy hole!" says Kate.

"Looks like it."

We storm out of the bathroom to be met by Renfrew clutching a handkerchief to his bleeding forehead. He pushes past us and starts bathing his wound in the wash basin.

"Peeping Tom!" accuses Kate. "Fall off your soap box, did you?"

"I don't know what you're talking about," blusters Renfrew. "I banged my head on a cupboard door."

"What's this, then?" I say, indicating the peep-hole.

"I haven't the faintest idea. You don't think I put it there, do you?"

"Do you mind if I look next door?" says Kate.

"Not at all."

We go into the bedroom and find that there is a small circular mirror on the wall at a point consistent with the position of the shelf on the other side. Kate reaches up and removes it.

There, for all the world to see – and be seen through – is a neatly bored hole.

"Remarkable. I never knew that was there. I'll have it filled in tomorrow."

I turn away from Renfrew and look round the room. There is a wooden stool but it is standing by the bed. I walk over to it, pick it up and one of the legs topples over.

Kate and I look questioningly at Renfrew who shrugs his shoulders.

"Inferior Australian workmanship," he says. "Things fall apart round here. Now let me show you my pride and joy." He starts walking towards the door as if that is the end of the matter and I can see that Kate is on the point of exploding. No one could blame her but I feel obliged to weigh in with some restraint. If Renfrew gets his kicks from watching girls do pee-pees, then he is so pathetic that I see no point in making a deal-shattering scene about it. We don't have to be nice, just tolerant. "Are you sure you're fit enough to go through with the rest of the tour?" I ask, taking Kate's arm and steering her towards the door. "What is your 'pride and joy'? Something to do with flying?"

"No, no. Something with a historical bent" enthuses Renfrew.

"The 'bent' does not surprise me," mutters Kate. "I warn you. If that Peeping Tom comes up with any more tricks, I'm going to crown him."

"Try and stick it out. Remember, this deal is important to us as well as the boys."

"How important does it have to be? He'll be coming into the loo with us next time."

Renfrew is limping down the corridor ahead of us and we see him produce a key.

"Uh, uh," breathes Kate. "What are we in for now? I don't like this one little bit. He reminds me of Manchester."

"Manchester?" The connection escapes me.

Kate puts on her lofty intellectual expression. "The character in Jane Eyre, silly. He had his mad wife locked up in the west wing."

"That was Rochester," I tell her wearily.

"This way, ladies." Renfrew waves us past him into the room. "I think my little collection will make you feel quite homesick."

Well. He is half-right. It does make me sick. The first thing that strikes my eye is what looks like the cast of a dressmaker's dummy lined with spikes. Next to it is hanging a hideous flail with knotted thongs and a pair of thumbscrews. It soon becomes obvious that Renfrew collects instruments of torture.

"I not only have a bed chamber but a torture chamber," he croons.

"I should think they're the same place," whispers Kate.

"Look." Our host lovingly slips a set of manacles over his wrists, like a woman trying on a precious bracelet.

'They really suit you," I say.

"Feel free to try anything on that appeals to you," says Renfrew. "I find there is comfort in the kiss of cold metal."

"I've read about guys like this," says Kate.

"Most of this stuff comes from the old country, though I have one or two items from Germany – very well made, they are."

"I find it all rather horrifying," I say. "I don't like to think that these implements were used to inflict hideous pain on innocent people."

"Not always innocent" says Renfrew, reluctantly removing the manacles. "Many of them deserved to be punished. I think a certain amount of corporal chastisement is good for all of us, don't you?" He goes up to a gnarled wooden cross and spreads his arms along the horizontal timber, so that his fleshy back is exposed to us. "I don't mind pain. It can be therapeutic." He nods towards a riding crop that is lying nearby. "You can try if you like." He tightens his grip on the cross-piece and I feel a wave of nausea sweep over me.

"I think I'd like to go back to the others now," says Kate with a slight catch in her voice.

Renfrew turns to us and shakes his head bitterly. "You don't understand, do you? None of my wives were able to. It's sad when there is no one to share your pleasures."

"I don't think your pleasures are many peoples' cup of tea," observed Kate.

Renfrew does not seem to hear her. "The Japanese understand," he says. "They'll take over this country in a few years. They can cater for any demand. Not like these insensitive clods. Living with sheep for so long has made them mutton-headed."

"You're very bitter, considering the debt you owe to this country and your uncle," I say.

"Take the Yoshihari Spanker," continues Renfrew, as if

talking to himself. "No western nation could conceive of such refinement."

"The what?!" says Kate incredulously.

"The Yoshihari Spanking machine. Look." He throws open another door and I find myself gazing at what looks like a padded sofa standing on end before a contraption with a car aerial sticking out of it at right angles. "I defy you to show me any article manufactured in Britain which has been put together with such loving care. Just look at the bevel on these flange mountings."

"Get me out of here. This guy must be a refugee from the funny farm," says a worried Kate.

"Careful, young lady. I heard that," rasps Renfrew and there is a mean edge to his voice. "Do not scoff at things you don't have the wit to comprehend." He pats the machine as if trying to comfort it.

As I look closer I can see that the Yoshihari has a small screen set into it at head height and that the shape of the padding conforms to that of the human body. Renfrew steps towards it.

"Such divine pain, and she never answers me back," he says.

As we watch in amazement, he turns a control on the metal box and presses himself against the padding so that his face is against the screen. Reaching out with both hands he manoeuvres two adjustable arms into a horizontal position and grips what looks like the controls on a motor bike. Immediately bands of steel are released to encircle his arms and bind him securely to the padding.

"Let's get out!" hisses Kate.

But I cannot tear myself away. I have to watch. The pinioned Renfrew lets out a moan of satisfaction and begins to turn both the handles. As he does so there is a whirring noise and the 'radio aerial' begins to twitch from side to side, striking Renfrew across the buttocks. The Yoshihari Spanker is now fulfilling its prime function and the mind boggles at what Renfrew is watching on the screen. I find the whole thing very unpleasant, but Kate is incensed.

"Stop it!" she screeches. "You're sick!" Renfrew's only reply is to turn the right handle so that the spanking rate increases to an accompaniment of ecstatic groans.

"I'm not standing for this," snaps Kate and steps forward to the control. She obviously intends to switch the machine off but Kate never was very good with electrical gadgets. She turns the knob briskly and the Yoshihari starts flogging the living daylights out of the unfortunate Renfrew. His moans turn to yelps of pain and a cloud of dust rises into the air. The machine is lashing out with such vigour that we cannot get near it for fear of being struck and we look about us desperately. A length of thick flex goes to a socket in the wall and I seize it and give an almighty yank. There is a high pitched whining noise that gets higher, and it is not all coming from Renfrew. The machine gives a couple of relieved shudders and the switch stops beating. Renfrew is sobbing against the padding and the steel bands still hold him tightly. He twists the controls desperately but nothing happens. "Help me," he gasps. "I can't get out."

He may not be able to, but we can – and do. We leave the odious Renfrew clasped in the steel embrace of his Japanese Iron Maiden and flee into the corridor. The noise must have been fantastic because the rest of the guests are streaming up the stairs with a worried Peter and Bruce at their head.

"Are you all right? What happened?" says Peter.

"Mr Renfrew has had a little accident," explains Kate. "Is he all right?"

"I think so. We've ruined his 'pride and joy', though!"

Kate looks down the corridor to where the rest of the guests are gawping into the room we have just left.

"Don't worry," she says. "I expect his friends will have a whip round for him."

CHAPTER SIX

"O.K. I'll tell you the whole story," says Peter.

"The whole truth, and nothing but the truth, please," says Kate.

"I second that," say I.

We are lying on the beach staring into the embers of a wood fire after a quick splash in the briny – at least it was quick as far as Kate and I were concerned; just enough to wash away the slimy feeling we had when we left Renfrew's house.

"It's all to do with my father," says Peter.

The minute he says the words my heart sinks. Maybe daddy is not loaded after all. The same thought obviously occurs to Kate.

"He's gone broke?" she says.

Peter smiles ruefully. "Nope. He's got a way to go before that happens. The problem is that I don't want to have to rely on his money. Call it pride if you like but for a long time I've been fed up to my eye-teeth with people thinking that I've got nothing to offer but my father's name. 'Sonny' they call me. 'Honey's Sonny'. I want to show everybody – and most of all my old man – that I can make it by myself. You see, I know my dad. And I know that though he pays lip service to the idea of me standing on my own feet he really likes to feel that everybody in the family would fall flat on their face and stay there if he wasn't around to pick us up and dust us down. He likes to have us all sitting around thinking he's wonderful while he makes all the decisions and reminds us that he's the only one who could do it. I aim to prove him wrong."

"But doesn't he own the airline?"

"Yes. But he wants to sell it. That's what the argument is about. At the moment it isn't in great shape. I believe it could make money – a lot of money – but my father won't take the longer view. As far as he's concerned if you're not making money right now, you're dead. He won't invest in anything. I've told him he would be made to sell Outback and he doesn't like that."

"So he's disowned you?"

"No. Nothing as dramatic as that. He's just said that he thinks I'm nuts and that he won't put a penny into the company. He's given me six months to find some capital and get the whole thing off the ground. If I don't, then he's going to sell up and kick my backside."

"And you haven't got any backing?"

"I've put all my own money into it – sure, I know dad gave it to me, but it's still my own. Bruce has put in some cash and I've got some from the bank and a finance house. But it's proving a lot more difficult than I had anticipated. I suppose I had thought that the Honey name would be good enough for some cash, but the money is very tight at the moment."

"Perhaps your father is making it difficult for you?"

"No. He wouldn't do that. That's not his style. I think I made it difficult for myself in the past. I was a bit of a hell-raiser. I got into quite a few scrapes. A lot of people were jealous of the opportunities I had received and thought I hadn't done right by them. Maybe they had a point. Some people thought I had turned against my father. Some thought, like you, that he'd disowned me. For one reason or the other they didn't want to get involved. It hasn't been easy. That's why I was forced to turn to people like Renfrew. My father will throw a fit if he hears about it – and after tonight's fun and games he will, believe you me. News travels round this place faster than you-know-what in a fan."

"Why didn't you tell us all this right in the beginning?" I asked. Bathed in the light from the fire Peter looks like a Greek god with the water glistening at his temples and picking out the ridges of muscle across his chest. I feel more sympathy than reproach but there is no doubt that he has been less than totally straightforward with us.

"Two reasons, Penny," he says. "First of all I didn't want to put you off the idea by suggesting that everything was less than as it should be and, secondly, I honestly didn't believe when I first talked to you that there would be all these complications. Bruce and I have been running around like a couple of crazy wombats ever since we got back."

"But without any success?"

"Nothing that's going to start a bush fire. Look, I quite understand how you girls must feel, especially after this evening's shenanigans. If you want to go home we'll pay for a flight out tomorrow. Right, Bruce?"

"Straight up, Pete. Or you can stay a few weeks at my parents' place and then go back. At least you'll get a holiday out of the experience."

85

I glance at Kate but I know exactly what her reply would be. "We didn't come all this way for a holiday," I say. "Apart from anything else, we've burned our boots, as Kate would put it. I don't think our old airline would be in a hurry to give us our jobs back. No, we'll throw in our lot with you – provided you still need us. You did say that Outback was flying, didn't you?"

"Oh yeah," says Bruce. "But it's mainly charters and a weekly service to the back of beyond."

"Most of the planes were too old to be used as props in 'The Blue Max'," says Peter. "If they could fly as far as Europe they would be collector's items."

"What do you mean 'most of the planes' – both!" says Bruce emphatically.

"You only have two?" says Kate, and she sounds as depressed as I feel.

"That's why we need capital. The airfield isn't bad. You have to swerve to avoid the kangaroos occasionally and the sheep can be a menace but the buildings are good. The Americans built it during the war."

"Which one?" asks Kate.

"The little number against the Japs."

"In which, I recall, the Germans were also involved," I say, not wishing there to be too parochial a slant on things.

"So I have heard tell from my uncle who fought against them in North Africa," says Peter.

"What kind of staff do you have up there?" asks Kate. "Does the airline really employ stewardesses?"

"Oh yes. We've got a couple of really swinging chicks, haven't we, Brucie?"

"You mean Gracie and Ruthie? Yeah. They're really –" Bruce seems lost for words.

"Exactly. That sums it up perfectly. Gracie is one of the old school – "

" – she worked dirigibles," interrupts Bruce.

"And Ruthie. Well, Ruthie is just Ruthie."

"Nobody else would be her," observes Bruce.

"I can't wait to meet them" says Kate. "Do they know we're coming?"

"No. We thought we'd get everything finalised before we told them."

"Very wise," says Kate, sarcastically.

Peter clenches his fists in frustration. "It's all so bloody stupid because I know we're sitting on top of a goldmine. Oz is just beginning to go some and young people aren't going to sit in their own backyards all their lives like the older generation. This isn't a country, it's a continent and more and more people are going to want to get around it. There's a hell of a future for the airline business over here."

"O.K., O.K. You've convinced me," says Bruce. "Now go out there and convince the guys with some money to invest."

"How can I convince you two guys that I'm starving?" says Kate. "I may not have been looking in the right places, but I can't recall anything to eat at the party."

"The same thought 'renfrew' my mind," I say to a chorus of groans.

"And to think I was on the point of taking you all out to supper," says Peter. "I don't think I will, after that. You can get lynched around here for making jokes like that."

"Why do you think she was so keen to leave England?" says Kate.

"I promise to leave all the terrible jokes to Kate from now on. Now, can we please have something to eat. A hot dog would do me fine."

"We can do a bit better than that, I fancy. There's a few restaurants round King's Cross that are quite interesting."

"Authentic Australian cooking?"

"I don't think there is such a thing. These places are mostly Italian or Greek. Many of them have been opened by New Australians and they've really caught on."

"They don't have stewed kangaroo on the menu?"

"I hope not!"

"Can we drive over Sydney bridge?"

"Not until after dinner. Please, Kate. I'm starving."

So we scramble into the Jensen-Healey and head back into the bright lights of Sydney. As we purr along the highway I catch Kate's eye and wink at her. Whatever our problems there is no doubt that we are in the company of two of the most attractive guys any girl could wish to clap hands on.

"How much further is it?" asks Kate when we seem to

87

have been burrowing into the town for some while.

"Just a couple of blocks," says Bruce.

"Hey, look!" calls out Kate. "Do you recognise that place?" She is pointing to a restaurant called Gantino's, which has a crowd of people spilling out of the door.

"Has the guy opened in London as well?" says Peter incredulously. "He's making a small fortune over here. He's got four restaurants in Sydney and he's just opened in Melbourne and Canberra. I'd have taken you there but you have to book weeks in advance."

"I don't know what you're talking about," I say to Kate.

"Don't be thick, darling. Cast your mind back to that sweet old man from Leeds we met on the ship. Do you remember that he was going to stay with his daughter who had married the Greek – ?"

"– who ran the Italian restaurant. Jack Truman. Yes, I do recall the old boy now. This is his son-in-law's place, is it?"

"One of them, apparently. He asked us to look him up, didn't he?"

We turn to the boys. "Can we try this place?"

Peter shrugs. "Sure, but unless you've got a lot of pull you're wasting your time."

"Drop me here. I won't be a minute. I'll just see if the old boy is inside." I get out of the car in a hurry and reveal enough leg to win a fortnight's ration of wolf whistles. I do not have much hope that Mr. Truman will be inside the restaurant but once I have pushed past a few resentful people waiting for tables I see him sitting by himself at a table laid for four. He looks up and I am glad to see that he recognises me.

"I bet you didn't think I'd show up so soon." I say.

"Eeh, no, lass. Can't you find no one to feed you?"

"I was passing with some friends and we thought we'd look in. Any chance of a table?"

"You can have this one. It's for family. Eeh, but they're packing them in, aren't they?" His voice swells with pride and amazement. "This isn't the only one they've got, you know."

I tell him that I do know and go out to tell a surprised Peter and Bruce that we have got a table.

"Just a question of knowing the right people," I say loftily.

We get a few very old-fashioned looks when we return to the table and I am in a position to tell you that Australians do not take kindly to queue jumpers. The British will mutter under their breath but the Australians make their feelings felt in no uncertain manner.

"We've been waiting here for twenty minutes," says one outraged Aussie. "Why should you be allowed to push in front? What makes you so special?"

"We're friends of the management," says Peter cheerfully. "If you don't like it you can push off."

For a moment I think there is going to be a punch-up because a lot of fiery words fly around but luckily another table becomes available and our attacker stalks off to claim it. Such an incident in a British restaurant would bring all conversation to a halt but here everybody goes on munching and the waiters make no move to intervene. All through the argument dear old Mr Truman has sat looking from one speaker to the other as if watching a tennis match.

"He had a very unfortunate manner, that young man," he says, stressing the first and last syllables of the word 'unfortunate' in a characteristically northern way. "Most disagreeable."

"He was a stupid clown," says Peter dismissively.

"Is your son-in-law about at the moment?" Kate asks Mr Truman.

"Happen he'll be in later. He's at one of the other restaurants now. And to think that I was right set against him marrying our Elsie. It was the smartest thing she ever did. Just shows that father isn't always right. I suppose it was him being a Greek that set me against him. Stupid really. Like Elsie said at the time, 'Prince Philip is a Greek, dad, and you don't have anything against him.' I didn't have an answer to that."

"Have you got any grandchildren?" I ask.

"I've got thirteen," says Mr Truman, proudly.

"Thirteen?! Not all out here, surely?"

"Oh no. Mike and Elsie have got three kids. I have two more daughters and a son who produced the rest."

We chatter on amiably with Mr Truman, finding it difficult to stifle his pride at his son-in-law's achievements.

"Only had a penny when he stepped off the boat and now he must be worth well nigh a million pounds. Real ones – English pounds." I see Peter and Bruce exchanging a swift glance. "He's only in the restaurant business, is he?" asks Peter casually.

"Yes – at the moment. He's looking at other things, though. He's not content to sit back and take it easy. He's ambitious."

"Yes, I can see that," says Peter, looking about him admiringly. Certainly the decor of the restaurant is very attractive, with tropical plants and ferns climbing everywhere. The lighting is subdued but allows you to see what you are eating and the arrangement of the tables is such that the atmosphere is intimate without being over-crowded. Most important, the food is delicious. My pasta could not be better and my gamberoni are out of this world. The wine is good too and Peter proudly tells me that it is a native brew.

" 'A native brew' makes it sound as if it was mixed in a cooking pot," giggles Kate who is half way to being a very tiddly lady. Whenever she is nervous she drinks a lot and at Renfrew's house she was very, very nervous.

"Ah. Here he comes," says Mr Truman and we look up to see a tall dark-haired man of about thirty-five coming across to our table. I do not know why people are always talking about Greeks being blond. I have never seen a blond one yet. I have seen a lot of good looking ones, though, and Michael Papadoulis would come very high on the list. He draws his eyes sleepily across Kate and myself and smiles at his father-in-law.

"I am glad to see that you have not been too lonely," he says. "I respect your ability to find such charming company." Something about the twinkle in his eye tells me that he is not referring to Peter and Bruce who look wary, to put it mildly.

"You mean my two girl friends?" says old man Truman. "Aye, they're a couple of handsome lasses, there's no denying it."

"I would certainly never dream of denying it," grins Michael.

"I met them on the boat, you know. Penny Sutton and Kate – wait for it, it's on the tip of my tongue – Goodbody. That's right, isn't it? You can't say my memory is going."

"I wouldn't dream of doing that either. Michael Papadoulis." He extends a hand.

"We've just had the most delicious meal," gushes Kate, devouring Michael with her eyes. "It really was super, wasn't it?" She turns to the boys, who give a grudging nod.

"I'm glad you enjoyed it. Perhaps you will accept a liqueur with my compliments." He waves for a waiter.

"Peter Honey and Bruce Wilson," I say, feeling that someone had better make an introduction.

"Not Ross Honey's son?" I can practically feel Peter wincing.

"The one and only," he says. "You've got a very good operation here. Congratulations."

"Thanks a lot. I'm a great admirer of the way your father handles things. You work for him do you?"

"On some things. I have a few irons of my own, though."

"I envy you. I wish I could diversify more. It's not a good idea to have all your eggs in one basket."

I catch Kate's eye and she turns away sharply. Peter could not ask for a better opening.

"Well, we're always looking for someone who wants a healthy return on their capital. We've got more ideas than funds and there's a limit to what we can raise through banks." He manages to sound interested without being desperate.

Michael Papadoulis nods and returns his soft brown eyes to Kate and myself. "Sounds interesting," he says. "I would like to talk to you about it sometime if you are serious."

"I'm pretty heavily committed at the moment," lies Peter. "I'll get my secretary to give you a ring."

Michael nods without taking his eyes off us. "You must excuse me for involving you in my business affairs, ladies."

I think that most girls would settle for any kind of affair with Michael Papadoulis. Certainly Kate looks as if she is well and truly smitten.

"That's all right," says Kate. "We're involved in one of Peter's business ventures ourselves. We're air stewardesses."

"I'll make a point of flying with you in future," says

Michael. He turns to Peter. "I didn't know that your father owned an airline?"

"It's my baby," says Peter. "Fantastic potential. I'd like to talk to you about it when we can get together."

"Sounds interesting. I reckon there must be a lot of scope for internal air services."

Underneath the table I am hugging myself with joy. What a break! Of course, it is early days yet but Michael Papadoulis does seem as if he could be the answer to all our problems. He chats to Peter and Bruce for another five minutes and then excuses himself with renewed apologies for interrupting our meal.

"What a living doll!" exclaims Kate when we have retired to the powder room. "You know, I think I must be suffering from galloping nymphomania or something. Nearly every man I see these days seems to turn me on. I thought I was carrying a torch for Bruce and now that seems to be flickering."

"Control yourself," I urge. "He's got three children, remember. Don't break his father-in-law's heart. Remember your last little fling with a married man." Back in England, Kate had an affair with a flight captain that nearly ended in the divorce court. She winces.

"I know, I know. I'm an irresponsible bitch. But did you see the look in that man's eyes? If he was happy he wouldn't look at us like that."

"Of course he would. Any man looks at you like that if he fancies you. Often the happier they are, the more they do it. He was probably trying to make sure that you came back to the restaurant again. It was cupboard love."

"Romantic creature, aren't you? I think there was more to it than that. I bet you he says something before we leave."

As it turns out Kate would have lost her money. When we get back to the table, Peter is paying the bill and there is no sign of Michael. We say au revoir to Mr Truman and accept an invitation to visit him at the Papadoulis home – Kate accepts with alacrity.

"O.K. girls. Are you fit?"

"Delicious meal, Peter. Thanks a lot."

"I could see you liked the atmosphere," teases Peter as we go out. "Mick the Greek certainly knows how to pack them in. Maybe we need a few male stewards on Outback."

"Why don't you ask Michael? He sounded keen enough."

"Yeah. That was a fantastic break, wasn't it? And all thanks to you two girls. If it comes to anything I'll see you all right. We might have Outback hogging the airspace before you can say Amy Johnson."

"Not with a name like that, you won't," says Kate.

"Kate's right," I chip in. "It sounds terribly old fashioned. If you want to recruit your passengers from amongst the young and the new Australians you need a more swinging name. Outback Airways makes me think of Chips Rafferty."

"Who?" asks Kate.

"He was the Australian Laurence Olivier," says Bruce.

"He was in a film called 'The Overlanders' they used to show every term when I was at school," I add.

"I don't know about Chips Rafferty. But I think you have a point about the name," says Peter, thoughtfully. "Have you got any suggestions?"

"What Penny said made me think of something," says Kate. 'How about 'New Australia Airlines'? It sounds modern and should appeal to new immigrants. Also it covers the whole country and makes the airline sound important."

Peter thinks for a moment and then nods his head. "I like it. What do you think, Bruce?"

"I think it's great."

"Of course it may put off the older generation Australians," says Kate hurriedly.

"I'm not worried about them. We can't appeal to everyone," says Peter.

"People may think that it's run by New Australians and this may put them off," says Kate desperately.

"Are you saying that you *don't* think it is a good name?" asks Peter, sounding puzzled.

I know Kate's problem exactly. The enthusiasm with which everyone has received her spur of the moment idea has surprised her and made her have second thoughts. She has been brainwashed into thinking that any wheeze she has, must, of necessity, be a bad one and therefore worthy only of rejection and a pat on the head for trying. That somebody might acually accept one of her ideas and act upon it fills her with trepidation.

"I think it's a great name," I say encouragingly. "A million times better than Outback. Like you say, that makes the outfit sound like something from Nowheresville."

Kate shrugs and tries to look happy. "Well, if you think it's O.K.," she says, doubtfully.

"Provided we can register it you've just named yourself an airline," says Peter. "Cripes! This evening is getting better and better. A couple of hours ago I was considering shooting myself."

"I'm glad you decided against it," I say, squeezing his arm. Kate may be getting all worked up about Michael but dishy as he is I would still pick Peter if I had the choice. It is that old Anglo-Saxon hankering of mine, I suppose.

"Likewise," says Peter, smiling down at me.

"Jeeze," says Bruce, with a trace of disgust in his voice. "Hang on a minute and I'll get my violin."

"You're a romantic devil, aren't you?" complains Kate.

"I'm not slushy," protests Bruce.

" 'Slushy'?! I bet you've never seen the stuff."

"Come on you two. Pack it up," says Peter. "What do you fancy doing now?"

Kate yawns. "I'm feeling very sleepy. I don't think I've found my land-legs yet. Would anybody mind if we drove home via Sydney Bridge?"

"I second that," I say. "After all that delicious food I'm ready for bed."

I did not mean bed to sound like an invitation but I can sense Peter's eyes asking mine to look into them, and when I do there is no doubt what is in his mind.

"Do you want to stay the night with us, Pete?" asks Bruce.

"Yeah, why not? I don't want to drive back to the flat."

"Mum and Dad go to bed early," says Bruce and leaves us to interpret that remark how we wish.

He is right, because when we get back to the house there is only the porch light and the glow from the illuminated swimming pool. The rest of the building is in darkness.

"I fancy a dip before I turn in," says Bruce and the rest of us agree that this would be a good idea. The thought of swimming at night in an outdoor pool still seems unbelievably exotic and I remember my last excursion at The Banana's ill-fated house party back home. Certainly it is a zillion times warmer here.

"Anybody fancy a night cap or some Ovaltine?" asks Peter. We settle for Ovaltine and I volunteer to make it while the others get changed. I find myself hoping that Peter will follow me into the kitchen and I am not disappointed. He shows me where everything is and then slides his arms round me so that his hands are cupping my breasts.

"I want to make love to you," he says.

"But I'm getting the Ovaltine," I say, wishing that something more witty would escape from my lips.

"Later," he says. "But not too late. It's been a long time."

"But we can't do it here. Not with Bruce's parents about. Let me go. The milk is boiling over."

Peter releases me resentfully. "Come out to the changing room. Nobody can hear us there. When the others have turned in. Oh, Penny, I want you so much."

He makes another lunge for me and there is a danger that nobody will get their Ovaltine.

"For Heaven's sakes!" I squeak. "Carry the tray so that I know what your hands are doing."

"Only if you say yes."

"I'll think about it."

"That's not good enough." Peter kisses me passionately and his hands mould me to him.

"Stop it! Suppose Bruce's parents came in?"

"I don't care if the Bondi Surf Club come in. I want you." The way his hands are roaming over my body makes it difficult for me to disbelieve him.

"Let me go, Peter. The others will be wondering where we are."

"I doubt it. If I know Bruce that's the last thing he'll be thinking about."

Peter may well be right because when we get out on to the patio there is no sign of Bruce or Kate. "They don't call him 'Lightning Wilson' for nothing," says Peter admiringly.

"They've probably gone for a walk," I say, feeling irritated by the arrogant male assumption that Kate has submitted so easily. She probably has, of course, but this if anything contributes to my annoyance. "Their Ovaltine will get cold," I say primly.

Peter laughs. "Poor devils," he says. "I wonder if they realise what they're missing."

"Oh, shut up!" I walk across the terrace and look into the pool.

"Can you see them?" jokes Peter.

"You're not funny," I tell him.

"Then why are you laughing?" Somehow the thought of Kate and Bruce locked in each other's arms on the bottom of the pool tickles my funny bone.

"I'm not laughing," I lie, taking a sip of Ovaltine.

"Ah, that's better. I really go for you with a moustache." I wipe my mouth hurriedly. "I think I put too much powder in," I say. Peter tastes his drink and winces. "I'll say you did. Maybe the others aren't missing anything after all." He looks at me thoughtfully for a moment. "I suppose all the stuff you serve on the plane is pre-mixed?"

"Not all of it. But then I don't have passengers mauling me the whole time, so I can concentrate on what I'm doing."

"You amaze me. I find you very maulable." Peter's arms are making an encircling movement.

"I had noticed. Careful what you're doing. The Wilsons could be watching us."

"Their bedroom is on the other side of the house. I'm sorry, Penny, but if you don't come into that hut with me I'm going to have to rape you."

"I'll scream."

"No you won't. You might wake the Wilsons and you wouldn't like that."

"Don't bet on it." Peter takes me in his arms and I let him kiss me.

"I didn't hear anything."

"I don't call that rape," I say. He kisses me again and this time I am swept off my feet and borne away into the shadowy interior of the hut. "Put me down!" I hiss.

"Certainly, ma'am." With practised – possibly too practised – ease Peter hooks his foot round a lilo that is standing against the wall and flips it on to the floor. No sooner has it hit the tiles than I am deposited on top of it.

"Pete—" I don't get a chance to finish what I was going to say because Peter's mouth gets in the way. Not that I feel like complaining too much because it is a very nice mouth and certainly knows what it is doing. Now that I am away from the exposed terrace I begin to feel a lot more relaxed and start to enjoy the sensations that are building up inside my body. Peter is a good lover, because now that he has me where he wants me he does not exploit the situation but gives me time to come to terms with my surroundings. He strokes me gently whilst I watch the moonlight cutting swathes above my head and listen to the sounds of the night. Almost without being aware of what I am doing, I find myself entwining my fingers in the soft curls behind Peter's ears and running my finger along the line of his firm, strong mouth.

"I don't hear you screaming rape," he murmurs.

"It's a woman's prerogative to change her mind."

"You'll have to stop wearing tights."

"Is that one of the rules of the aidline?'

"Absolutely."

"That's all right then. I thought you might have some ulterior motive."

"I can't even spell the word. No, the decision was made on medical grounds. Tights are very bad for the circulation."

"You must be wearing them, then. Your hands are terribly cold."

"I'm sorry about that. I have a very low heart beat."

"So you have lots of stamina?"

"That's right."

"How lucky."

As the more astute of my readers may have realised, Peter's hands have not been idle during our conversation and, with a little help from my increasingly eager fingers, he has prepared us both for the pleasure to come.

"Oh, Penny. You're fantastic," he breathes. "You have the most moreso torso." He rises above me and for a minute his shoulders block out the moonlight. I am trembl-

97

ing with excitement as I feel him poised at the threshold of my body.

"Go on, go on," I murmur. A cry of pleasure breaks from my lips as he enters me and begins to mould our separate motions into one. "Oh, Peter. It's beautiful." I mean everything – him, what he is doing to me, the house, being in Australia, the excitement of a new life in a new world. Peter's powerful body is probing the very substance of my being, flooding me with new sensations, awakening in me a realisation of just how wonderful life can be.

I cannot remember a greater happiness.

CHAPTER SEVEN

"You kept him at arm's length, of course?" says Kate. It is next morning and she is sitting on the end of my bed, looking at me accusingly. "I mean, after all those things you said to me you could hardly do otherwise, could you? 'Prejudicing our position as employees.' That was it, wasn't it? So true. I remember commenting at the time."

"What about you?" I say, evasively.

"Oh, I'm different. I don't have your firmly defined moral scruples and sense of propriety. Also, I didn't have such an exciting trip as some people, remember? It's not so easy for me to retain my Anglo-Saxon cool."

"So you made love. I hope you enjoyed it."

" 'Made love'? We started down the bottom of the beach and practically churned our way back to the car. There were moments when I thought we were going to disappear. Have you ever seen a crab burying itself in the sand? I've never known a fellow like it. I don't know what they feed them on out here but I'd like to take some back for the fellows at home. How did you get on?"

"Peter took me into the changing hut."

"Yes. He won the toss, didn't he?"

"What!?" The thought of my lovely experience having been set up on the toss of a coin is not one that appeals.

98

"Oh, yes. Didn't you know? Maybe I shouldn't have said anything." Kate can be very tactless, and she keeps talking to prove it. "Bruce was saying that he reckons that Pete must have a double-sided coin the number of times he ends up on the beach."

It dawns on me that I must be quite smitten with Peter, because I experience a definite pang of jealousy at the thought of him making love to a steady procession of girls. Kate is right. I should have taken my own advice and steered clear of entanglement. Maybe these two Aussie love pirates tossed for girls as well as love-making venues! Peter has never said anything serious about his feelings for me. It may be because the Australian male thinks this is 'soft' or because I am merely girl number two thousand and one on a soon-forgotten list. Certainly his love-making of the previous night was a hundred per cent physical. It was as if I awoke in him an almost animal hunger.

"What are you blushing about?" asks Kate.

"Never you mind," I say.

"Thinking about last night, were you?" says Kate perceptively. "Oh dear, I suppose I'm the most awful slut but I can never see the point of saying no. Life is so short, isn't it?"

I try and look mildly disapproving, but in my heart of hearts I know that I am exactly like Kate. More hypocritical, that is all.

The next few days are spent in blissful ease at the Wilsons, but there is always the disturbing thought of the finance for New Australia hanging over our heads like the sword of Thingumybobs. Mrs Wilson must be completely in the dark because though she knows that Kate and I are connected with one of Peter's business ventures, she has no idea what it is.

I am slightly annoyed because, though I had intended to be cool with Peter and show him that I was not always going to be available at the drop of a lilo, I get very little chance to register my feelings. Peter is hardly ever around. He works from a flat in Sydney and spends his whole time chasing finance. Bruce looks in to snatch a meal but he too is seldom available for longer than twenty minutes. Kate and I love it at the Wilsons and could not ask for kinder

99

hosts but we are getting desperate for some work. One of the main reasons for becoming an air stewardess is that one likes people. Maybe, 'likes' is the wrong word. One finds people interesting. There is always the chance that one will have to grapple with some totally new human problem every time one takes off. Living with the Wilsons, Kate and I are like two racehorses confined to a stable. We want to be out and about.

Most of all we want to see Outback Airlines. However awful it is, we have got to face up to it some time. Peter argues that our presence will excite speculation and disturb the existing employees but I think he is being over-sensitive. What about the effect sitting around doing nothing is having on us?

One afternoon, when we are lying by the pool, there is a screech of tyres against gravel and I look up to see Peter and Bruce striding towards us. They are not alone.

"I've brought an old friend to see you," says Peter, cheerfully. I notice him looking at me rather closely and realise that my bikini top is still lying beneath me. I lower myself hurriedly and put it on.

"I don't know why this girl bothers to wear a costume. She's always popping out of it," jokes Peter. The man he and Bruce are with is Michael Papadoulis and I watch Kate putting on her most welcoming smile.

"We are the bringers of glad tidings," says Michael.

Bruce produces something from behind his back which I recognise as a bottle of champagne.

"You mean – ?!"

"Exactly. It's lift-off for New Australia. We've just signed the papers."

"Hurrah!" Kate and I hug each other.

"The deal will probably cripple me," says Peter, "but at least it will get us off the ground."

"Don't believe him," laughs Michael. "I have been very generous. I must try and protect my investment. That is only common sense."

"Come on. Let's open the plonk and forget the sordid details," says Bruce.

" 'Plonk'? The Widow Cliquot would turn in her grave. I hope you don't believe in that old adage about Greeks

100

bearing gifts?" Michael favours Kate and myself with a charming smile.

"Anybody who produces champagne is O.K. with me," I say.

"You just have to produce yourself," says Kate, scorching him with her eyes. I must say that when Kate fancies someone they are seldom left in the dark about it.

"Boy!" says Bruce. "You've made a hit there, sport."

Michael clicks his heels and nods at Kate. "Let's drink a toast to New Australia Airlines," he says.

"Coupled with the names of Penny and Kate without whom it might never have been possible" adds Peter.

The bottle of champagne disappears in no time and another is opened as Mr and Mrs Wilson arrive to hear the news.

"So this is what you've been up to," says Mrs Wilson. "I thought perhaps you were going to open a club."

"With Penny as a topless waitress," says Peter amidst laughter.

"How has your father responded to the idea?" asks Mr Wilson.

"He's been in Perth all week so I haven't had a chance to talk to him about it. I'll get in touch with him when he comes back." Peter shoots a glance at Michael and I wonder exactly what the Greek has been told about the senior Honey's involvement.

"I'm looking forward to meeting your father so much," says Kate.

"He's a fantastic character," agrees Mr Wilson.

Poor Peter! I can see his eyes glazing over as the familiar refrain is taken up.

"I didn't think your father was keen on the airline" says Mrs Wilson. There is an awkward silence.

"He's come round a lot," says Peter, finally. "He always sees a good business proposition."

"In the end," says Bruce.

"He's certainly a hard man to budge when he's made his mind up," says Mr Wilson.

"Maybe that's where I get my stubborn streak from," says Peter firmly. He turns to Kate. "I'll introduce you to

Dad when we go and have a look at Outb– I mean New Australia."

"How long before we're really operational?" I ask.

"It will be a continuous process. With the finance we can raise, thanks to Michael, we'll get two more planes and improve the facilities. If that works out we'll plough back the profits and expand from there."

"It's not going to happen overnight," says Bruce cautiously.

"What do you want us to do?" asks Kate.

"I'd like you to have a look at the set-up as it stands. Fly with Gracie and Ruthie and see what suggestions you feel like making.

"I'm certain that something will occur to you," says Bruce pointedly.

"Yeah. I think their operation could be tightened up a bit," says Peter.

"Congratulations. You have just won first prize in 'The Understatement Of The Year Competition'," says Bruce. "I wonder if Gracie still wears carpet slippers."

"Carpet slippers?" I say incredulously.

"You'll see," says Bruce.

"When can we go? I'm itching to get into a plane again."

"You'll be lucky if you're not itching when you get off the crates they've got up there at the moment," says Bruce.

"Bruce!"

"Sorry, Ma."

"Bruce is prone to exaggeration – or he will be if he doesn't watch his P's and Q's," says Peter, waving his fist under Bruce's nose.

"I think I'm going to have a swim," says Bruce defensively.

"The same thought was occurring to me," says Peter. "Michael, could you give me a hand for a minute?"

Before Bruce can move the two of them have picked him up and thrown him in the swimming pool! Most people might take exception to this, but not Bruce. His only comment is that it is a good job that he is wearing his drip dry suit! He does not even bother to change when we decide to carry on our celebration at Gantino's and enjoy another fantastic meal. Looking back on it, I was so smashed that

I would not have noticed if he had dressed in a diving suit.

After dinner, Michael invites us back to his home and I spend a happy couple of hours talking to his wife Elsie, and Jack Truman. Elsie Papadoulis is very natural and un-affected and I am surprised to find Michael married to someone so unsophisticated. She is happiest when talking about her children and seems delighted to have her father with her. From her conversation it is easy to realise that she misses England a lot and adores hearing about all the goings-on at home.

I have a pretty hazy recollection of what took place but I do remember some dancing and the expression on Elsie's face when she saw her husband in Kate's arms. Even though I was pretty pickled it brought me up with a start. She looked really hurt and very vulnerable. With Michael away building up his fortune I wondered what kind of life she led. Her manner did not suggest that money was very important to her, and I felt that she would probably be very happy living a much simpler life and seeing more of her husband. I also seem to remember that Kate and Michael disappeared together for a sufficiently long time for their absence to be noticed, but perhaps it is hindsight giving the recollection substance.

To my surprise, Kate says very little about the evening when I talk to her the next day. Even then I do not attach too much significance because I am completely wrapped up in describing the multiple agonies of my hangover. Also, there is our impending trip to Coolburn, home of New Australia, to occupy our attentions.

Peter and Michael pick us up at half past ten on a typically lovely Australian day without a cloud in the sky. Just to be driving anywhere on a day like this would be a pleasure. We motor through the outskirts of Sydney and I enjoy a pleasing prospect of large family houses standing amongst trees and surrounded by what seems like acres of garden. There is so much room that no one needs to live in his neighbour's back pocket. After a few miles of these pleasant suburban residences we are in open country and I marvel again at the feeling of space that is so much a part of the country.

"You could make a western out here," I say.

103

"They're always trying," says Bruce, "trying to package Australia and sell it to the rest of the world as a kind of Wild West with kangaroos and cowboys in slouch hats."

"How far is it to the airport?" asks Kate.

"It's six miles to Coolburn and we turn off before then. A few miles is no problem in this country. There are places where if your car broke down you could die of thirst or heat exhaustion before anyone found you."

"Thanks a lot, Cheerful. I'll get out here," says Kate.

"One thing I've been thinking about is uniforms," I say. "Do you intend to continue with the ones the girls are wearing at the moment?"

"That's a very good question," says Bruce, a smile puckering the corner of his mouth. "What say you, Chief?"

"I think the girls had better make that part of their re-commendation," says Peter. "I want them to be responsible for all aspects of stewardess training and recruitment."

"Imagine me telling girls to keep their tunics buttoned up and not serve their hair with the soup," says Kate. "I never thought I'd see the day."

"There we are. That's my beauty."

I follow Peter's pointing finger and there, on the horizon, I can see the unmistakable outline of a hangar.

"Bleak, isn't it?" says Kate.

"You didn't expect it to be in the middle of a wood, did you?" Bruce and Kate stick their tongues out at each other. I am busy looking at the peeling sign by the roadside: OU BAC AI LIN S! At first I think it must be in Gaelic and then it dawns on me that it is Outback Airlines with a few letters missing.

"That's a great introduction to the place," I say to Peter.

"Don't worry. That's on my list of priorities. I didn't see any point in doing anything until I had the finance worked out. It's no use having an illuminated sign out there if the rest of the place is not up to scratch."

"And talking of scratching," chips in Bruce.

"Don't," says Peter.

"I can see a plane," says Kate.

"Well, it was a plane," I agree with her. Standing on the edge of the runway is the flame-gutted shell of what looks like a Dakota, a plane I remember as being long past its

104

first flush of youth when I was a child.

"What a beautiful way to say 'Welcome to New Australia,'" says Kate sarcastically. "The passengers must be fighting each other to get up the gangway when they've driven past that."

"Yes, and the smoke doesn't help, does it?" I am referring to a smouldering bush fire which is filtering thought-provoking wisps of smoke through the blackened fuselage.

Peter looks embarrassed. "Yeah. It isn't very good for business, is it? That old bus came from the Cameroons in West Africa, you know. Luckily they got the engines out before it went up in smoke."

"About the only thing it ever did go up in, I should think," says Kate. "Why did they want to take the engines out?"

"To use them, of course."

"What!? For flying?"

"Naturally. The fuselage was a bit draughty but Sandy says the engines are some of the best we've got."

"Who's Sandy?" asks Kate.

"He's our chief mechanic. He's a real whizz with engines."

"He must be," says Kate. "Do my tiny quaking ears deceive me or did you say that the engines from that Wright Brothers' revival are still flying?"

"Take a look above your head if you don't believe me," says Peter. I do as he says and there, circling the airport, is a twin-engined passenger plane.

"Is that it?" says Kate. "Hadn't you better drive into a hangar in case we get hit by a shower of nuts and bolts?"

"Not too many jokes, please, girls," says Peter and there is a firm edge to his voice that makes us shut up.

"Let's watch this flight check in and then you can get some idea of the system," says Bruce.

We agree that this would be a good idea and drive round the back of the hangar and park between two sheds looking out on to the airstrip.

"Here she comes," says Peter and there is a hint of fatherly pride in his voice. One feels that, whatever its deficiencies, he has a genuine affection for poor old Outback.

The undercarriage is down and the pilot is beginning his

105

approach when suddenly the plane's nose turns sharply upwards and it starts to climb. I can understand anyone turning their nose up at the home of Outback Airlines but surely the pilot must have seen the place before.

"Oh, look," says Kate. "Kangaroos. Aren't they sweet?" She is right. There, loping across the landing strip, are one, two, three – half a dozen kangaroos of varying sizes. The pilot was obviously taking action to avoid them.

"Don't they move fast?" I say admiringly.

"They'd move a bloody sight faster if I had a gun with me," says Peter, grimly.

"Oh, no. You couldn't hurt them," says Kate. "Look at that little one. It's so sweet."

But nothing Kate says seems to cut much ice with Peter who continues to cuss and blind about his ground staff and 'bloody 'roos' as he chooses to call them. Eventually the kangaroos bound away towards their appointment with the horizon and the pilot makes an indifferent landing. Maybe he was disturbed by the reception committee.

"Quaint, isn't it?" says Kate. "I've heard of planes hitting birds but never a kangaroo. You wouldn't think, in a country this size, there was a danger of bumping into anything."

The plane taxis round to a single storey prefabricated building beside the hangar and the exit door opens fractionally before the ramp is pushed into position. Fortunately a hand reaches out and restrains the passenger who is about to step into space.

"This should be interesting," whispers Kate. "I bet they kiss the earth when they get down those steps."

She is wrong. The passengers seem very unconcerned as they stroll towards the reception area. All two of them.

At first I imagine that there is a hold-up inside the plane. Some passenger making an effusive farewell to the stewardess, perhaps. But after the two guys have gone into the building and no-one else emerges, it dawns on me that I have just seen all the passengers.

"You can't stay in business with a passenger list like that," I say.

"Exactly. That's why we're doing something about it," says Peter.

106

"That's twice as many as we had on the last flight," says Bruce. "Maybe things are picking up."

"More like packing up," says Kate.

"Don't be so pessimistic. I can remember when the captain rang up and said he didn't have any passengers and was it worth proceeding with the trip."

"And did you?"

"Yes. It was fantastic. Do you remember, Peter? It was you and me and that girl from Adelaide. We had a real ball, didn't we? Whatever happened to her?"

"I've no idea. Look. I'm not interested in what happened in the past. We want some action now."

"Fine, fine. I couldn't agree with you more." I am flattered to think that maybe Peter's keenness to change the subject has something to do with me.

"Maybe we should take a closer look," says Bruce.

"Yes. I'm fed up with watching those guys trying to beat the luggage to death," says Kate, referring to the way the plane is being unloaded.

We step into the reception area and what I first think is the noise of a fan is the sound made by thousands of flies circling around the hot stuffy room. Airport lounges never rank amongst the first five hundred places I would choose to celebrate a passionate love affair with Richard Burton but this dump would automatically be rejected as the venue for a hobo's convention. Shabby is the right kind of word but does not do the place the injustice it deserves. There is dust everywhere, wire mesh windows with lizards running up them and a peeling foliage of posters that must have been stuck on top of each other since the first printing press came to Australia.

There is a gnarled old man waiting in an armchair that has the springs bursting out of it like worm casts. I imagine that he is waiting for one, or both, of the new arrivals but this is not the case. He does not move until the baggage arrives, and then calmly makes off with a live sheep!

"Now I've seen everything," I say.

"It's given me an idea," says Kate. "There are probably more sheep than people in Australia. Why don't we give them their own airline?"

"Black Sheep Airlines," I suggest.

107

"Maybe those kangaroos were waiting for a flight," says Kate. "Now there's a market for you."

"Stop it, you two! It may surprise you but you're not that far out. Animals are very important out here and we'll carry anything that pays for its seat – or whatever space it takes up."

"I wonder if Air India feels the same way about elephants," says Kate.

Peter does not bother to answer that one because a woman of about fifty comes into the room from the direction of the airfield. For a moment I wonder where she has been hiding and then I notice the carpet slippers. Even so, I am not certain. She is wearing a skirt that finishes too far above the knee to be acceptable to most airlines and far too far above that for a woman of her age. Her zip has burst open to reveal a pair of purple knickers and her blouse has large damp patches under the armpits that match in well with the contrasting swatches of colour that give the garment the appearance of a soldier's camouflage jacket. Her face brightens when she sees Peter and Bruce. "Hello, boys," she says. "Thank God you're here. Have those two perverts gone yet?"

It takes me a moment to realise who she is talking about. Both of the passengers looked to me as if they got their kicks from going to bed early with a mug of creamy Horlicks, and have driven off in dust-covered Holdens. They must have had guts if they had made a pass at this lady. With her mouth a slash of scarlet across her over made-up face, she looks more than a match for any light-hearted philanderer.

"What happened, Gracie?" says Peter humouringly.

"The same old story," says Gracie, grimly. "Both of them were eating me up with their eyes from the moment they got on the plane. I knew I was in for trouble when I started serving the lemonade."

"What happened, Gracie?" says Bruce, patiently.

"Oh, the usual thing. His fingers brush against mine. I could sense it was the prelude to a crude pass. Especially the way he was talking. Suggestive stuff, it was."

"Such as?"

"He said the lemonade was lukewarm."

"Is that all?"

108

Gracie shudders. "It was the way he said it, more than anything. It was obvious what he was getting at. Then the other joker chips in and says that his glass has got lipstick on it. I think they probably work as a team. That's why I hung behind in the plane. I thought they might be waiting for me in here with a chloroform pad."

"They'd be taking a bit of a chance, Gracie."

"Don't you be so sure. Things like that happen all the time. They could have bundled me into a car and carried me off before you can say Roger Carpenter."

"If you were worried why didn't you talk to Ashley or Ken? After all, the crew outnumbered the passengers."

"They were too busy flying the plane. Anyway, those two insensitive bastards would step over their own mother if she was being raped."

At that moment two world-weary figures appear looking hot and tired. "Did they get away, Gracie?" says one of them. "I think you're losing your touch. Why didn't you ask them to give you a lift into town?"

"You see what I mean?" hisses Gracie.

"I reckon a flight with only one passenger is what Gracie needs. Then the poor bastard could scream for help and there'd be no one to hear him."

"You two can come the raw prawn, but those two sex maniacs virtually assaulted me."

"I'll send their medals on to them," says one of the pilots.

"Come off it, Ash," says the other. "You know it's all in her mind. The only thing that is. Pure wish fulfilment."

"You're no gentlemen!" squawks Gracie indignantly.

"You're dead right we're not. There's no future in it with girls like you about."

" 'Girls'!?" says Ash. "You silver-tongued bastard."

"How dare you!" says Gracie, in tones of mighty outrage. "I don't have to stand here and be insulted."

"I know. You can stand anywhere and be insulted," says Ken.

"Oooooh!" Gracie sounds as if she is about to commit murder.

"Gracie! Gentlemen! Please!" Peter moves in and not before time. "Knock off your arguing, Ken Goodall and Ashley Banks, I want you to meet Penny Sutton and Kate

Goodbody who are joining us from a famous British airline."

There are a few moments of incredulous silence, and then Ken speaks. "I don't want to sound less than one hundred percent totally enthusiastic, but what in God's name for? Surely, it's passengers we're after. "

"The girls are part of a new deal for Outback. A hell of a lot of money is being pumped into the company. We're going to have more planes, a new name and a new image. We're going to grab ourselves a healthy slice of the internal air traffic in this country." Peter's stirring words must have some effect because Gracie starts tucking her blouse in to her skirt.

"Real, new planes?" says Ashley, incredulously. "Not just new, second-hand planes?"

"New, new planes," says Peter. "You'll be receiving an official statement of our plans in a couple of days. Very soon there are going to be some big changes around here."

"I never thought your father would put money into this outfit," says Ken. "I thought we'd be wound up."

"You're going to be wound up all right," says Peter. "You won't recognise the place, or yourselves."

An hour later we are driving to meet Peter's father and Peter asks if Outback was as bad as we had expected.

"Worse," says Kate with characteristic frankness. "I could see why your father didn't want to put money into it. Has Michael seen it?"

"I showed him some photographs," says Peter, defensively. "The buildings are in good shape. They need a spot of paint, that's all."

"I think everything could do with some colour," I say. "It's so drab. I think Kate and I should get together and design a really snappy outfit for the stewardesses."

"And do something about that morgue of a reception area," chips in Kate. "I wouldn't mind painting it myself."

"Get some trendy interior designer to give it the works and capitalise on the publicity. Maybe Pierre Cardin would do the uniforms. Is there an official one at the moment?"

"I believe there was but the girls hated it and had to buy it themselves, so they started wearing their own stuff."

"With results the like of which I have not seen in many a

110

long day," says Kate. "Tell me, are there really men in Australia so desperate that they would make a pass at Gracie?"

"I haven't met any," says Bruce. "No. It's sad but, as far as we can work out, she's always been like that. I think if a guy put his hand on her knee she'd die of shock."

"So would I," says Peter. "Frankly, I'm a bit worried about Gracie. I think we may have to let her go. She should have been retired years ago. I don't think she's right for the New Australia image."

"You can say that again," says Kate. "More like the Old Devil's Island image. Still, she's probably got a heart of gold. It seems to be a bit unkind to hoof her out. Is she married?"

"You must be joking," says Bruce.

"I hope we're not being employed as hatchet women," I say. "I don't fancy the job of getting people the sack."

"Nobody will be sacked who can perform to the standards we expect of them," says Peter, "and they'll all get a chance to show what they can do. If they can't make a go of it after a reasonable time then they're out. This place has been run as a sloppy benevolent society for too long. It's not fair to anyone, especially people who have invested money in the enterprise."

"Yes Sir!" says Kate, cheekily delivering a mock salute. "Permission to make a suggestion?"

"Granted, Miss Goodbody."

"Why don't we paint the planes a bright, cheerful colour? They did it in the States and it was a big success. That way the old planes wouldn't stick out like sore thumbs."

"I think it's a great idea," says Peter. "Sandy and the pilots will probably throw a fit but they'll just have to get used to it."

"Let's paint a smile on the nose," I say. "You've seen all those smile buttons?"

"Good thinking," says Peter enthusiastically. "I reckon the old man should be quite impressed with the way we're tackling things."

"He'll only be impressed when he sees the profit statement," says Bruce shrewdly.

"Well, we'll soon find out," says Peter, "Welcome to the home of the Honeys."

There is a simple sign by the roadside saying 'Eastern Springs' and Peter swings the wheel over and takes us down a dirt track. After about half a mile we enter a magnificent grove of eucalyptus trees and through them I can see what looks like the façade of a luxury hotel.

"Is this it?" says Kate, a note of awe in her voice.

"Yeah. The locals call it Sydney Town Hall," says Bruce. "Nobody can understand why they have the seat of government in Canberra."

"I didn't know they had houses like this in Australia," says Kate; once again demonstrating her rare sense of tact.

"You imagined we were all in corrugated iron shacks, I suppose," says Bruce.

"I didn't mean that," says Kate hurriedly. "You know how impressed Penny and I were by Sydney. It's just that this place looks like an English gentleman's country seat."

"And there aren't any gentlemen in Australia, I suppose? That's nice isn't it, Bruce?"

"Very nice, Peter. It didn't take her long to get our measure, did it?"

"Too true, sport."

Kate is still trying to explain what she meant when we pull up at the front door. We go up a flight of steps, past two great wooden doors and are in a spacious high-ceilinged hallway. There to greet us is a very pretty girl called Jean Hawks who is introduced to us by Peter as his father's personal assistant. She certainly looks very cool and efficient but I sense a trace of resentment in her manner which it is difficult to put a finger on. Peter, too, seems cool in his attitude towards her. I know that Peter's mother died a few years back and I wonder quite what the role of personal assistant entails.

"Ross is in the middle of a conference at the moment," she says. "Then he's got a few telephone calls to make. He hopes you can all stay for lunch."

"I said we'd be around for lunch," says Peter, stiffly.

"Excellent." Jean Hawks smiles an efficient smile and suggests that we might like some coffee or a drink. The boys

112

settle for a couple of 'tubes' and we go through to the garden at the back of the house.

"When I was a kid I had to make an appointment to see the old man," say Peter. "He was always somewhere else." There is a note of genuine regret in his voice and I sense that he is thinking about his mother. Certainly, he looks about the garden as if remembering scenes from his childhood. There is still a swing hanging from a beautiful flowering banyan tree and Kate and I take it in turns to be pushed to and fro, and watch the suspicious peacocks eyeing us warily. The contrast between this place and the home of Outback Airlines is quite something.

The boys are well into their second beer when a tall distinguished figure can be seen hurrying across the lawn towards us. From a distance his most noticeable feature is the shock of white hair, flowing almost like a mane. It is most unusual for any Australian male over the age of forty to wear his hair long but, on closer inspection, the newcomer's leonine features are well-suited to the style. A glance is enough to tell that this must be Peter's father. If anything, even more attractive than his son. He has a craggy face with deep-set blue eyes and a lot of lines sprinkled about them. It looks like a face that has experienced pain and happiness and knows that neither can exist to the total exclusion of the other. He looks at me and I suddenly feel naked. Not exposed by a lecher's stare but laid bare by the experienced eye of a man whose stock-in-trade is the ability to read character in a man's or woman's face. He is looking at me not as an older man might do but like someone of my own age who might want to be my lover. I had painted myself a picture of Honey senior as being a hard-headed business man interested only in making money, probably fat and balding. Well, there is not a spare ounce of flesh stretched across his lean, gaunt frame and the hair situation I have already commented on. Something tells me that his interests also extend beyond making money.

"Peter, Bruce. Sorry not to have greeted you but I had a trade delegation from Japan on my hands. Are these the two young ladies you were telling me about?" The tone is firm and incisive.

Peter makes the introductions and Ross Honey turns

to Kate and myself. "I hope that you two girls know what you're letting yourselves in for. I'd sell Outback tomorrow if I could find a buyer and I didn't have Peter, here, begging me not to. Remember I'm going to give you fellows six months from the time you're operational under the new regime to get things straight. If, as I imagine will be the case, nothing has happened to suggest that you're going to make money, then that's it. I'll put the whole caboodle on the market. I hope you made this clear to your new backer. What's his name? Papa Doc?"

"Papadoulis, Dad. How did you hear about that?"

"Not very much happens around here that I don't know about. People who like me tell me things, and people who don't like me tell me things. Which reminds me. What in God's name were you doing at Renfrew's party? I'm amazed to hear that you even bothered to go."

Peter explains quickly what took place and Ross Honey nods.

"Typical! You won't be surprised to hear that Renfrew is putting it about that you tried to compromise him."

"He must be mad," says Bruce. "There's not a word of truth in it."

"It was my fault, Dad," admits Peter. "It was a damn fool thing to do, I know. I was getting desperate to raise some finance and when Renfrew expressed interest and said he would like to meet the girls I didn't think there would be any harm in taking them along."

"Well, don't do anything like that again or I'll sell you out tomorrow."

"No, Dad."

Peter is obviously uncomfortable at being bawled out in front of us and I can almost hear him wishing that he had passed up the visit. Ross Honey is an old-fashioned father in some ways, despite his youthful appearance.

Kate and I sit on either side of him at lunch and he is a most sophisticated and amusing companion, able to converse on a wide range of subjects and listen as well as talk. He has the ability to sound interested in what is being said to him, unlike some very amusing men who switch off when someone else is talking. The meal itself is delicious and served with wine, so I am soon feeling completely at my ease. I notice that Jean Hawks, sitting at the other end of the table, seems preoccupied and keeps trying to catch Ross's eye, but he avoids her.

Kate and I do a grand job trying to make Ross enthusiastic about the New Australia concept but, though he listens politely and bows to our professional knowledge on a couple of points, he seems a great deal less than totally won over.

"One thing you're going to have to do is make your own business if you're going to stand a snowball's chance in hell," he says, addressing Peter. "If you sit around waiting for the passengers to roll up you'll be dead ducks."

"We were hoping you'd be able to put some business our way, Dad."

"If what you're offering fits in with my requirements, I'll be glad to. But I'm not subsidising an inefficient operation."

"Nobody is going to ask you to do that. Bruce and I have been working on some plans to extend the charter side of the business and we don't intend to fill the air with empty planes."

"I'm glad to hear it. And I wish you luck." He raises his glass.

"Here's to New Australia."

"And good luck to all who fly in her," says Kate, gaily.

"I think you might have put that better, but I believe I know what you mean," says Ross. "Cheers!"

An hour later, we have had coffee and liqueurs on the terrace and are preparing to leave. I am standing a little apart from the others when Ross comes up to me.

"Are you staying with the Wilsons?" His voice betrays more than casual interest.

"Only until we start work. Then I expect Kate and I will share a flat."

"If you have any problems finding one, let me know. I have a few interests in property." He takes my hand and gives it a gentle squeeze. "It was great fun talking to you. I look forward to our next meeting."

I make what I hope are the right kind of noises but I can feel an ill-suppressed excitement running through my body. I believe that this rich, powerful and attractive man fancies me. It is a thought that remains with me, long after Eastern

115

Springs has faded from view behind its entourage of eucalyptus trees and the Jensen-Healey is purring back towards Sydney.

CHAPTER EIGHT

The next few weeks pass in a blaze of activity and one blazing row when Kate comments on how sexy Peter's father is.

"Sexy," snorts Peter, "he's an old man ! He'd be better off acting his age than trying to turn your heads."

"He wasn't trying to turn anyone's head," I say. "He's a very attractive man, that's all. You sound as if you're jealous of him."

Peter turns scarlet through his tan. "There are certain things about my father I am not jealous of. I don't admire everything he does."

"What do you mean?"

"Oh. It would take too long to explain. It's family business. I don't approve of my father's moral attitudes. I know it sounds pretty smug, saying that, but I guess sons are sensitive where their mothers are concerned".

"He had other women, did he?" asks Kate, never one to beat about the bush.

"I told you. I don't want to talk about it. If you want to know the details, there are plenty of people around Sydney better placed than me to give you the low down."

"You don't like Jean Hawks, do you?" I ask.

"I don't like her living in my mother's house."

"But your mother has been dead for years," says Kate. "You can't expect your father to remain celibate. He's not an old man, whatever you say. How old is he?"

"Fifty-two."

"That's not old. He looks ten years younger."

"You may like old men," storms Peter. "Maybe you've got a father fixation. I think it's disgusting that you should ever think of using a word like 'sexy' about him."

I have never known Peter get so worked up about anything and his argument seems unreasonable to the point of being hysterical. Instead of us having father fixations it seems as if he is obsessed by the memory of his mother. We try and reason with him but soon give it up as his mood becomes more and more unyielding.

On the New Australia front things move far more smoothly. Bright yellow is selected as the colour for the planes and we have uniforms designed to match. Yellow is a bright, sunny colour and fits in ideally with the smile motif. This idea we carry much further than was originally intended. In addition to the smile on the front of the planes, we have the emblem on all printed material – letter headings, timetables, notices – and also in advertising. Bruce gave up a job in an advertising agency to work for Peter and has a lot of bright ideas which he knows how to put into practice. Our whole sales pitch is based on making New Australia seem as friendly and welcoming as possible and our slogan is: 'Make new friends with New Australia, the friendly airline'. Alongside these words appear photographs of Kate and myself looking as 'welcome aboard!' as we can manage.

Gracie is a little disappointed that she has not appeared in any of the advertisements but we tell her that we are saving her up for the second phase, without being too specific as to what this means. Gracie is thrilled, if a little over-awed, by her new uniform, although she expresses the fear that it may inflame the rapist tendencies of the already highly sexed passengers who are attracted to her like moths to a candle.

Kate and I overhaul all the cabin equipment and settle down to our major task of recruiting new staff and instituting a training programme. In the course of this we come across the other half of Outback's fleet of stewardesses – Ruthie.

If Gracie has a tendency to be brash and outspoken, then Ruthie is quite the reverse. She can hardly look one in the eyes and wears the merest trace of make-up that looks as if it has survived the attentions of a tidal wave. This is a great pity, as we soon discover when we encourage Ruthie to be a little more adventurous in her presentation of herself. We send her off to have her hair cut and styled by the most swinging hairdresser in Sydney and Kate has a big session with her, explaining that to wear eye make-up does not automatically mean that one is embarking on a career as a street-walker; also, how to apply same. The result of our transformation is that Ruthie begins to attract wolf whistles and her confidence soars. Bruce certainly notices the change.

"What a fantastic looking girl that Ruthie is," he says enthusiastically. "I think I'll have to take her out and buy her a few beers."

"That's marvellous, isn't it?" says Kate, bitterly. "All that hard work and I stand to lose my fellow."

"Well, at least Gracie doesn't seem to be giving us any competition yet."

Kate shakes her head. "Poor old Gracie. What are we going to do about her?"

It is a sad fact that Gracie is performing right down to our expectations and has already earned an official complaint from a passenger who was threatened with physical violence because he commented favourably on her uniform.

"I could see what was lurking behind his eyes," she says defensively. "It was my body he wanted."

"I wonder what for?" says Kate to me afterwards. "I suppose you might use it if you ran out of horsehair half way through stuffing a sofa."

"She'll have to go," I say. "I flew with her the other day and she took off her shoes and started cutting her toe nails."

"Well at least she took her shoes off first," says Kate.

"Don't make jokes. This is serious. I don't want to be responsible for getting her sacked."

"Neither do I. Yet she is hopeless. Worse than hopeless – a dead liability."

"Oh, dear. It is difficult, isn't it? It makes you realise how nice it is just to be a stewardess and not to have to worry about decisions like this."

"Absolutely. Well, what are you going to do?"

"I'll speak to Peter. Perhaps he can say that New Australia has different retirement rules to Outback."

But when I next see Peter it is he who is doing all the talking.

"How do you fancy a round trip of Australia?" he says

118

enthusiastically. "I've just landed a very nice piece of business, ferrying this Rugby League team round the country. Chance to meet up with some of your compatriots if you're feeling homesick."

"A British Rugby League team? They're going to be pretty tough characters, aren't they?"

"That's why I'm going to send Gracie with you. She knows how to handle herself. Who knows? She might actually have something to complain about this time."

I am about to express my reservations concerning Gracie when it occurs to me that this trip might well save us from the embarrassment of having to give her her marching orders. If these rugger players are anything like the ones I have come into contact with back home, then Gracie could be wishing she had a parachute with her half an hour after take-off.

"How long will we be away for?"

"Two weeks and you'll be back in Sydney for the first test. I'll change crews then because I reckon you will probably have had enough."

"You could well be right. At least it will give me a chance to see some of the country. I imagine they'll be playing a couple of games a week?"

"Something like that. I haven't got the itinerary with me." Peter takes my arm and puts his hand over mine. "I haven't seen much of you lately, we've both been working so hard. What are you doing at the moment?"

"I'm free until after lunch and then I've got to go and interview some of the girls who answered our advertisement for stewardesses."

"Where are you doing that?'

"I've booked a hotel room in Sydney. There's so much work going on around here that the place is looking even more of a shambles than usual."

"Great. That means I can buy you lunch before you go into battle. Would you like that?"

I say 'yes, please' and we end up at the hotel in which I have booked the room for the interviews. I think that lunch is one of my favourite amorous meals because it is slightly unusual to be chatted up in the middle of the day, and I do like a spice of difference occasionally. Peter asks if Kate

119

and I have found a flat yet and I tell him that we have looked at a number but not found anything we really like. I do not tell him about his father's offer because something tells me that this would not go down very well.

"There's an apartment coming up in the same block as mine," says Peter. "I can have a word with the manager if you like."

The offer puts me in a spot because, much as I like Peter, I feel that living under the same roof may be too close for comfort. If our relationship is to develop it needs space in which to do so.

"I shouldn't think we'd be able to afford the rent," I say.

"I expect the airline could be persuaded to give you a living allowance," says Peter.

"It's very sweet of you, Peter," I say, "but I know that Kate has found something she is very keen on and wants me to see. If that falls through then perhaps we can take you up on your offer."

"I thought you said you hadn't seen anything?" says Peter looking puzzled.

"Yes. It was stupid of me. I'd forgotten about this place. Kate only found it yesterday."

"Where is it?"

"I can't remember," I say vaguely. "We've been sent so many particulars."

Peter looks in to my eyes for a moment and then asks if I would like a liqueur. I do not think he believes what I have said about the flat but he is keeping his feelings to himself. "We'd better check your accommodation, hadn't we?" he says.

For a moment I do not know what he means and then I realise that he is talking about the apartment for the interviews. It is now two fifteen and the first interview is scheduled for three. Something about the glint in his eye tells me that he has more on his mind than the interests of New Australia.

"It's all right," I tease. "I don't want to put you to all that trouble."

"I feel a responsibility to make sure that everything is in the right condition to receive these very important young ladies," says Peter, draining his coffee cup and putting it down firmly on the table. "First impressions are very important."

I am wearing my new uniform and I take pleasure in the admiring glances I receive as we go to the lift. The hotel is one of the swankiest in Sydney and from the public relations point of view it is obviously a place to be seen looking your best.

The apartment comprises two rooms, one of them a bedroom and the other a small sitting room. I have decided to conduct the interviews in the bedroom and use the sitting room as a waiting room. I feel I can hardly ask applicants to wait in a bedroom, and that room contains a large table which will be ideal for interviewing. I pin a notice to the sitting room door saying 'New Australia Stewardess Interviews. Please enter and wait until called' and go into the bedroom.

Peter is so close behind me he is almost in front of me. "You told reception you were here, did you?" he asks.

"Of course I did," I say, indignant that my efficiency should be questioned over such a detail.

"O.K. Keep your wool on. Sorry I asked." He stretches out an arm and gently strokes the side of my cheek. "How are you going to keep yourself occupied until the first one gets here?"

"I'll re-examine their application forms."

"Very conscientious." Peter's hand slides round my back and he pulls me against him. "It's been a long time since we made love."

"A couple of weeks," I say, trying to stop a stray hand slipping under my skirt. "Come on, Peter. The first girl is going to be here in a minute."

"Forty minutes to be precise, Angel. It seems a shame to waste the company's money by hiring this tastefully furnished bedroom and not putting it to its proper use."

"I can't. I'll get myself all muzzed up. Oh!" The latter exclamation is occasioned by me being lax in taking protective measures against those roving hands.

"Come on," says Peter. "You know you want to. Think how much you enjoyed it last time. We'll take great care not to ruckle your uniform." And with those words he starts unpopping the buttons of my tunic.

Now, I know that any girl reading this would immediately say 'nix on trix' and probably dust his darn cheeks with the flat of her hand for good measure. But I am a creature of depraved appetites and on certain occasions a most unenviable weakness of the head. No sooner has Peter undone all my jacket buttons than I am obediently extending my arms for the article to be removed. Next to vanish, without any resistance from me, is my blouse. Peter punctuates his work with deep kisses and I can feel the wine we had for lunch lulling me into a state of drowsy contentment. My arms cross behind Peter's neck and his skilful fingers remove my Biba bra. He slips it from my shoulders and immediately begins to squeeze my nipples gently between finger and thumb. This always makes me feel incredibly sexy and in no time I am fumbling for his zipper. Most of the men I make love to are well practiced in the art of removing a lady's clothes but I am afraid that I cannot match their skill. Even the simplest zipper becomes an obstacle course when I get my fingers on it and as for what lies beyond, that is up to you, gentlemen. A pair of Y-fronts sets me a greater problem than being asked to crack the vaults at Fort Knox with a hairpin.

Fortunately Peter does not require my services as a disrober and merely interprets my wishes correctly. He unzips my skirt and, as it falls to the floor, pushes me back on the bed. As I lie there wearing only panties and tights – I have tipped off my shoes long ago – he stands back and goes into a quick-strip routine that baffles the eye with its speed. Jacket, shoes, socks, shirt, trousers and pants. I am glad he does it in that order because the sight of a man standing naked except for a pair of socks always reminds me of a set of blue photographs I was once unfortunate enough to be shown. Shabby and rather pathetic.

There is certainly nothing pathetic about Peter. Talking to Kate I don't think either of us has ever experienced any lack of ardour in the Australian male. I have never found the male sex organ a thing of great beauty but it can be impressive. And, believe me, Peter is very impressive. No sooner is he naked than he drops down on his knees beside the bed and kisses me tenderly, sending down his hand to explore beneath my panties. Drawing back from my eager arms he peels off my tights and panties and joins me on the bed so that we can lie side by side and let our hands give each other pleasure. Soon I can be denied no longer and pull hungrily at Peter's lean flanks, urging him into me. He rises up and, as our mouths melt against each other, he buries himself in me like a velvet dagger. Oh, what sweet murder ensues in the following minutes and never was there a more willing victim! I close my eyes and lie there, feeling the heavenly sensations running through my body, as if I am floating on my back in the sea and being borne shorewards by a series of mounting waves.

"That's gorgeous," I moan. "Absolutely gorgeous."

Peter is no 'wham, bam, thank you, ma'am' artist and the controlled fury of his love-making envelopes me in a kind of trance in which I lose all sense of time.

This, as it turns out, is unfortunate.

Our love-making is interrupted by a sharp tap on the door leading into the corridor, and almost before we can spring apart the door opens and a pretty girl is looking down at us with an expression of amazement and embarrassment on her face. Even worse, two more girls are craning over her shoulder.

I pull a sheet over Peter and myself and the girl blushes scarlet. "I'm sorry," she gasps. "We thought – oh, it doesn't matter." The door closes hurriedly and I look at my watch. Eight minutes past three! Never was the phrase 'time flies when you are having a good time' more convincingly proved.

"Oh, no!" I shriek, leaping off the bed. "This is disastrous." No sooner have I started struggling into my tights than there is a knock at the room next door.

"We're surrounded," groans Peter. "They probably thought that what we were doing was part of the interview."

"Don't! What are we going to do?"

"I'm going to get out, and you've got to get on with the interviewing," says my gallant employer. Boy, if I thought he was a fast undresser I had never seen him when he was making the return journey and the chips were down. He has slipped on his shoes and is turning the door handle before I have buttoned up my blouse.

"Hey! You can't leave me like this," I squeak, but he is

gone. Outside in the corridor I hear him clearing his throat and directing another aspiring stewardess to the room next door. In a hopeless fluster I do something to my face and listen to the buzz of chatter coming from the sitting room. No doubt newcomers are being regaled with stories of the interview technique being employed next door. I straighten the bed, drag the tables into the centre of the room – of course it makes a loud squeaking noise – and arrange my papers. I never did get around to checking through those application forms. I have half a mind to follow Peter's example and make a bolt for it but there is no turning back now. If the applicants feel that they have been hoaxed when nobody appears to interview them, then New Australia's reputation will be harder hit than it has been already. After all, I try and comfort myself, we are supposed to be a fun airline. With sinking heart I take a last look at myself in the mirror and open the connecting door on five girls who run their eyes up and down me as if searching for finger prints.

"I'm so sorry I kept you waiting," I say sweetly. "I'm afraid things got on top of me after lunch." Somebody giggles and I realise that the remark could have been better phrased. "Is Miss Birkin here? Good. Come inside, please."

My first interviewee follows me into the bedroom and I make a mental note to avoid filling in one of the sections on the interview form. It is headed 'Estimation of applicant's moral standards.' Somehow, I just don't feel equipped to comment on that at the moment.

I find out later that my notice had fallen off the sitting room door and not been seen by the interviewees who had been given the number of the suite in reception. Hence those bright, eager faces peering round the bedroom door. My interviewing becomes less nervous as the afternoon proceeds and by the end of it there are three girls that I think are excellent stewardess material. One of them, unfortunately, is the wench who discovered me in Peter's arms and there is a temptation to reject her on the grounds of being a future embarrassment. However, my better nature comes to the fore and I decide that I have to add her to the list. I wonder what she will think when she sees Peter. Perhaps she will not recognise him.

The plan is that Kate and I will give the girls three weeks intensive training which will, of necessity, be combined with flying experience. This will now have to start when I get back from my rugby tour. I am pretty apprehensive about this tour of duty and my first glimpse of the customers does nothing to reassure me. Having flown out from England they have found their feet – and according to local newspapers, their fists – against a local team and are now raring to go. I am introduced to them in our brand new airport lounge but their eyes seem to have no time for the decor. A low, appreciative growl breaks from twenty-one pairs of lips as I appear and I feel like a Christian stepping into the lions' pit. Gracie does not go down quite as well and I see one of the team cover his face with his hands and shake his head disbelievingly.

'This is Mr Driscoll, the team manager," says Peter who is in charge of introductions. "The next couple of weeks will give you plenty of opportunity to get acquainted with the rest of the boys." There is a menacing rumble of agreement from behind him. Sam Driscoll is the ugliest man I have ever seen and hairy as a monkey. He must be about fifty and his head looks as if it has been hammered down into his shoulders so that there is virtually no sign of a neck. His features are sprinkled haphazardly around his face as if he has walked into an electric fan and it is obvious that he has played a lot of rugby league football in his youth – either that or wrestled sharks. 'The Boys', as he chooses to call his charges, are cast in the same mould and mount a terrifying battery of muscle. They tower over Gracie and I – and it takes something to make my flying companion look petite, believe you me.

We pose for some publicity pictures beside the plane and immediately rough hands start goosing me from behind as I try and look svelte and demure for the photographer. God knows what they will be like once we have taken off. I soon find out. An ingenious range of ploys are invented in order to make me lean across as many seats as possible and the jokes and ribald comments would make the script writer for a blue movie blush. Half the team organise a daily sweepstake on the colour of my panties and the other half explore ways of finding out in advance. I had thought that

125

these guys were supposed to be highly trained athletes but the amount of booze they put away is nobody's business. Every single one of them seems to have a flask of spirits stowed away somewhere and Gracie and I get no peace until they begin to fall asleep like babies who have had their bottles.

Gracie has fared better than me in the groping department but confesses herself amazed at the manners and appearance of my countrymen.

"They're like animals," she says, not without a certain grudging admiration creeping into her voice. "I've never seen anything like that Driscoll." I watch the team manager wrapping his false teeth in a handkerchief and have to agree with her.

By the end of the first week my bottom is black and blue from the pinching it has received and I announce the colour of my knickers automatically every breakfast time to avoid speculation. 'The Boys' have clocked up another mammoth victory over a team drawn from a number of widely spread districts and Gracie has made a number of boobs which would have been serious if we had been carrying more demanding and less good natured passengers. Her ability to get her uniform dirty is unrivalled by a toddler coming to grips with its first ash tray and there is no one quite like her for getting announcements wrong. She even confuses the name of the plane we are flying in. There is no doubt about it, I think to myself, you have got to go, Gracie.

Not all our passengers are mauling hulks. One, especially, called Jim Ransome, is a really nice guy. He appeals to me because he has a tremendous physique but a very gentle face and manner. I can imagine the rest of the party tearing the opposition limb from limb but not Jim. He also appears shy and that makes him stand out from the rest of the party. I learn that he is training to be a teacher and that he comes from a town in the north of England called Dewsbury. I attach myself to Jim, both because I like him and because to be seen to have singled out one member of the team affords me some protection from the others.

It is strange but the fact that I have a very successful sexual relationship with Peter makes me more eager to experience sex with other men. My whole appetite for

126

physical relationships has been increased. It can work the other way too. An unrewarding sexual encounter with a man will often blunt my sex drive for a number of weeks. During our flight to Rockhampton I look into Jim's sleeping face and wonder what he would be like as a lover. Would he be as gentle as his expression suggests? Or, as forceful as the hard, firm lines of his body? It is difficult for him to share a seat with anyone else because his shoulders are so broad.

The game in Rockhampton is an important one and the team are ordered to bed soon after supper. I cannot really see that it is going to make a lot of difference to these rough-hewn muscle mountains to be tucked up early but at least it prevents them breaking up the hotel as has apparently happened before.

"Are you going to take a turn round the town?" I ask Gracie who has made herself 'comfortable' as she calls it. In other words she looks like an unmade bed.

"I don't think it would be safe for us to wander around there by ourselves," she says.

"It will be with the team in their rooms," I say. "They're the only danger I can think of."

"There'll never be any trouble with Mr Driscoll in charge," says Gracie. "He won't stand any nonsense."

Gracie is clearly impressed with dour Sam who rarely addresses a word to anyone other than his trainer. I think it may have something to do with his ugliness. Certainly, in the area of beauty Gracie rarely has the advantage over a man and it is a novel experience for her to be so clearly the superior that she does not have to protect her inferiority complex by indulging in rapist fantasies. Later that evening I see her in the lounge standing beside Sam Driscoll's chair as he plays draughts with his trainer. He is staring thought-fully at the board and she is staring thoughtfully at him rather in the manner of a mother gazing down upon her sleeping child. She turns, sees me, waves, and knocks Sam's drink across the board as she turns back. Typical, I think, as I go on my way.

'The Boys' do some light training on the morning of the big match and eat an early lunch. I can see that they are tensed up because there are hardly any jokes about the food or Gracie and myself. I am no sports fan but I feel a kind of

127

loyalty to the team and so troop along to the ground with Gracie and Sam. Sam disappears for a last minute pep talk and I take a look at the opposition team as they run out on to the pitch. In all respects they seem identical to our lot and I would have difficulty in telling the difference if it was not for their jerseys. Things are made worse because a lot of rain has fallen during the night and the pitch is soon reduced to a quagmire. In no time both teams are indistinguishable, covered from head to toe in mud and often confused as to who to give the ball to. In these conditions it is not surprising that tempers are soon lost and the referee's whistle orchestrates the baying of the crowd. I try to watch Jim but I cannot tell him from anyone else. I know nothing about the rules but there is a lot of cheering when one of the home team kicks the ball between the posts and over the bar and a chorus of whistles followed by silence when one of our team does the same thing. Gracie, who I had imagined would be fiercely partisan, is strangely silent and occasionally looks at the phlegmatic Sam to see how he is reacting to the game.

"Who's winning?" I ask when the whistle goes for half-time and the two teams separate like a piece of black pudding being broken in half.

"It's a draw. Two-two. I'd better go and put some ginger into the bastards". Sam leaves us and I turn to Gracie.

"I thought you'd be shouting your head off for the locals," I say to her.

"I don't feel I can, really when I'm sitting next to Sam. He takes it so seriously."

I do not care too much who wins as long as no one gets hurt, but two minutes into the second half a fight breaks out on the field in front of us and I recognise Jim, for the first time, when he is carried off bleeding at the temple.

"Boo! Dirty foul!" I shout immediately becoming totally committed to the British cause.

From that moment on the game becomes rough, to put it mildly. To me it seems pointless that the tourists should have travelled twelve thousand miles to indulge in a tedious brawl in a mud bath when one purpose of sport at this level must presumably be to foster better, rather than bitter, international relations.

Two men get sent off and when the tourists go ahead by a hotly disputed try there is nearly a riot, both on the pitch and off it.

Jim comes and sits beside us with a bandage round his head and is quite clearly concussed. This does not stop him from becoming involved in a slanging match with some home team supporters sitting nearby and I am relieved to hear the final whistle. A further boost to Anglo-Australian relations is supplied by one of the tourists who delivers a defiant V-sign to the crowd as he leaves the field.

"Good win," says Sam, sounding cheerful for the first time that I can remember.

"Is it always like that?" I ask.

"The boys weren't holding their passes today. They're not usually that sloppy."

"I meant the violence."

"Oh, that. Yes, I'd say that was about average to hard."

On the way back to the hotel I learn that there is going to be a 'celebration' dance in the town later in the evening. After what I have seen, I imagine it must be to celebrate the fact that no one got killed.

"It's usually better if we have a get together later in the evening when everybody has had a chance to cool down," explains Sam. "You'll see. There'll be a real nice atmosphere tonight." I have my doubts, and – boy! – are they vindicated.

When the team gets back to the hotel they are in truculent mood and boasting openly about the blows they struck. Indeed, to look at their faces, one would think they were boxers, not rugby players. I had imagined that Jim would be put to bed but he is soon in the bar with the rest of the party. That is one place you can always be sure of finding most of the team.

"You're not going to this dance tonight, are you?" I say, looking at the ugly gash on Jim's forehead.

"Try and stop me, sweetheart. I want to find the bloke who put the boot in."

"I'm not coming if there's going to be violence."

"Oh, there won't be any violence. Just a bit of sorting out, that's all."

I do not regard Jim's words as offering much reassurance

and it is in a mood of considerable trepidation that I climb aboard the coach that is taking us to the reception and dance. I seem to be the only member of the party who is sober and I notice that Gracie has let her hair down sufficiently to sit on Sam's knee. What a couple they make! Unkind as it may seem, they look to me like two battered Toby jugs.

The coach pulls away with everybody singing loudly and the half-bottles much in evidence. I peer out of the window and try to listen to the words. There is a certain kind of – usually undersexed – man who gets a kick out of shouting four-letter words in the presence of a woman and I do not want to give any of them the satisfaction of seeing my blushes. The embarrassment I feel is not caused by the sexual nature of the songs but the infantile banality of the creatures delivering them.

The reception is at the Town Hall and when we get there the opposition are already getting stuck in to the booze. Again I am struck by the similarity between the two sides and how incongruous some of them look, bulging out of ill-fitting suits or sporting blazers that hang over their shoulders like horse blankets.

The Mayor says a few words of welcome but is obviously pushed to find anything good to say about the game. 'Hard' is the best adjective he can muster. When he has finished Sam gets up and grinds out a speech of thanks which is loudly barracked by his own team. The social graces completed, everybody settles down to some serious drinking. The two teams keep firmly apart and I am reminded of The Jets and The Sharks facing each other in West Side Story. There are a few wives present at the reception but they are mostly on the frumpish side, which is probably just as well knowing how some of the tourists can behave.

Soon the sound of music manages to make itself heard above the noise of popping corks and drunken chatter and the crowd in the room begins to thin out as people drift off to dance or examine the action.

"Do you fancy a whirl, girl?" says a very pronounced Australian accent and I find myself being led on to the floor by one of the local team. Whatever his skill on the field, it certainly does not extend to the dance floor and my feet are in constant danger of being crushed. Neither is it the only part of my body that is suffering. My partner's hands wander over my limbs as if suspecting that they might conceal a secret compartment and I am literally being assaulted to music. No sooner have I struggled free from this customer than another appears in his place and the mauling continues. Both the guys stink of booze and it is no surprise when male number two suddenly slides to the floor and stays there! Unfortunately, this incident coincides with the appearance of Jim who has come to rescue me. Another Aussie reckons that Jim has felled his mate and swings a vicious haymaker that provokes instant retaliation and in no time the dance floor is a mass of milling bodies.

Jim is clearly still suffering from the after-effects of his concussion and I see him deposited on the seat of his pants by a blow that leaves him shaking his head as if he does not know where he is. A boot whistles past his nose and I realise that I must stage a rescue act. Behind me is a small broom cupboard and, as a bottle shatters against the wall above my head, I pull open the door and drag Jim inside. For a few moments we sit there listening to the battle raging on the dance floor and then Jim's hand reaches out and touches me.

"Ah, there you are. What happened? Where are we?"

"You got another crack on the head. I thought it would be a good idea if we sat this one out. We're in a broom cupboard."

"I wondered what that smell was. I didn't think it could be your perfume."

"Thanks a lot. I don't usually use floor polish!"

"It's cosy in here, isn't it?" Jim's hands reach out in the darkness and pull me to him. A body crashes against the door and it is clear that the brawl is continuing.

"Cosier than out there."

"I'm glad I've got you alone at last. I don't like having to share you with twenty men." Jim's fingers feel for my face and he gently tugs at the lobes of my ears.

Wicked as it may sound I feel myself titillated by the thought that Jim and I are alone in the darkness just a few feet away from hundreds of people. It invests the whole scene with a kind of delicious danger.

"You're huge, aren't you?" I say, as I run my fingers over the expanse of Jim's back.

"Too big for some. I had a tart once – or, more like I was going to. She gave me my money back."

"What do you mean?"

"I was too big for her."

"Are you warning me?"

"I thought I ought to tell you." He pulls me closer to him and I can feel what he is talking about. At first, I think he has taken advantage of the darkness to play a trick on me by putting something down the front of his trousers but I soon discover that this is not the case. Kissing me hard on the mouth he slides his hand up underneath my skirt and swiftly tugs down my panties and tights.

"Just making a recce," he says, putting his fingers to work. "I don't want to hurt you."

He seems satisfied because I can feel him freeing himself and my inquisitive hands close about what feels like a hot cucumber. Maybe it is the darkness inflaming my imagination but the size of the thing really is remarkable.

Jim changes his position so that he is leaning back against the wall. "Kneel across me. Then you can take as much as you need."

I finish removing my underwear and do as I am told. Jim's huge hands enclose the cheeks of my behind and he gently settles me across his lap.

"Now. Easy does it."

His mouth seeks mine and as we kiss I lower myself gingerly on to his giant pestle. I can honestly say that I have never experienced anything like it. I do not wish to appear crude, but I feel like a sausage skin that has been filled to bursting point. Big men often have very ordinary implements but in every respect Jim is larger than life. Once he has ascertained that I am safely mounted I feel his muscles flex as he takes the whole weight of my body and moves me slowly up and down. My whole being thrills to the sensations that explode within me and I hear myself cry out in pleasure.

"Oh, that's heaven. Heaven!"

Jim is an experienced lover, as well he might be with such a gift from nature, and he reads my wishes well. Moving

132

me up and down with increasing speed he probes me to greater depths than I would have believed it possible for my body to sustain. I feel myself borne away on a whirlwind of lustful delight and am so overcome that I burst into tears. Shaking with emotion I attain an orgasm that breaks through me in waves and renders me practically unconscious. My pleasure is doubled because I hear Jim release a long moaning sigh and know that we have attained the ultimate together. For long minutes we quiver in each other's arms and slowly the noises from outside begin to impinge upon our exhausted silence. Foremost amongst them is the band playing 'The Lady Is A Tramp' – not dedicated to me I hope! The punch-up is obviously over.

"We'd better get out and see what's happening," says Jim, in a voice that suggests he is eager to join the fray once more.

"Wait till I get my panties on." I beg him.

This is easier said than done because it is very dark in that broom cupboard. Eventually I am in a position to kiss Jim and thank him for one of my most pleasurable experiences ever, and scuttle out of the cupboard in front of an amazed man who is engaged in sweeping up a pile of broken glass.

No sooner have I escaped from him than a distraught Gracie heaves into view. "Thank God! Where on earth have you been? I thought somebody had slipped you a Mickey Finn. I was so worried!"

"Relax. I was hiding up with Jim. Where are the others?"

"Half of them have gone to hospital, half have gone to the Police Station, and the rest are waiting in the coach." This is pretty typical of the way Gracie's mind works but I ignore it.

I look about me and the dance floor appears like the set of a low-budget war movie. Notwithstanding the debris that is still littering the floor, people are dancing and the leader of the band is conducting with a crimson handkerchief held to his nose. That is what I like about Australians, they know how to take things in their stride.

"We chose a good one to sit out, didn't we?" says Jim, coming up beside me. "Jeeze, but I still feel muzzy."

"Me too," I say with feeling. "Very, very muzzy."

CHAPTER NINE

By the time I get back to Sydney I am completely exhausted. Not, unfortunately, for the first reason that might spring to my readers' minds. I do not enjoy another encounter with the formidable Jim Ransome. No more broom cupboards present themselves and, without such fortunate accidents of fate, there is no chance of me escaping from my responsibilities as nursemaid to twenty-one men.

I might as well add a woman to that list. Gracie becomes more and more helpless as the tour proceeds and I have grave doubts about leaving her with Ruthie when I take up my duties as administrator of what Kate and I, with new found efficiency, call the S.T.P.: The Stewardess Training Programme. I confide my fears to Kate who tries to offer encouragement.

"From what you tell me about 'The Boys', I don't think that they would notice if you gave them a female gorilla as a stewardess," she says. "Why not let her finish the job and then break it to her tactfully that she ought to retire. Maybe Peter will do it."

"Do you think that Ruthie will be able to handle things virtually by herself?"

"I'm certain of it. She's come on by leaps and bounds. She's so pretty too. Damn her."

This business of prettiness is something I am brought into contact with when I start supervising the Stewardess Programme. When Kate and I were being trained, all our instructresses seemed incredibly glamorous. Now it is the trainees who are the beauties. Maybe it has something to do with the way that policemen appear younger as one gets older, or perhaps I am self-conscious after my embarrassing experience at the first interview. I stand by my lectern and yacker on about safety regulations and emergency exits while I look down upon three really snappy young chicks who need no help from me in the matter of dress sense and deportment. One of them, Astrid Roberts, was a fashion

134

model before applying to join New Australia, so it is no surprise that she always looks like a million dollars. The other two girls, Lynn Western and Jill Wood, are typical of the new generation of young Australians who borrow their dress sense from the increasing contact that their continent has with both the western and eastern hemispheres.

The new additions to the flying fleet require the services of two stewardesses, and number three has been selected to take Gracie's place. I feel pretty sneaky knowing that, while poor Gracie is toiling in the back of beyond, her replacement is being groomed to step into her shoes but I can think of no alternative. At least, I tell myself, I will face up to the job of breaking the bad news to her on her return. I only wish there was a ground job we could offer her but I would have qualms about employing Gracie as a cloakroom attendant.

I pass a sleepless night before my meeting with Gracie and when she comes into the office I am feeling quite sick. It is some comfort to me that she has dyed her hair a streaky blonde colour that makes it look like dirty hay. I must be doing the right thing in asking her to resign. She looks unusually apprehensive and I wonder if she suspects what is in my mind.

"How did the trip go?" I ask her, deciding that it is impossible to come straight to the point without being spectacularly unkind. "I see that they started losing games after I left."

"Yes. They said you were their lucky mascot. I expect you read about the fire in the hotel?"

"No! What happened?"

"I'm surprised they were able to keep it out of the papers. One of the boys fell asleep with a cigarette in his hand. Nobody was hurt."

"Thank goodness for that. How terrifying, though. You must have been shocked out of your wits."

"Not as shocked as when they tried to take over the plane. We dropped like a stone for two thousand feet."

"Gracie!" I feel really guilty that all this should happen when I am thousands of miles away preparing to jettison Gracie. Still, maybe it will help me in my unpleasant task. "Gracie. You must feel that you never want to see another plane?"

Gracie shrugs uncomfortably. "Well, it's not that so much."

"It must be so tiring," I prompt. "You've done so much for the airline. It seems unfair that you should have to keep on undergoing the strain of assignments like that."

"I've always enjoyed my work." There are tears in Gracie's eyes. "Of course there were the men."

"The men," I say eagerly. "That must have been awful for you on the last trip. Some of them were so coarse, weren't they?"

Gracie burst in to tears. "I – I – I've – "

I decided to seize the opportunity with both hands. "I understand. You don't have to say anything. I know the strain it must have been for you. Someone with your sensitive temperament. And I believe it's going to get worse. Some of the charters that Mr Honey has been forced to book to make ends meet are fraught with the same kind of problem. I think everyone would understand if, in the circumstances – "

"Please!" Gracie holds up a silencing hand. "Don't say any more. There's something I've got to tell you." I freeze in mid-sentence, wondering what on earth Gracie has to confess. Maybe she used salt instead of sugar again. "I want to leave Outback – I mean, New Australia."

"What!?"

Gracie manages to misinterpret my amazement. "Yes. You must think I'm awful, but I want to leave. You see, I'm going to get married."

"Married?"

"Yes. I'm sorry leaving you in the lurch at a time like this but I've got an opportunity and if I don't take it I may never get another one."

"Gracie! Who – ?" And then the penny drops. All those introspective silences. The spaniel eyes at the card table. The sheer unbeatable ugliness of the man. "Sam Driscoll," I say.

Gracie nods. "It was love at first sight. The minute I saw him, I knew. He told me that he did, too. It was while we were waiting outside the hotel for the fire engine to come."

"I'm glad some good came of the incident," I say.

136

"The whole tour was planned in heaven. He proposed while the plane was plunging through the air, completely out of control. 'If we ever get out of this alive, will you marry me?' That's what he said. He wanted me to know, you see."

"Gracie! It's so romantic." So convenient, too. What a godsend that we will be able to say goodbye to Big G. without any embarrassment. There are tears pricking my eyes and it is not just because I always cry at engagements and weddings.

Soon after I hear the news I bump into Kate and Bruce, and Bruce is swift to add another dimension to our enthusiasm.

"What a fantastic publicity angle," he exults. "The Friendly Airline sparks romance between stewardess and manager of touring rugby team. I can just see the headlines."

"And the photographs," says Kate grimly.

There is a moment's horrified silence.

"Cancel the photographs!" shouts Bruce. "Cripes. That would be a disaster, wouldn't it?" He shakes his head sadly. "What a pity it isn't one of you two getting married."

"Nobody has asked us," says Kate, tartly.

Bruce looks uncomfortable. "No, well-er. We'll have to think of something else, won't we?"

"Like banning all photographers from the wedding," I say.

"You couldn't do that. Poor old Gracie would have nothing to remember the great day by."

"I wasn't serious, you fool" I snap.

"We need to do something," says Bruce thoughtfully. "I wish to hell I knew what."

So do I. But nothing comes to me and I am beginning to reconcile myself to the sight of the world's unloveliest couple doing a slap down advertising job for New Australia when Ruthie asks if she can see me.

The moment I clap eyes on her I fear the worst. She looks worried and ashamed of herself. Classic symptoms of the girl who suddenly finds herself in the family way.

"I'm sorry, Penny," she says. "I'm afraid I've got some bad news for you."

My heart sinks. Just as I thought, stupid girl. I did not think it was possible for anyone to be caught out these days. But, no doubt something can be done about it.

"I want to get married. I feel awful about it after all that Kate and you have done for me. I know I'm letting New Australia down."

To say that the news comes as a bombshell represents the understatement of the year. For a few moments I can think of nothing to say.

"That's all right," I blurt out eventually. "It happens all the time. One of the hazards of the profession."

"I know, but coming so soon after Gracie. I wish it could have happened another way. There must be something about those limey rugby players."

My ears prick up. "Limey rugby players?"

Ruthie nods. "Yes. It was a flight to romance, wasn't it?"

"Which one?" I ask, my mind running through a catalogue of broken-nosed pug-uglies.

"Jim Ransome. Do you remember him? He's the big one with the nice smile."

Bombshell number two explodes above my head. "I do recall him," I say, trying to make it sound like an effort. "He got hurt in that game at Rockhampton, didn't he?"

"Yes. It was after that I really got to know him. Oh, Penny, if only you knew. He's so – I just don't know how to put it."

'Don't bother," I say hurriedly. "I know what it's like. When you're in love, I mean."

I must confess that my first reaction to the news is to feel a pang of jealousy. I don't think that any girl likes to see an old beau snapped up by someone else. Maybe Jim does not exactly fit into the category of a beau but you know what I mean. I secretly hope that all my ex-lovers will pine away and die rather than succumb to someone else's embrace. There is always the uncomfortable feeling in the back of my mind that they have found someone with more to offer than myself.

My second reaction is the one Ruthie alluded to: a feeling of disappointment that we should be losing a girl of Ruthie's increasing capabilities. Our slogan seems to be going to everybody's head.

Bruce is swift to see a more cheerful side to the picture.

"This could save the day," he says. "What a break. If we can organise a double wedding we can direct all the pictorial coverage at Ruthie and that bloke she's marrying. They make quite a handsome couple, you know."

"I had noticed," I say, not without a trace of bitterness. "But do you think they're going to want a double wedding?"

"By the time I've finished with them, the whole team will be looking round for someone to marry."

Bruce is nothing if not a very accomplished hustler when it comes to generating publicity. He talks to the Australian Rugby League authorities about the effect on gates of stimulating widespread newspaper and radio coverage of the wedding – Australia seems to have hundreds of radio stations – and gets them to contribute to the cost of a joint honeymoon at a posh hotel in Tasmania – not too far away to write off future opportunities for commercial exploitation. New Australia, of course, are very prepared to chip in some money in order to publicise themselves and soon Sam and Gracie and Ruthie and Jim – sounds like a movie about wife-swapping, doesn't it? – are lined up as recipients of a sizeable dowry.

Only one problem remains: Sam and Gracie stand a good chance of being the ugliest couple to reach the altar since the last version of 'The Bride Of Frankenstein'.

"It doesn't matter so much about Sam," says Bruce. "He doesn't reflect on New Australia. If only there was some way of making Gracie wear a sack over her head."

I pay no particular attention to his words until a few nights later. I have come back from one of our, now regular, flights to Melbourne and Peter has taken me to the cinema. I cannot remember the name of the film and it is pretty lousy, but it is all about Spanish noblemen indulging in bouts of acrobatic sword-fighting. I am on the point of dozing off and hoping that Peter is not feeling too sexy because I am tired, when there comes a scene where the heroine is in a church with her duenna and the hero wants to get a message to her without the old bat realising that he is in the vicinity. The plot is unimportant. What grabs my attention is the veil that the heroine is wearing.

"I've got it!" I shout so that everyone within five rows turns round. "We'll dress her up in Spanish costume with a veil!" Peter must also be on the verge of sleep because it takes him a few minutes to realise what I am talking about. "Gracie!" I shriek. "If we put her in a costume like that, nobody is going to be able to recognise her."

"I like the idea, but supposing she doesn't want to wear it?"

"Bruce will persuade her. He'll think of some marvellous reason why the two of them should dress up as señoritas."

"A couple of Spanish fly girls?" suggests Peter, while I groan and the audience hisses at us to shut up.

But, for once, Bruce's blandishments cut no ice and Gracie is determined to be married in white.

"My mother wouldn't have it any other way," she says. "What would people say in Yarrah if I turned out not wearing white?"

"We thought a little bit of mystery would add a certain je ne sais quoi," says Kate.

"I don't think my mother would like that either" says Gracie, suspiciously. "She's very conservative. She likes everything to be done just as it should be. She wants my sisters to be bridesmaids."

Somehow I had never thought of Gracie as having a family and news of their existence does nothing to cheer me. "How many are there?"

"Six."

"Six sisters!?"

"That's right. Six sisters and four brothers. Mother used to say we ate her out of house and home."

"Some of the sisters will have to be maids of honour, won't they? I mean they're married I imagine?"

"No," says Gracie proudly. "I'm the first."

At this point words fail me. What can the other six sisters look like? And as bridesmaids. The thought is too horrible to consider.

"Can't we persuade Gracie to get married in England?" I ask.

"Not now. Sam is so keen on Australia that he and Gracie are going to live here when the tour is over. It's one of the heart-warming angles on my press release."

"Oh, well. There's nothing for it. We'll have to let her do what she wants," says Kate. "After all, it is the happiest day of her life and all that kind of thing."

"And the most miserable day of mine," says Bruce.

But soon, we have a stroke of fortune. Gracie's sisters are apparently part of a juggling act touring Europe and cannot be released. "I never had the balance, myself," says Gracie and nobody who had seen her trying to serve coffee to a cabin full of drenched passengers could disagree.

We swallow our disappointment concerning the sisters bravely, and prepare for the big day. One awesome figure we come into contact with is Gracie's mother. Mrs Segal is of Hungarian extraction – or beef extraction as Peter puts it when he claps eyes on the lady's generous frame – and is very determined that her daughter will not miss out in the joint ceremony.

"Down the aisle side by side they come," she says firmly.

"There isn't room for them to come down the aisle side by side," says Bruce bitterly. "Has the old bag taken a look at her daughter lately?"

On the morning of the wedding Kate and I have been pressed into service as maids of the bedchamber under the elderly but still eagle eye of Mrs Segal. Gracie's wedding dress is not one I would have chosen myself but has apparently been in the Segal family for hundreds of years.

"About twice as long as Gracie," says Kate, unkindly.

One interesting light it throws on the physical development of the Segals is that it is too small for Gracie. "They're obviously geting bigger and bigger," says an awed Kate.

Mrs Segal is not deterred. "With the needle and cotton anything is possible," she says, positively.

We make running repairs as we stitch Gracie into her nuptial finery but I have the feeling that at any moment the dress may explode. Deciding to play safe I take a needle and cotton to the church with me.

The wedding guests must represent some of the largest people on the Australian continent. Looking down the aisle I can see the bull-necks of the British rugby league contingent and, on the other side, plentiful evidence that Gracie will not be without family support on her big day.

"Look at Sam!" hisses Kate as a nervous face gazes up the aisle towards us.

Never the most beautiful of men, Sam is looking positively horrific and does not appear to have slept for three days. I later find that he really hasn't slept for three days! Sam's stag party was held two nights before the wedding in order to give him time to recover but no sooner was he in a position to escape from the attentions of his team than he was nobbled by Mr Segal. That gentleman introduced him to an old Hungarian custom in which the bridegroom takes his prospective father-in-law out and buys him enough liquor to render him insensible. Small wonder that poor Sam looks as if he has difficulty in standing up.

We are about to advance down the aisle when Gracie suddenly stops and clutches her bosom dramatically. "It's gone," she says.

She is obviously not referring to her bosom which would require a small pick-up truck to carry it a hundred yards.

"It's coming apart at the front," she hisses.

Feeling impressed with my foresight I produce my needle and cotton and step forward to render assistance. Gracie has still got her veil drawn over her generous features and has not been exposed to the bevy of photographers swarming outside the church.

"Do something!" People are beginning to look back up the aisle towards us and the vicar is hovering nervously. I exchange a glance with Kate and I think the idea occurs to both of us at the same instant.

Gracie's blouse is bulging apart, unable to contain her formidable breastwork. As Kate pulls it together, I swiftly insert a few stitches and make sure that I tack the veil to the dress so that it cannot be freed without jeopardising the safety of the rest of the creation. With any luck Gracie will now be shut away behind her veil for the rest of the ceremony.

This, in fact, proves to be the case, although there is a nasty moment when Sam tries to reach his bride's uncluttered lips and almost succeeds in inserting his head underneath the veil in order to attain this end.

"Brilliant, girls," says a satisfied Bruce as we watch the cameras clicking away happily outside and Gracie's veil is still held firmly in place. "Now I can really begin to enjoy this wedding."

He is not the only one! I do not think I have ever been to a more swinging reception. Everybody gets happily drunk and there is a great deal of good-natured horseplay from the rugby tourists without things getting out of hand.

After the speeches the champagne continues to flow and people begin to dance. I am high as a kite and take a turn round the floor with anyone who cares to ask me. Sam and Gracie perform a kind of waltz and everyone cheers. I have apologised profusely for my clumsiness in stitching Gracie's veil to her dress and the incident has been forgotten by everyone except Mrs Segal who keeps shooting me baneful glances as if she suspects the truth. Ruthie is looking radiant and Jim, to my mind, looks even better. I still feel a slight pang of jealousy and disappointment when I see him cradling Ruthie in his strong arms. He dances with me and I cannot resist telling him what a two-timing Romeo he is.

"I should be very angry with you," I tell him. "You treated me very badly."

"I treated you beautifully, and you know it. Nobody forced you to drag me into that cupboard."

"I was saving you from being beaten up."

"Well, I think I said thank you as nicely as I could." He kisses me gently on the cheek as Ruthie comes up.

"Look at him," she jokes. "Married for a couple of hours and he's misbehaving already. I bet you had your hands full with him, Penny."

I cannot remember how I answered that but I know that my reply was a good deal tamer than it might have been!

Talking of misbehaving, the revelation of the day concerns Kate. The wedding turns into a party with the departure of the brides and grooms and the dancing continues unabated. Very tiddly, but very happy, I decide to find Peter and make him dance with me. I remember him going upstairs just before Gracie and Sam left and imagine that he is comforting Mrs Segal who was too overcome to leave her daughter's dressing room – "Booze and relief," says Kate unkindly, diagnosing the causes of the condition in her usual malicious fashion.

I go upstairs and make my way along a corridor, keeping

my ears open for the sound of Mrs Segal's unmistakeable voice. A couple pass me hand in hand, giggling, and I wonder what they have been up to. I look into one bedroom but there is no one there. I am about to go out when I hear noises coming through a door which presumably connects with the adjoining suite. I open it and then close it swiftly.

In the room Kate is lying on the bed in a position that suggests she could be making love to the man stretched out beside her. I do not look long enough to be certain. Neither of them see me, though the man looks towards the door as I close it. The man is Michael Papadoulis.

CHAPTER TEN

What I have seen casts a blight over my enjoyment of the rest of the wedding celebrations and I wonder what I should do about it. Normally Kate and I discuss our love affairs with each other and the fact that Kate has kept this one secret suggests that it is serious, as well as that she fears my disapproval. I do not believe that what I saw was the celebration of an instant attack of passion. What Kate and Michael were doing on that bed suggested that they were mature lovers.

After giving the matter a lot of thought I decide that there is nothing I can do until Kate raises the matter with me. To my increasing alarm she shows no sign of doing so. I notice that her affair with Bruce seems to have cooled to friendship point and that she often goes out by herself, giving only a hazy idea of her whereabouts. She even disappears for a weekend, saying that she has discovered some long-lost relation who has invited her to the family home. It all sounds very suspicious and I cannot resist doing some detective work to discover where Michael Papadoulis is. It comes as no surprise to discover that he is away 'on business' at exactly the same time as Kate. Quite a coincidence!

Several times I am on the point of raising the matter but on each occasion I check myself. It is none of my business and I know that if Kate is deeply embroiled in a passionate love affair, no words of mine are going to change things. She will come to me when she needs help – I hope.

It is about this time that something happens that helps to turn my thoughts away from Kate's presumed love affair. Having put Peter's nose out of joint by turning down his offer of accomodation, Kate and I have still not found a flat that we really like and several times I have been on the point of taking up Ross Honey's offer of assistance. Two things have deterred me. Firstly, the fear of further irritating Peter, and secondly the feeling that there was more to Ross's offer than a simple desire to help a couple of damsels in distress. I feel that if I ring him up it will be tantamount to saying: 'O.K. Come and get me.' Maybe I am reading too much into my last exchange with the dynamic paterfamilias of the Honeys but I do not think so.

My quandary is resolved when, one day, the telephone rings at New Australia and a secretarial-type voice tells me that Mr Ross Honey would like to talk to me.

"Penny? I hope you don't mind me being informal. I wondered how you were fixed accomodation-wise?"

"It's awfully kind of you to ring, Mr Honey," I gush. "We have had a bit of difficulty finding exactly what we want."

"Come and have dinner with me and we can discuss it. I'd like to talk to you about the airline, too; I don't seem to see much of Peter these days."

I accept with alacrity, but hope that Honey Senior does not intend to pump me for a lot of inside information that he cannot get from Peter.

On the evening appointed for our meeting a chauffeur-driven Rolls arrives outside our very unexciting apartment and, at first, I cannot see Ross through the tinted glass. He steps out to greet me and I restrain from commenting on the ostentation of the transport. I would like Ross Honey to think that I spend my whole life climbing in and out of expensive motor cars.

"You're looking very beautiful," he says. "One of the few good things about not seeing you for so long is to be reminded of how attractive you are. You're even prettier than I remember."

What girl could resist such blandishments? Certainly not one called Penny Sutton. Peter may disapprove of his smooth-talking father but I think he is sweet. As I have said before Australian males are not exactly lavish with the compliments and a few appreciative words make a welcome change.

I leap into the Rolls and notice Ross's eyes flitting over my legs as I settle back in my seat.

"I hope you like fish," he says, and immediately I am reminded of Peter. They obviously have a lot of tastes in common.

The restaurant compares to any that I have been to in the world, and is built on stilts rising out of the sea, so that you feel that your meal was swimming around beneath your feet a few minutes before it arrived on your plate. I notice that most of the clientele are on the mature side which may be an indication of how expensive it is to eat there. Ross orders us a martini in the sumptuously appointed cocktail lounge and lights a cigarette with something that looks like a small gold bar. Half an inch of crisp white cuff protrudes from his sleeves and I think how pleasant it is to be in the company of someone with more sophistication than the faded denim brigade. I have almost forgotten what it is like to see a man wearing a tie.

"I see that young Wilson has been drumming up some useful publicity from all this wedding activity you've been having," says Ross, blowing a thin column of smoke across the room.

"Bruce is very good at that kind of thing," I say. "I believe he used to work in an advertising agency."

"Yes. He used to work for me. We have an advertising agency in the group. I was sorry to lose him. Peter made a shrewd choice there."

Honey Senior seems to have a finger in every pie.

"Did you get that dress in England?" The sudden change of subject throws me for a minute.

"Er-yes," I stammer.

"It suits you. From what I have seen you have a very good dress sense. You were responsible for the New Australia stewardess uniforms, weren't you?"

"I made a few suggestions."

"I think they must have been listened to. How are you getting on with Peter?" Another switch of direction and a difficult one to cope with. I will have to assume that he is talking about the job.

"Very well, when I see him. He's been terribly busy lately. I think he's doing a very good job. Business is getting better all the time."

"You don't find him rather dour?"

"He has been a bit preoccupied lately but I think that's all to do with the job. It matters a lot to him, you know. He sees it as a chance to prove himself in your eyes."

"Show the stupid old fool he was wrong, you mean?"

"No, not that. I think he has a very genuine respect for you."

"Do you really believe that? I always thought that he thoroughly disapproved of me. Sometimes I feel as if I'm the son and he's the father."

"Well," I try to choose my words carefully, "I don't know all the background, obviously, but it does seem pretty usual to me that boys go through a period when they resent their fathers. In your case it must be very difficult for Peter to compete with you on your own terms. He's always Honey Junior, the boy who has to work twice as hard to prove to everybody that he isn't where he is just because his father is called Ross Honey."

Ross nods his head understandingly. "There's a lot in what you say, I know that. What I object to is his holier-than-thou attitude. I think he would like to chain me to a bath chair."

"He was very fond of his mother, wasn't he?"

Ross leans forward intently. "So was I!" he says with feeling. "Nobody in the world could tell you any different. I suppose he's been saying that my drinking and whoring drove her into the grave?"

"He hasn't said anything of the sort," I parry, surprised by his vehemence.

Ross shakes his head as if angry with himself for his outburst and pats me on the arm. "I'm sorry. I feel too much sometimes." He waves for the waiter and I wonder if his anger may hide a guilt that is directed at himself rather than Peter.

"Maybe you are both more like each other than you imagine," I say, trying to pour oil on troubled waters, "It's

147

not unusual for members of the same family to rub each other up the wrong way."

"I suppose not." Ross breaks off to order some more drinks and then starts asking me questions about the New Australia operation. From what he says I sense that he has already done a considerable amount of background research amongst his business cronies and wants to check out some details. Although he gives nothing away, I sense that he is secretly quite pleased with the way his son has handled things so far.

I answer his questions truthfully, but obviously take pains to ensure that a good impression is left of the New Australia operation.

"I think you're doing a grand job in more ways than one," says Ross when I have paused for breath. "Peter should be proud of you." He looks at me intently. "Tell me if I'm being presumptuous, but was he the reason you came over here?"

"He was one of them," I say, deciding to remain truthful. "I had just emerged from an unhappy love affair and felt like a complete change of scene. Australia could not have been further away from my old stamping grounds."

Once again my conceit makes me query the reasons for Ross's interest in my relationship with Peter. I would like to think that he was probing the depth of my feelings for his own ulterior motives. Not that I would respond if he made a pass at me. Or would I?

"So there is nothing particularly serious between you?" Do I detect a note of hope in his voice?

"Not at the moment, no. We're good friends, of course."

Ross declines a menu and orders cold lobster. I say that I would like the same and he takes my arm and guides me to a secluded table overlooking the water. I notice that a waiter is standing beside it as if to welcome the master home. I wonder how many girls have been here before me.

Ross waits till I am seated then sits down, spreads a spotless napkin over his lap and considers a packet of cigarettes before deciding that he does not want one.

"I think I ought to say something about my relationship with Peter's mother," he says, still staring at the cigarette packet. "I loved her very much, but after a while we had virtually no kind of physical relationship in our marriage. Elsie had a bad time bringing Pete into the world and I think that turned her against the whole sex thing." Peter certainly takes after his father, whatever he may say about him, I think to myself. "She never minded what I did. She never thought about it. But, whatever anyone says, I bet we had a better marriage than most of the couples who used to throw up their hands in horror when my name was mentioned. I don't think I ever lied to her in the whole of our marriage."

"How did she – "

"Cancer." Ross Honey spits out the word as if he has snapped it in two between his teeth. "It took her six months to die. That's too long." His voice trembles. "The biggest criminal in the world deserves a speedier death than that." For a moment I think that he is going to burst into tears. Fortunately the arrival of the sommelier helps to restore his equilibrium.

"Peter was engaged until quite recently, wasn't he?" I say, anxious to change the subject.

"I think he still is, officially. But I don't believe that Miss Celia Richmond would have been a great success. A good first marriage, maybe."

"That sounds very cynical."

"It's probably only an indication of how ancient I am. You don't need to get married these days, do you?"

'I want to get married – one day. Maybe I'm old-fashioned, too."

"I'm always surprised at how many people still do. It makes me think that the permissive society exists only in the minds of feature writers."

'Surely permissiveness is more likely to be found inside marriage these days rather than out of it. Take your own, for example."

"You may well have a point there." Ross tosses back his head, so that his shaggy white mane hangs in whisps over his ears, and rests a hand on top of mine. "You're a real pleasure to have dinner with. You're beautiful, stimulating and I can pour out my heart to you." His eyes burn into mine and I have to look away. "Still, you must be thinking that I got you to have dinner with me under false pretences. I invited you out to discuss accomodation, didn't I?"

"Whatever the reason, I'm very grateful for a delicious meal."

"Thank you, Penny. And I'm grateful to you for the reasons I've already mentioned." He pats my hand and waves for a waiter. "Look. I hope you won't misunderstand me, but I think that rather than me rambling on like a third-rate estate agent we might have a look at one or two apartments after dinner. I asked one of my people to see what was on the files and there's something rather special I'd like you to see."

"That's very kind of you," I hear myself saying, while my mind races away to consider the multiple implications of Ross's offer. Is it usual for the senior executives of large companies to show females round apartments late in the evening? Not in the normal course of their duties. Any self-respecting girl would say 'no thank you' firmly. Trouble is that I am in my usual slightly sozzled condition, when my discretion disappears faster than snow on a hot griddle.

"Brandy?"

I find myself nodding. "Two large Cordon Bleus, please."

I have absolutely no recollection of leaving the restaurant but I do recall resting my head on Ross's shoulder as we speed along a broad highway, feeling a sea breeze on my cheek, and hearing the roar of the surf. "Thank you," I murmur. "I had a marvellous evening."

"It isn't over yet, I hope." Ross's words make me open my eyes and look up into his impassive face. Just what does he have in mind for the rest of the evening?

"The place I mean is along here." He sounds as if he is about to ask his chauffeur to pull into a roadside snoggery, or maybe it is my imagination – or wish fulfilment.

"You mean the flat?" I ask.

"What else? We've only just completed it. The development, I mean."

"You're in the building business, are you?"

"Very much so. It's probably the sector of my interests that takes up most time, especially at the moment."

"You'll be able to build New Australia a nice city terminus."

"If they can make it a financial proposition, I will." He leans forward and speaks to the chauffeur. "Take us up to the Miramont, Carpenter."

As the Rolls turns off the highway I have difficulty in reconciling my charming, and slightly vulnerable, dinner companion with the tough dollar-conscious businessman who is now sitting beside me. He is obviously used to getting his way, by one means or the other, and I wonder what his plans are for me.

"Here we are. What do you think of it?"

We are pulling up outside a tall white building that seems to glow in the darkness as if moonlight is shining right through it. It has very graceful lines and looks like a superior country hiuse of another generation, with elegant wrought-iron balconies.

"It's fabulous," I breathe. "Is this really a block of flats?"

"They haven't finished laying out the gardens yet." Ross is looking about him, checking every detail.

"Is anyone living here yet?"

"I think a couple of apartments are occupied. Do you want to look inside?"

"Yes, please." It occurs to me that maybe I am sounding a bit too enthusiastic but my desire to get inside really is prompted by the beauty of the structure. "The rents must be prohibitive," I say, preparing myself for the inevitable disappointment.

"Company employees always get a subsidised rate and I guess you come into that category."

I suppose I should make some token argument but I would be a hypocrite to pretend that I am not knocked out by my surroundings and prepared to do almost anything to get a permanent foothold in the place.

There is subdued lighting in the foyer and what appears to be a marble floor. A porter comes towards us and nods respectfully when he recognises Ross – and believe me you have to be someone in Australia before you find anyone going out of their way to be subservient. Most Aussies don't give a damn.

"Good evening, Mr Honey. What can I do for you?"

"Good evening, Bevan. I want to have a look at some of

151

the apartments we haven't let yet. Can you give me the keys?"

"Certainly, Mr Honey."

Bevan looks me up and down in a way that I do not particularly like. I wonder if he thinks that I am a tart. Perhaps I am being over-sensitive. Ross takes me by the arm and walks me over to the stone pillars that command the entrance.

"Do you like it?" he asks. There is a note of pleading in his voice that makes him sound genuinely keen to receive my approval.

"I think it's fantastic, really I do. It's like a temple. All this stone and high ceilings. You haven't spared any expense, have you?"

"We've tried to make it as attractive as possible." His voice tails away. "It was an idea of my wife's. She was an architect, you know. She was working on it when she died. I tried to finish it just as she would have wished." He looks out towards the ocean. "She was the one with all the artistic talent in the family. She used to channel everything into her work. It was strange, but when she was dying she did some of her best work. She had so many plans." He seems a thousand miles away and I wish there was something I could do to comfort him. But somehow it seems an impertinence to reveal my presence at a moment like this. His grief is obviously a very private thing.

"I've got the keys, Mr Honey. There are two suites on the top floor and one on the second."

"Thank you, Bevan." Ross takes the keys and stalks swiftly towards the lift as if eager to disrupt his thoughts with movement.

I always find it awkward to travel in a lift with someone, even if I know them quite well. There is always the desire to find some insignificant topic of conversation that will fill in the gap between three floors, rather than stand in an uncomfortable silence waiting for the other person to speak. Tonight the strain is even worse than usual. I can sense Ross's preoccupation as the lift powers smoothly upwards, and I wish I could find some object or event to comment on. Words do not often fail me but tonight, when I need them most, my mind is blank. The lift comes to a halt almost imperceptibly, like a jewel settling back in its padded box, and the doors slide open.

"Turn left." Ross guides my arm and I am conscious of what a tactile person he is. It is as if he constantly needs the reassurance of my presence. I sense that in this temple of memory to his dead wife he wants to be protected against too many ghosts.

We walk along a wide corridor and Ross stops and inserts one of the keys in a lock. It is strange, but the action takes on a sexual connotation in my mind. I feel myself flinch as the key turns and the door swings open.

The beauty of the wall coverings is the first thing that strikes my eye and, without being told, I know that Ross's wife must have chosen them. The whole apartment is fitted out in a very feminine style with many skilfully blended patterns and colours in its decor. Having been used to existing in the tiniest of kitchens, I am amazed by the spaciousness of the facilities at the Miramont. Normally I have to put a turkey in the oven from outside the kitchen. Here it would be possible to eat Sunday lunch round a table in the middle of the room. The bathroom, too, is quite splendid, with onyx fittings and a sunken bath which is the last word in luxury.

"This is marvellous, Ross," I say. "But we couldn't possibly stay here." He looks up sharply as if surprised by my words. "I mean, Kate and I. It's just too grand. I couldn't believe that any company subsidy could bring it within our reach.'

"I want you both to stay here." Ross's tone suggests that there is going to be no argument. "This place was made by someone I loved very much and I want it to be lived in by people I find sympathetic to her memory."

He walks across the spacious living room and throws open two doors that give on to a bedroom, as large as the flat Kate and I are currently living in. I gaze upon the sumptuous needlework of the counterpane and am almost frightened to cross the threshold. The moonlight pours through the window and plays on the bed like a spotlight. I dare not look at Ross. If I felt it would bring him happiness I would gladly sleep with him but I sense that his anguish cannot respond to any physical solace within these walls.

153

The place has taken him over, robbed him of his natural vigour and turned him into a figure waiting at a deathbed, looking near to death himself. He seizes my arm and feels down it to my hand. "You will take it, won't you?" he pleads. "It would mean a lot to me."

"Provided that we can pay as much as we can afford towards the rent." He nods. "Whatever you wish. I respect your integrity." He smiles for the first time that I can remember since we have been in the building and squeezes my hand. "Make a note of the telephone number and you can make your own arrangements with Bevan about moving in. Do you think your friend will be prepared to come?"

"I think she'll jump at the chance. I can't tell you how grateful I am."

Ross holds up his hand. "It's me who should be grateful. Say no more about it. I just hope the place will give you the pleasure it was designed to give."

I take a last look round the beautiful apartment and, hardly able to believe my luck, follow Ross to the lift. How strange the turn that things have taken. There I was, anticipating a seduction attempt, and instead of that I have been presented with this beautiful flat because the owner finds me sympathetic to the memory of his dead wife.

"Bevan, Miss Sutton will be moving in to number twenty-seven at her convenience. Give her all the help she needs."

"Yes, Mr Honey." Bevan looks me up and down again and I feel like a kept woman.

We say goodnight to Bevan and go out to the Rolls. Carpenter springs forward to open the door but Ross has ushered me into the back seat before he can get his fingers to the handle. We purr through the silent streets and I can hardly believe my good fortune.

"I don't really want to go home now I've seen that place," I say.

"Don't worry. I'm certain you'll soon be settled in. Ah, here we are." Ross does not need to remind me that we are back in Dragsville. He presses open the door and I wonder whether it would be a good idea to invite him for a cup of coffee. I do not get the chance to find out.

"Thank you for having dinner with me. I enjoyed it very much. I hope you'll be happy at the Miramont. Now, I'm afraid I've got some work to catch up on." He squeezes my arm, wishes me goodnight and is gone without so much as a kiss on the cheek.

The absence of the latter upsets me much more than it should.

CHAPTER ELEVEN

The next few weeks see a rapid upsurge in business and for the first time I get the feeling that I am part of an organisation that is really going places – and I do not just mean the ones featured on the timetable. People stop saying 'who?' and start saying 'oh, yes' when I mention I work for New Australia and the morale at Coolburn is sky-high.

"I'm making arrangements for us to fly to every major city in Australia," says Peter. "When that happens, we've really arrived."

I have been dreading him finding out about our super new flat because he would be certain to put two and two together – and, knowing Peter, probably make five. But, luckily perhaps, he is working so hard that we hardly ever date. On a couple of occasions I spend the night at his flat but he does not come round for a return visit.

As I had anticipated Kate is knocked out by the flat and cannot believe that I did not get it for services rendered. "I can't see how you could have held out for so long," she says. "I would have gone to bed with him before he had time to open his mouth."

"It wasn't like that all," I tell her for the fiftieth time. "Ross was a complete gentleman about the whole thing. Would I hold anything back from you if he hadn't been? We don't have any secrets from each other, do we?"

This is the nearest I have ever got to prompting Kate about her relationship with Michael Papadoulis but, though she blushes, she reveals nothing. The only answer my question receives is a few mumbled words of agreement. Kate is embarrassed but clearly not prepared to spill the beans. I feel hurt, but also – and much more important –

worried that the relationship between Kate and Michael may be getting dangerously deep.

My feelings are thrown into relief when I bump into Elsie Papadoulis and she invites me round for a cup of tea. Once again her love for her husband is made patently obvious and I feel a great sadness as I listen to her chatter on about how she always knew that Michael was going to be successful. Her father is there too, and I learn that it is the day before he leaves to return to England by ship. I am reminded that it is thanks to him that New Australia got off the ground. Also, that Kate and Michael were brought together. Two events that may have very different consequences in terms of human happiness.

The news about Mr Truman puts me in a quandary. I am certain that Peter would like to be involved in any farewell party that is being organised but, on the other hand, such an event will surely bring Kate and Michael into contact, for I know that my flat-mate is not on duty. However, does that really matter? If Kate and Michael are engaged in a love affair of long-standing their passions can hardly be fanned by a meeting 'in the open', and I need not feel guilty about organising it. It might even provide me with an opportunity of raising the matter with Kate.

I track down a harrassed Peter but, bless him, he is not too busy to be reminded of the debt he owes Michael's father-in-law.

"Thanks for telling me," he says. "I'll give Mick the Greek a ring and see what's been organised." He runs his fingers through his tousled hair. "I'd be glad of the excuse for a party. I've been working too darn hard lately."

He rings me later in the day and tells me that the Papadoulis family are having a farewell meal for the old boy in Gantino's and that there is going to be a party at Mike's house afterwards.

"We've been invited to both events," says Peter. "Mick was very keen that you and Kate should attend. I think you've made a hit there." Little do you know, I think.

That evening I watch with interest as Kate gets ready for our date. She has received the news of the party with less enthusiasm than I would have anticipated. Maybe she is trying to play it cool. However, the care with which she applies her make-up suggests that she has more than old man Truman in mind. Even though our bathroom is large enough to cater for a ballet company I can hardly get near a mirror or find a surface not littered with Carmen rollers and tissues.

"Are you trying to give the old boy increased blood pressure," I say sarcastically, as she struggles into a dress that practically shoots her breasts out of the top like a pair of cannon balls.

"I think I must have put on a bit of weight," sniffs Kate. "This used to fit perfectly."

"From a man's point of view it still does," I say. "I'd wear something round your shoulders, if I was you. At least until you get to the restaurant. You walk through King's Cross looking like that, you'll either be asaulted or arrested."

"Can I choose?" asks Kate innocently.

When I eventually get her out of the bathroom we are running behind schedule and by the time we get to Gantino's we are running – literally. The place is jammed and it is obvious that a lot of Michael Papadoulis's relations have followed him from the old country. The way their dark eyes cling to every contour of my body makes me feel that I have forgotten to put something on. In Kate's case this is more or less true. Jack Truman is also glad to see us.

"Hello, my dears," he beams. "How nice to see you again. Eeh, you are looking well. I can see that the climate agrees with you. I'm going to miss all this lovely sunshine when I get back to Leeds."

"Ah, but you'll have Leeds United," says Kate. "They don't have a football team like that out here, do they?"

While Kate is revealing surprising signs of an interest I never knew she had, I look round the restaurant to size up the male talent. Peter is present but a girl can never have too many beaux to her string, can she? I have always been partial to Greek men ever since my trips to the beautiful island of Cyprus and there are some stunning examples of the race present tonight.

"Can I give you a glass of wine?"

The man standing beside me makes George Hamilton look like a prime contender for the world's ugliest man contest. Such deep-set flashing eyes I have never seen. The bone structure is impeccable – as if the flesh has been stretched over a framework of finely chiselled features – and the dark, curly hair invites my browsing fingers.

"I'd love some Retsina."

My companion's eyes widen with a new interest. "You like Retsina? That is most unusual. I do not find that it is greatly to the Australian taste."

I explain that I am not Australian, and we are getting along famously when Peter appears. I have seen him shooting the odd glance in my direction and he has presumably decided that it is time to intervene. I am quite flattered because in my experience Australian men and women seldom mix at parties. The men stand at one end of the room discussing football or cricket, while the women group at the other chatting about matters domestic. For a man to go and start talking to a woman is seen as a confession of either degeneracy or rapist tendencies. The Australian male seems to be able to consider the act under either heading, according to whim.

I introduce Andreas, and Peter nods stiffly. "We've brought the old boy a present," he says to me. "I think it would be a good idea if you two girls handed it over. I don't want to make a big thing of it because I think this is a family party and I don't want to turn it into a press conference for New Australia. Probably better to do it now before everybody gets too tanked up."

Peter can be surprisingly thoughtful sometimes, and generous too, as I realise when I see the present. A beautifully sculpted solid silver aeroplane that becomes a cigarette lighter at the touch of a finger.

"I don't think he smokes but it was the most appropriate thing I could get him," says Peter.

Kate and I take the old boy aside and he is tickled pink with his present. So much so that for a moment I think he is going to cry. "Eeh, but it's beautiful," he keeps saying. "I've never seen nowt like it." He goes off to show it to everybody and I notice that Michael Papadoulis moves in to claim a few words with Kate. I see him whisper something in her ear and give her hand a quick squeeze and I wonder what he is saying. He certainly is a very attractive man and

I wonder if any of my resentment of Kate's affair is conditioned by jealousy. The return of my own private Greek prevents me from dwelling on the question too much and I am concentrating on being as beguiling as possible when there is a commotion by the door.

A tall, statuesque blonde is complaining bitterly because she has been told that the restaurant is closed.

"How can it be closed if all these people are here?" she wails. She has a very high-pitched voice which is inclined towards a whine.

"I'm very sorry," says Michael. "I'm afraid we're having a private party. We normally only accept pre-booked reservations anyway and we informed everyone who rang us."

The lady is just explaining to her slightly embarrassed escort that she refuses to leave without being fed when she suddenly claps eyes on Peter.

"Peter, thank goodness you're here. For old times' sake, can you make this man see sense and give us a table?"

"I was never able to make you see sense, Celia. What makes you think I have the gift with anyone else?"

Celia? The name is known to me. Where have I heard it before?

"Don't be impossible, darling. Surely you carry some weight around here. Tell the silly little man to give us a table."

Michael is hardly an inch shorter than Peter and I can see that he is having difficulty keeping his fiery Greek temper in check.

"I have told you once that tonight we are having a private party. You were not invited and I must ask you to leave." He steps forward and throws open the door with a flourish.

"And I've told you that I'm not leaving until I get some food."

"Celia. Don't make a scene." Peter is sounding strangely conciliatory. "A friend of ours is having a farewell party before returning to England. Don't spoil it for him."

"I don't want to spoil anyone's party. I only want some food." Celia continues to rant and rave and I rack my brain to remember why the slightly unusual name means something to me. And then it comes to me. Celia Richmond! That was the name Ross Honey mentioned when he was talking about Peter's unsuitable fiancée. I examine the statuesque lady with even greater interest. She has a large aristocratic nose and, in fact, all her features are constructed on the generous side. Peter usually looks a pretty muscly guy but standing beside Miss Richmond he appears no more than average. Not that the lady is unattractive. Oh, dear me, no. Try as I might I cannot find a lot to criticize about her appearance. Her dress must have cost a bomb and it is obvious from her bossy manner and the few pieces of jewellery that I can see, that she and money are no strangers to each other.

The more I look at her the more I dislike her and the more attractive Peter becomes. I suppose I have been taking him a little for granted lately but the minute some competition shows up I begin to sharpen my nails.

Is Celia Richmond still competition? I had a feeling that she was all in the past. But something about the way Peter looks at her tells me that she can still exert a powerful fascination. I imagine that he respects her aggressive temperament and I wonder if this has anything to do with his attitude to his father's personality.

Whatever it is – possibly all the Retsina that Andreas has been plying me with – I suddenly find myself feeling quite aggressive towards Miss Richmond. It is probably an indication of my deep-rooted insecurity but I want to crown her with something. I can see dear old Jack Truman beginning to register that some kind of commotion is going on, and my number-one male standing helpless on the sidelines, and all this spurs me to action.

"For the very last time, I am not going to move until I get some food," says Celia, haughtily.

Right! I say to myself. You shall have some food! At the moment that the evil impulse springs to my mind a waiter carries past a large dish of spaghetti which is to form part of a buffet supper. Before any one can stop me I snatch it up and – whoosh!! Celia Richmond suddenly looks like Medusa – the Greek lady with all the snakes in her hair. It seems terribly appropriate.

"Is pasta all right?" I say, sweet as sugar ice. "It's what we call a take-away meal. You can eat it on the way home."

I must confess that I have to hand it to Celia. Kate says

160

that if I had crowned her with a tureen of spaghetti she would have tried to scratch my eyes out. Celia is far more lady-like. She draws herself up to the limits of her not inconsiderable height, destroys me with a look, brushes aside Peter's offer of assistance and sweeps out, followed by her spluttering escort throwing threats of legal action over his shoulder.

The minute they have gone I feel humble and contrite. Both Peter and Michael are furious which does not help.

"With respect, Penny. That was a very stupid thing to do," says Michael, barely able to control his anger. "Under no circumstances would I expect anyone to be treated like that in my restaurant. I will have to offer the most humble apology and that will double the pain the incident has caused me."

Peter is even more adamant. "You must have taken leave of your senses," he storms. "Do you know who that girl was?" I dare not say that I know very well. "That was the girl I was engaged to. It was embarrassing enough bumping into her without you doing that. She comes from a very important family round here. This incident could have all kinds of repercussions for Michael and me."

Because I am feeling guilty and on the defensive I immediately have to take exception to that remark.

"That's the only thing that worries you, of course," I sneer. "The fact that some mud might stick to your precious businesses. You don't think about Mr Truman."

"Don't be ridiculous," snarls Peter. "If you were leaning over backwards to avoid a scene you wouldn't pour spaghetti over someone."

Fortunately, the arrival of a bemused Mr Truman prevents any further discussion on the subject and we disperse to eat. I feel awful because I know that I was in the wrong and only acted as I did because of a mixture of jealousy and drunken bravado – a deadly combination which I advise anyone to be very wary of.

After we have eaten I apologise to Michael and say that I will write to Celia Richmond and offer to pay for any damage that I caused to her dress. It occurs to me that this could cost me a pretty penny because the dress looked a very original creation. Michael is sweet and says that he thinks that this would be a very good idea and that he will go halves with me on any bills that are incurred.

Peter is more difficult to come to grips with and I fear that I may have driven him back into Celia's arms by my irresponsible action. From the way he looked at her it was clear that he still felt something for her and I should have guessed that his previously stated protestations of indifference were not as firmly rooted as I had imagined.

The party moves on to Michael's splendid new house on the outskirts of Sydney but, though everyone else seems to be enjoying themselves, I find myself standing alone on the terrace, unable even to give the ardent Andreas any good reason to talk to me.

As I look out across the garden I feel that there is someone standing behind me and turn to find Peter uncertain whether to come or go. On an impulse I run to him and throw my arms round his neck.

"Forgive me," I say. "I did know that girl was your fiancée. I think I was a teeny bit jealous."

"Good job it was only a teeny bit. You might have killed her." He strokes my hair and kisses me gently on the lips. "I'm sorry I flew off the handle. I wasn't really worked up about New Australia."

"I knew you weren't," I interrupt him. "I was being bitchy. I'm sorry, too."

Everything is pointing towards a spendiferous reconciliation when I remember that Peter does not know about the new flat. No sooner has the thought struck me than he speaks the words I least want to hear.

"I'd suggest we cut out of here and went back to my place for a coffee, but I've got the painters in and the flat stinks to high heaven."

There is a pause while he waits for me to suggest that we go round to my place and I try and think of some credible excuse not to do so.

"Of course, I could be tempted to go round to your place. It looks as if your friend is going to be quite happy here for a while." Kate, indeed, is exhibiting signs of her 'I could have danced all night' syndrome.

"Are you living in your flat at the moment?"

"Not with that smell. I'm staying with the Wilsons."

162

"Fabulous. Let's go and have a swim. That's just what I feel like at the moment."

"They've had to empty the pool. The water turned green."

I feel as if I am going to turn green. Why does everyone else have all the good excuses?

"Oh, dear. What a shame."

Peter holds me with both hands just below the shoulder and looks into my eyes. "Penny. I'm trying to say I want to be alone with you. Do you know what I mean?"

"Yes, of course. It's just that . . . Well, we've moved flats now."

"You're still living in Sydney?"

"Yes."

"And you haven't moved into a convent?"

"No, of course not."

"Well, I don't see what the problem is."

I breathe a deep sigh and decide that Peter has got to know some time. "Come and have a cup of coffee," I say.

"Did you take that flat Kate was looking at?" asks Peter as we drive along the coast road towards the Miramont.

"No. It wasn't really what we wanted." I feel guilty at giving a second version of the same lie.

"Very expensive property round here." Peter sounds impressed but a little perplexed, as he has every reason to be considering that he pays my salary.

"Turn right here". I see Peter shoot a glance at me and wonder if he suspects where we are going. If he does he says nothing.

We drive along the gently curving road which rises gradually through clumps of shrubs and eucalyptus trees and I sense that Peter is beginning to relate to his surroundings.

"You don't live in the Miramont, do you?" I nod. "How did you find that place?"

The silence that follows that remark seems to last for minutes and must serve as an answer to Peter. "Did my father put you in there?"

Once again I take exception to the tone of the remark.

"What do you mean, 'put us in'? Are you suggesting that your father is keeping us?"

"It wouldn't be the first time. You must have had some reason for preferring his offer to mine."

"Oh, Peter, don't be silly. Don't let's have another argument. It was pure chance that your father was able to help us."

"I've heard that before, too. I can see why you didn't want to bring me round here. Is he coming round later?"

"The way you are behaving now is the reason I didn't want to tell you before I had to. I knew you'd throw a ridiculous scene. It's very sad but I think you're jealous of your father."

If I wanted to ensure that I enraged Peter I could not have chosen a better means of doing so. "Jealous!?" he shrieks. "I'm not jealous of that pathetic old womaniser. If you want to be his latest mistress that's all right by me but I'm not paying your wages while you do it!"

"Right. Stop the car!" I snap. "I'd rather walk the rest of the way."

Peter stands on the brakes. "Good! Because I don't want to see my father's whore walk into something my mother designed."

That does it! "When you've let me out of this thing I suggest you take your scrambled brain to the nearest psychiatrist. Why I should bother to tell you this I don't know, but your father loved your mother more than your petty little mind will ever understand. He had tears in his eyes when he was talking about her and the reason he wanted us to stay here was because he thought that she would like us to."

I do not wait for the door to be opened but get out and slam it behind me. Peter does not say anything so I do not know what he is thinking. I do not care very much, either, as I crunch up the gravel towards the house. In my present mood I can think only about getting into bed and waiting for the blessed relief of sleep. Everything I can remember about the evening has disaster written over it in capital letters. Come the morning and I will have to have a serious talk to myself.

I say a terse goodnight to the trusty Bevan and almost fall asleep in the lift. It is not so much that I am tired as that I am emotionally drained. I suppose I should be thankful, because whenever I get involved in a very bitter argument I am able to sleep it off; unlike Kate who will toss and turn all night worrying about what was said.

164

I do not even bother to remove my make-up but strip off my clothes and flop into bed. Seconds later I am asleep.

The next thing I respond to is the pressure of someone sitting on the edge of the bed and a voice calling my name. Imagining that it is Kate I make the kind of noise that will tell her I am half asleep and do not wish to be disturbed.

"Penny. It's me. Are you awake?"

The voice is not Kate's. It belongs to Peter.

"Peter?" Even in my drowsy state a note of asperity has little difficulty in creeping into my voice.

"Yes. I came to say I was sorry."

"It's too late for that, now. You said some terrible things."

"I know. I didn't really mean them. I've been working pretty hard recently and the liquor got through to me."

"You didn't call me all those names just because you were drunk!" I turn my head and can see Peter's profile as he perches on the edge of the bed.

"No. There was some truth in what you said, I guess. I do get a bit twitched up about the old man. There was a girl once. One of my girl friends. She made a tremendous pass at him and everyone knew about it. I've been a bit sensitive ever since."

"There was no need to turn on me like that. I know I've behaved stupidly tonight but – "

"It was nothing to do with that. It's probably a kind of back-handed compliment. I'm pretty fond of you, Penny. I was being jealous like you said."

There is a silence in which I try to wake myself up and decide what I really do feel. Peter's hysterical outburst did shake me up but, on the other hand, I know enough about men to realise that he must be a very feeling guy who easily gets screwed up about things. Also, he has been under a lot of strain lately. In addition, and most important, I am very fond of him. He must be sorry for his behaviour otherwise he would not have come back to apologise. I wonder how he could have got in. Perhaps he bumped into Kate or maybe he got round Bevan to lend him a pass key.

"How did you get up here?"

"I climbed up."

"Climbed up!? You might have been killed."

"It didn't seem to matter very much at the time." His

voice sounds so genuinely contrite that I cannot resist the wave of sympathy that sweeps over me. He seems so miserable that all my mothering instincts are aroused and I stretch out a hand to touch his. A strangled sob breaks from his lips and he snatches me into his arms, pressing me to him so that the breath is driven from my body. I can feel his skin, moist with sweat, and his sinews straining as his mouth fights its way to my own. He drinks from my lips and his fingers knead into the small of my back. It is as if his rage was a disguise for the passion that now engulfs him. His body arches and his mouth begins to descend the length of my trembling body. I am naked and vulnerable, yet powerless to resist the mounting fury of his love-making. Instinctively I cover myself with my hands but these are snatched aside and with a low, trembling sigh I thrill to the sensations as he begins to tongue me.

It is as well that Kate never returns that night, because I would not want any girl friend of mine to hear the words that I used in the passionate period that followed. The tension, the anger, the uncertainty were all swept away in a maelstrom of emotion that made us gnaw one another like ravenous dogs, and batter each other with our bodies, until we were left exhausted and contented as the first rays of the sun began to lighten the eastern sky.

It was a night I will always remember.

CHAPTER TWELVE

One way in which the average Australian does not differ from his opposite numbers throughout the world is in the matter of being an aeroplane passenger. I would like to be able to report that my experience throws up a number of individual character traits but it does not. O.K., so New Australians, especially those hailing from hot climates, are more inclined to suffer from an attack of the deadly 'wandering hand' but this is merely a throwback to their native inclinations.

On the whole they gripe, groan, grab and complain just like any other bunch of passengers anywhere you care to mention. Where there is a difference in our dealings with passengers comes about from the fact that Kate and I are British.

I had always imagined that the English miss was considered staid and a little drab by most foreigners. A bit of a push-over perhaps because – poor dear – she was stuck with the even more unappetising English male and desperate for romance, but in the main pretty dull. Such an impression, if it ever existed, did so before the 'swinging Britain' image was exported to Australia. On our travels I can see passengers looking at Kate and myself out of the corners of their eyes as if they are waiting for us to suddenly tear off all our clothes. Old ladies look us up and down nervously and business men hear our accents and look us up and down lecherously.

What does surprise me is the number of times we are mistaken for Americans. I suppose it is because many Australians have never heard an English accent except on the radio, and because the American influence is very strong 'Down Under', and has been since the last world war when a lot of American servicemen passed through Australasia.

One 'first' that is chalked up during our Australian adventures is possibly of a kind that should not be mentioned. But, knowing me – and my readers – you will not be surprised that I mention it! When talking to a friend about our first book ('The Stewardesses', published by Sphere), he told me that he was very surprised that I had never 'made it' – that was his expression – in mid-air. I thought about it and he was right. There was that occasion with the hijacker in Beirut but the plane was firmly on the deck at the time.

My lack of flying experience – you know what I mean – was due both to lack of opportunity and also my disenchantment with becoming a member of the Mile High Club. I could never see what benefit height – i.e. altitude – could bestow upon the sexual act. As far as I was concerned it depended totally upon one's feelings for the man concerned. It was going to take a disastrous lack of facilities at ground level – or an incredible hunk – to make me change my mind about airborne sex.

When my eyes light upon the person of Brian Keegan I realise that I *am* in the presence of an incredible hunk. A man who could easily turn my ideas about most things up-side down. I would describe him as Australia's answer to Errol Flynn, if Errol Flynn had not been an Australian in the first place. Brian comes to us with our new planes and conforms to every girl's star-struck dreams of the incredibly handsome, charming and debonair captain whose calm, re-assuring voice is coming to her over the tannoy system. Every stewardess, too. Brian, according to Brian, has flown with every major airline in the world and has come to New Australia out of love for his native Oz and on account of the enormous salary that he hints made it impossible for him to refuse the job.

"Everyone has their price, don't they, darling?" he says, minutes after we have met, as he runs his fingers lightly up and down my arm. "I'm putty in the hands of a beautiful woman or a shrewd financial wizard who knows how to pander to my basic susceptibility to large sums of money." He gazes deep into my eyes and shakes his head. "I never realised that I was going to meet anyone like you when I came back to this place. I thought it was going to be a case of plain Janes in lame planes."

"Very witty," I say, trying to retain my fast disappearing cool. "In fact, you will find that our girls are as attractive as any stewardesses flying today. You do your country-women a disservice."

"That's something I wouldn't want to do to any woman," husks Brian. "My, but I'm looking forward to flying with you, and – " he pauses and his eyes smoulder like coals "– and everything." When he says that I feel like a tray of ice cubes that have been left on top of the oven. He is so devastatingly good-looking that I would stand a good chance of being hypnotised if he started reading from the Sydney telephone directory. Few men make such a strong physical impact on me from the first moment and my feelings alarm me.

In fact it is not until another two weeks have passed that Brian and I take to the skies and in that time Captain Keegan has become a legend. As far as I can make out none of the other stewardesses has actually capitulated but not for lack of trying – on their part.

"He's got a fantastic body," says Kate, describing a flight

168

she made with Dream Boat. "He's skinny but it's all muscle."

"Are you leading me to believe that I should congratulate you?" I asked her.

"No such luck. He took the whole crew swimming when we were in Perth. He was in the pool from which the Australian Olympic team was chosen, you know. Fantastic swimmer. I could sense that he wanted to get me alone but the others kept being gooseberries."

"How unsporting of them. Maybe we should have a competition to see who can get him first."

"What a good idea! Open to all-comers."

"You could put it like that. What shall we have as a prize?"

"Surely Brian is a prize in himself, isn't he?"

"Probably, but we still need something else. I know. Leave it to me. I know just what to get."

Kate tries to make me reveal my idea but my lips remain firmly sealed. There is a surgical appliances shop in town and I have noticed that they sell a number of items advertised as promoting sexual harmony. Foremost amongst these is a vibrator-massager that bears an unmisakeable resemblance to a familiar part of the male anatomy. The vulgar side of my nature responds to the idea of this object being offered as a prize in our competition. Screwing up my courage and wearing a pair of dark glasses I rush into the shop with exactly the right money, intent on making the world's quickest purchase.

Unfortunately, the shopkeeper has different ideas. Imagining that I am a very sex-starved lady, as well as a very embarrassed one, he tries to sell me half a dozen other products too blush-making to mention, and ends up by offering his own services should all else fail! In the end I am so desperate to get out of the shop that I pay my money and leave the Frottibalm – yes, that is what it is called – on the counter! By the time I have plucked up my courage to return and claim my purchase and returned to the flat I am shaking like a leaf.

Captain Keegan may know nothing of our plans for him but he approaches every woman as if she is a prospective conquest. In this respect his style is slightly cramped by his co-pilot. Arthur Blunt has been with the airline since way back. In fact, since its Outback days. His attitude to women must have been shaped by long exposure to stewardesses of the Gracie type, if he ever had an attitude in the first place. He never looks up when we bring him a coffee and winces every time Brian makes a joke that acknowledges the existence of women. I think that Peter must have teamed him up with Brian on purpose, in order to stop the aircraft becoming a flying four-poster bed.

Brian calls Arthur 'Laughing Boy" and makes no secret of his feelings for the man. "The only time I saw him smile was when your friend poured a cup of coffee over my lap," he says. "He soon stopped when she started to mop it up. So did she!" He smiles happily at the recollection. "But you're the pick of the bunch, Penny. You're the girl I really want to make an impression on. With my body, ideally."

He is always saying slightly outrageous things like that but somehow they never sound bad coming from his lips. What could be bad that came from his lips?

"If it wasn't for Laughing Boy I'd make a play for you the minute I could get this crate on to the automatic pilot. That's the irony of having that long streak of pièce de resistance on board. He's only here as a chaperone. I wonder if I could persuade him to sit with the passengers."

But when we take off for Perth there would be no room for him. The flight is fully booked and every seat is taken. "Marvellous for the airline but useless for my tortured libido," complains Brian.

I do not say anything but feel a secret nostalgia for the time when amorous crew members could have lost themselves in almost empty planes.

We have been flying for about an hour when Brian buzzes me to say that he has a headache and do I, by any chance, have any aspirin. In fact I have a brand that I swear by, but when I go to get them I find that I have picked up Kate's handbag which is almost identical to my own. I am furious, and not a little embarrassed, because the monstrous Frottibalm is in my bag and I hope that Kate will not find it if she starts rummaging through my effects.

I tell Brian what has happened and mention that the only pills Kate seems to carry are sleeping tablets.

"Don't take any of those, for God's sake," says Arthur Blunt, grimly.

"Absolutely right," says Brian and with a large wink he virtually snatches the handbag from me.

"Could we have some coffee, please, Miss Sutton?" says Blunt. "And could you ensure that this time it is hot? The last cup was tepid."

"What a good idea," says Brian, and again he gives me a big wink. I toddle off to perform my masters' bidding and when I return Brian and Blunt are arguing about the stars that are now beginning to appear in the skies.

"Do you know anything about astronomy, Angel?" says Brian, cheerfully. "I'm convinced that those bright little chaps are the Southern Cross. What do you say?"

"Regardless of what Miss Sutton may say, there is absolutely no doubt that you are looking in completely the wrong direction." Blunt sounds both censorious and pleased. "I'm amazed that someone with your experience could make such an elementary error."

"Very well," says Brian. "Where is the Southern Cross?"

"We can't see it at the moment. It's behind us at about seven o'clock." Blunt turns round to indicate and as his attention is diverted Brian's hand rises to one of the cups I am holding. Cool as a cucumber he calmly tips a handful of tablets into it. So many that the surface of the liquid starts to froth! I stand there dumb-founded but Brian takes the cup and presses it into Blunt's hand. "I suppose you could be right," he says taking an encouraging sip from his own cup. "Ugh! This stuff tastes a bit funny, doesn't it?" He grimaces and looks to Blunt for an opinion. I have to admire his cool cheek, and his cunning. Blunt obviously hates agreeing with him about anything and shrugs his shoulders once he has taken a sip. "It's no worse than usual," he says. "At least it's hot this time." He takes a hearty swig as if to prove that, once again, Brian is talking nonsense.

"Thanks a lot, Penny." Brian gives me a big smile. "We'll give you a buzz if we need anything."

I depart wondering what on earth – or maybe I should say what above earth – is going to happen. The number of tablets that Brian poured into Blunt's coffee seemed enough

171

to put him to sleep for far longer than the time it takes to get to Perth, Western Australia – or even Perth, Scotland! The man is obviously totally irresponsible as well as totally irresistible and I should have nothing to do with him.

While I am wrestling with my conscience a few minutes later, the call button from the cockpit starts flashing. Wondering what I am going to find I obey its summons.

"What's happening back there?" says Brian, coolly.

"They're all beginning to fall asleep."

"Snap!" Brian indicates Blunt who is leaning back in his seat with his eyes closed and his mouth wide open. He is breathing heavily.

"Is he all right?" I ask nervously. "You gave him an awful lot of pills."

"He's fine. They always understate the dose. I hate light sleepers."

"You're taking an awful risk. Supposing you suddenly fall sick?"

"I've never felt fitter in my life. Come here."

I let out a scream. Not because Brian has grabbed me but because I have been so busy concentrating on Blunt that I have not noticed that my captain is stark naked!

"Brian!" I hiss. "Are you mad? What about the passengers?"

"Let our needs come first for a change. Oh, Penny, just look at those fantastic stars. What a pity Laughing Boy isn't awake to tell us all about them."

"Put your clothes on, you fool," I yelp, trying to avoid his octopus arms. "We can't make love now."

"Why not? The plane's locked on automatic, Laughing Boy is having some much-needed shut eye and the view is out of this world – well, nearly out of this world. Besides – " Brian rises from his seat. " – I know you want to." His arms close about me and he turns me round so that he can fondle my breasts and nibble my ears. "This is what flying is all about," he murmurs. "You're Penny, let me fly you to Perth."

"You are stark raving mad," I tell him. "This could get us both the sack. Let me go!" But, even as I protest, I find myself sinking down on to Brian's lap as he subsides into his seat. This man is able to exert the most fantastic influence over me and I find myself powerless to gainsay him any-thing. I have met only a few men like that and they have all been rogues. It is as if there is a special compartment of my personality that will only respond to evil. I feel ashamed of myself for feeling the way I do, but there is nothing I can do about it.

"Careful with those beautiful legs. I don't want you flying the plane with your knees."

The cockpit of an aeroplane is not the roomiest place in the world and Brian is right to be worried about me brushing against the controls. He slides his hands under-neath my skirt and wriggles them into a position to start tugging down my tights and panties. Besides me Blunt gives and ugly snort and I have the nasty feeling that he is sud-denly going to open his eyes. The sight of him destroys the sexy feelings that are beginning to build up inside me.

"He does look a bit like a dead fish," says Brian under-standingly. He guides my panties over my heels and drapes them over Blunt's face.

"That's better. He makes a good clothes horse, doesn't he?"

"You're terrible!" I squeal.

"Absolutely right." Brians hands run lightly up and down the insides of my thighs. "Now, hop on to the old joy stick." With surprising ease he lifts me up and draws me closer to him before pegging me to his lap. "At least you're unlikely to fall off if we go through a spot of turbulence," he grins.

"It's much better than a seat belt," I agree with him.

"Now, look at those stars. Didn't I tell you that this was the only way to travel?" He begins to flex his legs so that a myriad new sensations begin to stir within my body.

"Fantastic." I put my hand down between my legs so that I can contribute to my partner's pleasure. He groans and begins to lick my neck. Before me the night stretches away, an unending glade of stars. I am gliding through space at six hundred miles an hour and I feel as if I am stretched out on the Milky Way being made love to by some figment of my erotic fantasies. Brian's hands cover every inch of my body, stroking and exploring, but they are so gentle that my mood of delicious sensuousness is sustained without reaching boiling point. It seems like hours before the rhythm begins to speed up almost imperceptibly and the pressure of Brian's fingers becomes more urgent. From what might be described as the movement of a lazy ocean swell he changes to that of a bucking bronco and suddenly my nerve ends are jangling and my body trembling with excitement. The stars outside fuse with the stars that burst within my body and I feel like a meteor burning across the heavens in a blaze of ecstatic movement. If I was told that the plane no longer existed and that I was flying through the air under my own velocity I would believe it at that moment. I cry out in my pleasure and squeeze the hand next to my own.

Regrettably, perhaps, it does not belong to Brian. Arthur Blunt blinks and opens his eyes. "Aaaargh!" he screams.

I feel like screaming too. But Brian is made of sterner stuff and holds me tight to prevent me trying to escape. "Have a good sleep?" he says calmly.

"You're naked!" says Blunt incredulously.

Brian shakes his head. "Pull yourself together, sport. Did you have a nightmare?"

"I think I'm having one now," says Blunt. "You are naked and there is an airline employee sitting on your – your lap."

"Naked?" Brian's voice combines interesting elements of amazement, disbelief and annoyance. "Did you have a few drinks before you came aboard?"

"Of course I didn't. I am cold, stoned sober." The slip of the tongue is accidental but Brian is on it like a flash.

"Stoned, eh?" he says. "I thought as much. I'm glad you have the grace to admit it. Miss Sutton, please get Mr Blunt a cup of coffee, it may help him to sober up." Blunt starts to splutter but Brian holds up a restraining hand. "It's all right, Arthur. Your secret is safe with me. I'm certain this is only a temporary lapse. Trouble at home, is there?"

Poor Blunt has now discovered my panties on his lap and is staring at them incredulously.

"These tumbled out of your breast pocket," says Brian sympathetically.

"Are you certain there's nothing you want to talk to me about? They do a very nice line in shock treatment these days, you know. Better remove them, Miss Sutton. And his tights. We don't want him to get over-excited."

I take my chance and escape as fast as my exhausted legs will carry me. When I return with a coffee Brian is wriggling into his trousers. "Tell Penny what you just told me," he says.

Blunt blushes and shakes his head. "I couldn't. I must have been dreaming – I mean, having a nightmare."

"He thought we were having sexual intercourse. Can you imagine?"

I shake my head. "How awful."

"Yes, isn't it? Arthur is going to have a check-up when we get down. You haven't been sleeping so well lately, have you, Art?"

By the time we get to Perth I am feeling quite sorry for poor Arthur Blunt. Brian has convinced him that he is on the verge of a nervous breakdown and has given him the name of a totally fictitious specialist in nervous diseases – Doctor Ivor Twitch. Blunt is so het up that he cannot see that he is being made fun of.

Brian is a complete bastard and has no compassion for anyone. Nevertheless I find it impossible not to like him. Whatever his other faults – and their number must run into thousands – he has the priceless gift of being able to make me laugh and that counts for a lot. Any man who can make me laugh is well on the way to winning my heart.

I have completely forgotten about the Frottibalm by the time I get back to Sydney and it takes me some time to associate Kate's slightly uptight manner with the fact that she *has* indeed been through my handbag. I can see that the packet containing 'the natural, sensuous way to soothe away stress and strain' has been opened and I can imagine Kate's shocked reaction to her discovery. One of the girls once came across a sex shop catalogue and we all had a good laugh at the weird appliances that were advertised.

"Some of them look as if they would be quite happy mating without any human assistance," says Kate and it is difficult not to agree with her. Now she must be wondering about me.

"I'm sorry I took your bag," I say. "I hope it didn't put you to much inconvenience. I see you found my Frotti-balm."

Kate blushes a deep scarlet. "Your w-w-what?" she stutters.

"My vibro-massager. It's deep, penetrating vibrations stimulate and revive tired tissues, increase the blood flow and massage muscles. And it's ideal for stirring junkets."

Poor Kate does not know whether to take me seriously or not. "Don't worry, darling," I tell her. "I haven't developed a whole new range of slightly unnatural tendencies. I bought the thing as a joke prize for our 'Get Keegan' competition. Trouble is that I'll have to present it to myself. I had a rather fantastic session with Brian on the way to Perth."

Kate counts her fingers. "That must make you number three. Nice going."

"Number three!? What do you mean? Nobody could have got to him before me."

"Not so. Jill Wood had an all-night party the night before your trip and apparently both she and Lynn Western snaffled him."

"Hussies! Is nothing sacred? How can you excuse behaviour like that?"

"It's absolutely appalling, I know," says Kate sarcastically. "These young girls have no discretion. I'd sue if I were you. Or better still, grab your Frottibalm and hobble to the nearest wheel chair."

My reply to that is unrepeatable and I am ashamed to say that I throw my prize into Sydney harbour. I can be a very bad loser sometimes!

CHAPTER THIRTEEN

The divine Keegan is too good to last and it comes as no great surprise when we hear that he is off to the States. Whether as pilot, gigolo or film star nobody is certain. On the evidence available he could perform very satisfactorily in any of the three roles. He is the only man I know who could be caught with his hands in your pocket and then blame you because it had a dirty lining. He is, without doubt, the most outrageous character we meet during our Australian adventures.

On the broader scale New Australia is doing very well and we now have flights to all the major Australian cities. Many of the shorter 'bus service' flights have proved to be financially impracticable but I am getting the opportunity to visit some of the more inaccessible parts of the country, by courtesy of the New Australia Touring Service.

N.A.T.S. is another bright idea that Bruce has dreamt up to fill aeroplanes and expand the market. You probably do not need me to tell you that the Australian continent is considerably larger than the whole of Europe and that its numerous places of historical and geographical interest take a bit of getting to. N.A.T.S. links up with both shipping lines and international airlines to provide a specially planned tour of Australia that flies passengers the length and breadth of the continent, taking in the sights.

Both Kate and I enjoy working on this assignment because it allows us to meet an interesting cross-section of people from all over the world. Also, because we get the chance to see parts of Australia we have only read about in books. Places like Alice Springs, for instance, thirteen hundred miles from Sydney and another thousand from Darwin at the top end of the continent.

I had thought that its only claim to fame was that it was slap bang in the middle of Australia and that Neville Shute had featured it in his famous book; 'A Town Called Alice', but I soon find that it has a lot of other things going for it.

Alice Springs first came to life as an overland telegraph station in 1872, just ten years after John McDougall Stuart became the first white man to cross the continent from south to north and name Central Mount Stuart – situated to the north of 'The Alice', as it is now known.

Alice Springs now boasts a population in excess of four thousand, including eight hundred aborigines who were once the only people who could exist in the arid wastes where the only water is that which collects in soaks or rock pools along the courses of dried up river beds. The town is growing fast and reminds me of something from a Hollywood western. Not surprising when you learn that it is the headquarters for a vast cattle industry and the rail head for the 'Ghan', the train that connects with the south a thousand miles away. Out of the north of the town stretches the Stuart Highway which connects with Darwin on the Timor Sea. You really do get a feeling of the great outdoors in 'The Alice'.

One of the town's main claims to fame is that it is the nerve centre of the famous Royal Flying Doctor Service. With isolated cattle stations covering areas of thousands of square miles it would be impossible to attend to the medical needs of such a far-flung practice unless help could be summoned swiftly in case of emergency. A net-work of short-wave wireless sets cover the area and these are used for consultation and, where necessary, to summon airborne aid. Both Kate and I feel that this must be one of the most rewarding ways to fly and we get a big kick out of being introduced to some of the dedicated men and women who work for this famed institution.

As I have said before, the aboriginal influence is very strong in Alice and we become firm friends with Albert who is our guide when we visit local beauty spots. Albert does have another name but it is so difficult to pronounce that I will not try and write it. When I say that he is a member of the Pitjintjantjara tribe you can get some idea of my problem! He also owns a camel and makes a lot of money from painting very accomplished oils of local views, so you can see that he is very much an all-round entertainer.

Another friend is Ron Springer who keeps the hotel at which our guests stay. He is a quiet well-mannered man with something of the feel of Gary Cooper about him. But, whereas you always felt that 'Coop' would explode into action when the time was right, Ron always keeps his emotions bottled up in a most un-Australian manner. We hear a rumour that his wife ran off with a travelling salesman and maybe this has made him withdraw into a shell. Kate, particularly, is keen to draw him out.

"Every time we come here I flutter my eyelashes at him and every time he blushes a deeper shade of scarlet and runs out of the room faster," she complains.

"Maybe he doesn't fancy you," I say.

"Don't be ridiculous. If he didn't fancy me he wouldn't

178

bother to blush. He's enslaved by my captivating charms like every other male. He's probably frightened by the depth of his feelings."

"No woman has ever aroused him like you," I prompt.

"Exactly! I can see that you've been exposed to my charisma before."

"Please! Watch your language. There may be fish porters present."

The only thing that blushes deeper than Ron Springer is a remarkable boulder known as Ayers Rock. This hunk of stone is two and a quarter miles long, one and a quarter miles wide and rises to a height of 1143 feet above the surrounding plain to the south-west of Alice. According to the angle from which it is seen the rock can look like a sleeping hippopotamus or a giant dachshund but the most unusual thing about it is the subtle changes of colour which it undergoes at various times of the day and in different weather conditions. At sunset this amazing monolith takes on an irridescent terracotta glow which makes it look as if it is being lit from the inside. As the sun sinks, so the intensity of the red glow increases until the shadows reach the base of the rock. As the light fades, so the glow dies.

To the aborigines the rock is known as Uluru and was once a very important gathering place as it provided them with the most reliable water holes – and hence game – for thousands of miles.

There is a landing strip and tourist lodges near Ayers Rock but one of the highlights of the N.A.T.S. tour is a night in the Australian wilds in which our guests can actually curl up on Ayers Rock and get the feeling of the primaeval heritage that stretches away on all sides of them. I have my doubts about this part of the tour and so do many of the passengers. Most of them have left their camping days far behind them and would much prefer to be tucked up in their beds in the hotel rather than swapping camp-fire pleasantries as they grill their steaks on an open fire.

Our camping trips also give the inevitable flight Romeos a chance to try their arms – and other parts of the body – and Kate and I frequently feel like indenting for fortified sleeping bags which lock from the inside. Kate, however, has taken it upon herself to take Ron upon herself and considers that our night in the wild will present her with her best opportunity to snaffle him.

"Have you noticed how he always seems much more alive once we get out into the bush?" she says earnestly.

"Frankly, no," I tell her. "He shouts at Albert a little more, that's all. He always parks his sleeping bag as far away from us as he can get it."

"More evidence of how crazy he is about me," says Kate, cheerfully.

"Think of all those guys who are so nuts about you that you never see them," I tell her.

"Don't try and be clever, it doesn't suit you," says Kate coldly. "Despite what you say, I see plenty of evidence that Ron is a different man when we get out of Alice."

"I think that's what you need. A different man."

"Read all about it! Air stewardess found murdered in middle of Australia," sings out Kate. "Don't push your luck, Sutton. I see portents of a great romance on this trip."

"And I just see tents."

Kate is nothing if not an optimist, but I find it difficult to see how she imagines she has a chance of getting anywhere with Ron Springer. Anywhere other than to Ayers Rock and back that is. Ron does put her sleeping bag in the Land-Rover but he is looking the other way when he does it and he shows a good deal more affection towards his red setter. Despite all that, I can see what Kate rates about the guy. With a briar pipe wedged between a set of perfect white teeth and big, brown, hairy arms sticking out from a plaid shirt he looks like something from an old-fashioned tobacco advertisement. His hair even curls forward in a cow lick over his forehead.

"Basically you're just an old-fashioned girl, aren't you?" I say to Kate as we watch the Land-Rovers being loaded up for our Australian safari. "You'd like nothing better than to be milking cows all day."

"Strange as it may seem my uncle did have a farm," says Kate. "He sold it to a man who promptly got planning permission and became a millionaire."

"What was his name?"

"Ben. Dear old uncle Ben. I can see him now – "

"Not him, you fool," I squawk, revealing my true personality in a tell-tale outburst. "The millionaire!"

I do not learn any more fascinating details about Kate's family on the way to Ayers Rock because I am being nice to the paying customers and chatting about the surrounding countryside as if I have lived there all my life. I feel a bit guilty about doing my continental guide bit, only having been in Australia for a matter of months, but at least I have been around longer than most of our passengers. It is when I have to address parties of native-born Australians that I start to get worried, although they are always very nice and never start asking awkward questions.

We get to the rock a couple of hours before sunset and I am amazed at the effect it has on me as we get closer and closer to it across the plain. Always I think of it as an animal and I would never be surprised if it lumbered to its feet and suddenly took off across the flat, red earth or slid below its surface, like a basking whale disturbed by the arrival of a boat-load of sightseers. I think that it is because it is the only object in the midde of the desolate plain that it seems to me like an animal that is resting before moving on, rather than a permanent landmark. There seems no good reason why it should be there. No attachment to any other feature of the place.

Albert is responsible for making camp once we have reached one of the gorges at the foot of the rock and Kate and I retire with our guests to watch the effect the changing light patterns have on the colour of the boulder. Kate is a veritable mine of information and does New Australia proud on such occasions.

"At the end of the rock you will see the Kangaroo Trail," she says pointing to a semi-detached length of rock which droops down towards the ground. "In the legend of the neighbouring Loritja tribe this signifies Ngaltawadi, the sacred digging stick." Nobody attempts to disagree with her. This party is even older than usual and many of them are already beginning to mop their brows and look weary. No sing-songs around the camp fire tonight. "The digging stick divides the initiated from those who have yet to pass through the ritual of the Mala. The Mala is the mythical kangaroo rat which is the totem of the group."

"Did you make all that up?" I say to Kate later.

181

Kate is indignant. "Of course not! It's all completely authentic. Albert told me about it."

"It's just that I seem to remember that last time that piece of rock was a ladder that led the spirits of the dead to the land of the hereafter."

"You're probably getting confused with another piece of rock," says Kate coldly. "Anyway, there are so many legends surrounding this rock."

"More every time we come here," I mumur to myself.

As the sun sinks beneath the horizon the clear air grows cool and the glory of the rock passes into memory. Now it looks eerie and rather menacing. As we shepherd our charges back to a jolly evening round the camp fire, I cannot resist asking Kate how she intends to seduce the resolute Ron.

"Just leave me alone with him by the camp fire and you'll see. I believe he's frightened off by my sophistication and worldliness. I'm going to show him that I'm just a simple child of nature at heart. Once he realises that I share so many of his interests I'm certain our relationship will blossom."

"But you know nothing about his interests."

"When I find out what they are, I'll share them," Kate can be very pragmatic sometimes.

Kate's plans are disrupted because not all our guests retire to their tents and sleeping bags soon after supper. One American gentleman has visited the Grand Canyon in Arizona and he points out in infinite detail how far superior it is to anything he has seen since he arrived in Central Australia. This is very fair comment, but it does begin to pall after the second hour.

Eventually it is left to me to beg to be excused and retire to the tent I am supposed to be sharing with Kate. That lady has been left sitting round the camp fire with a silent Ron and the American gentleman, still in good voice.

Ten minutes after I have climbed into my sleeping bag I am not surprised to hear Kate coming into the tent.

"Have a nice time?" I ask, maliciously.

Kate's first reply is unprintable. "Stupid old wind-bag!" she hisses vehemently. "My goodness, some people have absolutely no tact."

"Did you have a nice chat to Ron?"

"Don't be stupid. We didn't exchange a word."

"You ruffled his dog's ears. I saw you doing that. That must have gone down well. The quickest way to an outdoor man's heart is through his red setter."

"Don't be pathetic!" Kate has no sense of humour sometimes.

"He's gone to bed, has he?"

"He went before me. And do you know what? The minute he had disappeared that American wind-bag asked me for a date."

"Amazing. I wouldn't have thought there were a lot of places to take you around here. The odd burial ground I suppose."

"When we get back to Sydney, stupid! I don't know how I kept myself in check."

"Eager, were you?"

"Eager to bash him over the head with a rock."

"Maybe that's what you should do with Ron. When he came round you could be lying beside him shielding him from the cold."

Whatever Kate thinks of my ideas I never get the chance to find out because Springer's dog comes nosing into the tent. And when I say nosing, I mean nosing. "If Springer was this enthusiastic you wouldn't have any problems," I say, fighting off the brute's advances.

"Prince! Prince!" The voice comes from a long way away and belongs to Ron Springer who is obviously searching for his missing pooch.

"Push off, boy. Master is calling," I say, trying to force the totally disinterested dog out of the tent.

"Hang on a minute," says Kate. "I've got an idea." This could be bad news for everyone and I listen nervously.

"Ron dotes on his dog. If we keep it here and I go and help him search for it I will be creating exactly the right impression and have a great chance to get close to him. After about twenty minutes I'll come back here, collect the dog and say I found it."

"Ron will be overjoyed and you'll be married and live happily ever after. Yes, it sounds great."

"Don't be sarcastic. It's worth a try, anyway. You stay here with the dog, will you?"

"No thanks. I think it has dishonourable intentions and it's practically bigger than I am. Don't worry, I don't have designs on Ron. I won't get in the way. We can tie Prince to the tent pole. He seems quite happy now he's found your shoe."

Prince is chewing happily at one of Kate's brogues which does little to further endear him to the lady.

Kate pulls on a pair of jeans under her shortie nightdress and then takes them off again. I refrain from comment and lash the unresisting Prince to the tent pole.

"O.K., animal lover. Let's go."

"Don't get in my hair," warns Kate.

"I wouldn't dream of it," I assure her. "Are you sure you're not going to catch your death of cold prancing about like that?"

Before she can answer, a distraught Ron heaves into view "Have you seen Prince?" he says, totally ignoring the generous acres of flesh that Kate is flaunting. "If anything happens to him I'll never forgive myself. He's totally out of his element here. He's a city dog, really."

With all respect to Alice it hardly strikes me as having achieved city status yet, but that is a detail compared to the stark tragedy that is unfolding before me.

"Poor little chap," squeals Kate in a tone of such obvious insincerity that a wave of nausea ripples through my system. "We must help you find him. He was such a friendly soul, wasn't he?"

"Friendly, he was," I agree. "I'll go and have a look where we were eating in case he's clearing up there."

"I'd better stick with you," says Kate, shrinking to Ron's side. "I'm helpless in the dark."

In fact there is practically a full moon shining down out of a cloudless sky but Kate is not the girl to miss an opportunity for close bodily contact.

"I hope he hasn't tangled with a snake," says worried Ron. "He's quite likely to try and pick one up."

"Snakes!?" Ron's worry becomes catching.

"Yes. There's a few little fellows around here that could give you a nasty bite."

"See you later folks," I say, firmly. "Don't ring me, I'll ring you." I move off swiftly as I hear Ron suggesting to Kate that they should look in some nearby caves.

"You'll have to hold my hand," says Kate archly. "I'm terrified of confined spaces."

"That's amazing when you work on an aeroplane," says Ron destructively. "Don't worry about the caves. There's only a few bats. I do hope Prince hasn't got lost down one of the shafts."

Poor Kate really earns her thrills, I think to myself. If she can bring this romance back from the grave I take my hat off to her. I make my way back towards the tent and, of course, now that I have been told about snakes, every shadow on the path looks as if it is poised to strike.

I am gazing down at my feet so attentively that I walk straight into the American who was holding forth on the Grand Canyon.

" 'Trip no further, pretty sweeting,
    Journeys end in lovers meeting.' "

He beams at me and I apologise for my clumsiness without feeling at all contrite. In fact I feel even more bitter because I have had to compromise my principles by saying sorry to a jerk. People who have handy bits of Shakespeare up their sleeve for every occasion always makes we want to puke.

"Taking the night air?" he asks.

"I'm looking for Mr Springer's dog," I say, trying to keep a civil edge to my voice.

"I would be glad to assist you in that endeavour. What name does the creature go by?"

"Prince," I say. I soon wish I had kept my mouth shut.

"Prince! Here, boy. Good boy. Prince!" Uncle Sam gets involved with all-American enthusiasm and immediately the rotten pooch has to sit up and take notice. A muffled bark reveals that it is but a few tents away.

"Did you hear that?" My comrade starts forward and immediately trips over a guy rope and falls flat on his face. He lets out a howl of pain and surprise and this really goes to Prince's head. He starts barking fit to burst and there is a fiendish commotion from the direction of our tent. As I set off to the rescue I am faced with the remarkable sight of the tent coming to meet me! Prince has succeeded in pulling the tent pole out of the ground and is towing the whole contraption behind him. Not only that but anything else that gets in his way. He *is* strong, that dog. I have to hand it to him. Two more tents are collapsed and I catch a vision of a terrified female face covered in cold cream and topped by an electrical circuit of curlers. Screams fill the air and the doughty Prince ploughs on regardless.

In less than thirty seconds a peacefully sleeping camp site is turned into a disaster area. By the time Prince is towing so many tents that he cannot put one paw in front of the other, nothing exists at a height greater than ten inches above the ground that is not a human being.

"Prince! Thank God! Is he all right?" Ron Springer arrives at a fast gallop with a remark calculated to make him a lot of new enemies.

"Nobody has got close enough to check," I say coldly. "He seems healthy, though."

"Here boy, here. It's your old cobber, Ron." Ron scrambles into the welter of tangled tents as Kate arrives on the scene, panting.

"You can't compete with that kind of animal appeal," I tell her. "You don't have a wet nose for one thing."

"Do you want to bet? That cave was soaking. Everything I've got is wet."

"How was it going in there with lover boy?"

"Fantastic. He was on the point of exposing me to his favourite stalactite."

"Your cup over-runneth."

"Exactly. That's just what I said to myself. How can one girl get so lucky. Those were my exact words."

"All thanks to Fido, there."

"Man's best friend." Just at that moment there is a screech of pain from Springer as his ungrateful pooch sinks its fangs into its owner's helping hand. "And woman's too," says Kate vehemently. She can go off people very fast sometimes.

CHAPTER FOURTEEN

As the weeks pass it becomes clear that New Australia is not only established but successfully established. New planes are in the order book and there is no longer any problem about raising finance. Ross Honey, though never one to be effusive in singing his son's praises, shows by his support that he no longer has any thoughts of selling the airline, although I can sense him itching to get involved in the day-to-day running of the operation. To his credit, he is prepared to accept that it is his son's baby and leave him to nurse it, putting in only the occasional appearance at board meetings to keep himself in touch. He also takes me out to dinner from time to time, although I believe that this is more because he likes my company than that he wants to pump me for information.

My evenings with Ross, though I enjoy them very much at the time, are a source of some foreboding to me because I always fear that we might bump into Peter. Despite our passionate reconciliation and Peter's acceptance of his resentment of his father, this does not alter the fact that he still harbours all the feelings that were at the root of our explosive row. I know that he dislikes me living at the Miramont and it is ironic that both father and son seem inhibited by the place. I know, too, that he sees his father as a threat at a number of levels including that of pure male competition.

All in all, it is a very difficult situation and I do not know what I should do for the best. If I refuse to see Honey Senior I am denying myself a pleasant evening and running the risk of offending someone who has never been less than charming to me and is also the titular head of the airline for which I work. On the other hand, Honey Junior is something more than just a boyfriend and I can understand him not liking the idea of sharing me with his old man. I recall a stewardess called Madge Pennyquick and the problems she had when she got involved with a father and

187

son millionaire combination. Her trouble was that she did not know that they were related!

As usual in this kind of situation I decided to do nothing and let things sort themselves out while I concentrate on someone else's problems.

Kate and Michael Papadoulis still seem to be at it like knives and I am getting more and more worried about the long term outcome of the affair. Elsie Papadoulis is such an innocent, trusting wife that she must be the easiest person in the world to deceive, and thus plays into the lovers' hands. Whenever she has a weekend free Kate disappears on some half-explained jaunt and Jill Wood actually sees her on the beach with 'that good looking Greek who owns all the restaurants'.

This seems to present me with a first rate opportunity to raise the subject and being no angel I step in fast.

"I hear you've been swimming with Mike Papadoulis," I say innocently as we sit on our balcony at the Miramont and examine the South Pacific Ocean.

Kate appears to be considering for a moment. "Yes. So I did. I bumped into him on the beach. There was quite a party of us."

"Like who?"

"Oh, friends of his, mostly."

"Anybody I know?"

"I don't think so. It's difficult to remember. Why are you so interested?"

"I'm always rather intrigued by Michael. He's got a twinkle in his eye and I've often wondered how faithful he is to Elsie." This is really laying it on the line and I watch Kate's face with interest.

"I think he loves her very much" she says slowly. She pauses and looks at me and I think I can see her eyes glistening. "Very much."

And that is that. Apart from threatening her with a gun I cannot think of a lot more ways of getting her to talk about the subject. Her implied awareness of Elsie's feelings for Mike make me believe that she has thought about the matter in some depth and I only hope that she and Mr. Papadoulis are not planning on doing anything serious. Kate's last escapade with a married man was nearly a marriage-breaker and the affair did not last as long as this one.

I know that sooner or later everything will have to come out into the open but I have no idea of the circumstances in which all our relationships are going to be resolved.

I know that Ross Honey has some business interests in New Guinea and I am intrigued by the stories I have heard of that mountainous, heavily jungled country, populated by fiercely warring tribes of cannibals. I remember reading somewhere that it is the only place left in the world with tracts of jungle so impenetrable that no white man has ever set foot in them. Not a good place to come down in an aeroplane.

I am surprised one day when Peter calls me into his office and I find him sitting behind his desk with a cynical smile on his face.

"Guess who wants you to fly to Port Moresby?" he says. (Just in case you don't know, I should say that P.M. is the biggest town in N.G.)

"The king of the Head Hunters?" I query.

"Practically. Do you really expect me to believe you don't know?"

"I haven't the faintest idea," I say, suspecting from his tone that it must be Ross.

"It's your sugar daddy. My daddy and yours."

"Don't start that again," I say wearily. "I expect he had to go there on business and thought that I might like to see the place."

"Exactly what he said. My, you do understand him well. Anyone would think you had rehearsed the same story."

"Anyone with a damp brain and nothing better to occupy it. You do get on my nerves sometimes, Peter."

"Sorry about that. I've got some more bad news for you. I'm afraid you're going to have a chaperone."

"Not you. I couldn't stand it."

"No. Not as bad as that. My father's sense of propriety made him suggest that your friend Kate came along too. Or maybe he fancies her as well."

"He probably wants to have an orgy with both of us," I say.

As I talk, I feel my spirits foundering. Peter and I seem

189

to find it so easy to sink into this kind of bitter slanging-match which gets us absolutely nowhere, except into a situation from which it is difficult to escape without feelings of long-lasting mutual recrimination. I cannot put up with his petulant jealousy although I know in my heart that he has some cause for his resentment. I sometimes ask myself if it is not his attitude, more than anything else, that makes me so conscious of Ross as a man.

The thought is still in my mind when I report with Kate for the flight which is taking us all to New Guinea. Imagine my surprise when I find that we have a totally unexpected additional passenger: Michael Papadoulis!

"Did you know he was coming?" I say to Kate.

"Why should I have done?" Something in the tone of my voice makes Kate sound ultra-defensive.

"No reason," I say, looking at her levelly. "I just thought that someone might have said something."

It does not take us long to find out that Michael has approached Ross with a view to his helping finance a restaurant development in Port Moresby and has hopped a flight in order to show him the site and talk him through the deal. Whether the trip is also the excuse for a love idyll with Kate I do not know. As usual the lady is keeping very quiet on the subject.

The flight is a very long one and it is a relief to be on board in the capacity of a semi-passenger and not on duty all the time. I have to be woken up for my first glimpse of New Guinea and when I look down at the steaming jungle that is rising up towards us, as if on the prongs of a brandished trident, I get an immediate impression of just how rugged the terrain is. The mountain peaks rise up like needles from a pin cushion and I can understand why the jungle must be virtually impassable on foot. To traverse a few hundred yards as the crow flies could necessitate rising and descending several thousand feet. I do not normally listen attentively to the note of the plane's engines but in this case I am very relieved when we begin our descent towards Port Moresby without incident.

"Looks a cosy little place, doesn't it?" says Kate. "I hope you brought the picnic hamper."

"I packed it inside the first aid box," I tell her, grimly.

"If you see me venture outside my hotel room before it's time for take-off, ring my psychiatrist."

"If I go out you can ring my next of kin," says Kate.

Of course we are over-dramatising as usual and, when we get down, Port Moresby is like any other airstrip in a relatively under-developed part of the world. Discovered by the Coca Cola company, but not a great deal else. Kate picks up a copy of 'David Copperfield' on a bookstall and wonders if it is an original edition!

Ross and Michael are spirited away into an office the moment we have landed and we assume that this has something to do with customs because we have come in virtually as a private flight. We soon learn that their disappearance has a far more serious significance. When Ross returns his expression is grave.

"I'm afraid we're going to have to change our plans," he says.

"What's the matter?" We ask nervously, sensing that something serious has happened.

"A plane has come down up country and they've got nothing here that's in a fit state to take off. Apparently they've had the most fantastic storm. You probably noticed as we came in."

"I thought maybe it was like that all the time," says Kate. Certainly the scene on the airstrip had reminded me of my first glimpse of Coolburn but I had not attached too much significance to it.

"Have we got to bring them in?" I ask.

"That's the idea." Ross shakes his head grimly. "And it's not going to be easy."

"Why? Are there a lot of casualties?"

"There are some. We don't know how many. The control tower lost contact with them soon after they came down. The main problem will be getting to them. They're about ten miles from the nearest place we can bring a plane down in. They're also in a part of the bush where there has been a lot of inter-tribal warfare lately. If they get mixed up in that there could be trouble. I've been talking to a District Officer in there," he jerks his head towards the office. "He says that the natives have got a lot of superstitions about planes. Every time they see one going over they attribute all their bad luck to it. If they find one on the ground they could turn very nasty."

"I thought I saw someone sticking their tongue out at me when we flew over," says Kate.

"It could be a lot worse than that" says Ross. "As far as I can make out the longer we leave them there, the greater the danger on every count. It looks as if the weather is turning nasty again, too." As he talks, torrential rain begins to lash the windows of the reception area and I can see the palms being beaten down towards the ground across the landing strip.

"Are you going to be able to get this thing down in the jungle?" asks Mike. We are not flying one of New Australia's latest acquisitions and I know that in the old days it was Outback's boast that they could land on a cabbage patch. As far as I can recall it was their only boast.

"I have a lot of faith in Ken Goodall when it comes to handling this baby," says Ross. "They grew up together. In fact I think the plane may be older than he is."

Ken shakes his head ruefully. "I've had a look at the map, for what it's worth. It looks as if we should be able to come in by the river and the D.O. says there's some open ground there. It may have cut up after all this rain, though."

"We'll have to take that chance," says Ross.

"What happens then?" asks Kate.

"Shanks's pony. We've got a vague idea where they are but it's going to take luck to find them in that country. Unless they come up on the air again."

"When are we going in?" I ask.

"As soon as we're refuelled and got some medical supplies aboard. But you girls aren't coming. It's rough out there."

"I'm not being a hero," I say, "but I am a qualified nurse. I think you're going to need me along."

"If she goes, I go," says Kate. "Anyway, we come with the plane. We don't stand down when the going gets tough."

Ross thinks hard for a moment. "O.K. I respect you very much for what you've just said. I'll tell the D.O. you want to come. But don't be surprised if he vetoes the idea. You saw what the country was like."

In fact it is Ross that the D.O. tries to exclude from the

rescue party and for a moment I think that Honey Senior is going to explode!

"Young man," he snaps, "I would like to inform you that I could walk your legs off any day of the week. Furthermore it is my plane and I intend to remain in close contact with it and my staff until this operation is completed." He sounds like a boy telling the gang that they cannot borrow his ball unless he is on the team. I am so used to thinking of Honey Senior as much younger than his years that it comes as a surprise to be reminded of his age. What rather touches me is his proud assumption of the role of leader of the New Australia operation. I feel that all through the painstaking build-up of the airline operation he was taking a much closer interest than even I realised.

Of course, Ross gets his way and, in fact, all four of us find ourselves clambering aboard our plane for its most important ever mission. With us are a stalwart band of half a dozen rescuers including a doctor and the D.O. We are not taking too many people because nobody knows what the casualty situation is going to be and our plane is hardly equipped as a hospital unit.

One piece of luck, if such a word can be used in the situation, is that the D.O. who is accompanying us actually covers the region in which the plane came down so he will be able to guide us through what is some of the toughest jungle in the world.

As we take off it is difficult for me to believe that I am not dreaming. Only an hour before, my imagination was painting sinister pictures of a dense impenetrable terrain and now I am going to be plunged into it.

"Why did the plane come down?" I ask.

"We don't know," says the D.O. "Probably something to do with the storm. When it rains around here it can knock your hand down to ground level if you hold it out in front of you."

"Who was on board?"

"A party of missionaries. I knew most of them. Fine bunch of men. There were some wives and children with them."

"What do you think their chances are?"

"Frankly, I'm amazed they got down in one piece. That

193

was a chance in a thousand. It also gives me some idea of where they might be. If they are not in too bad a state and they keep their heads, they should be all right." The D.O. winces as if he has just thought of something unpleasant.

"What's the matter?" I ask.

"Didn't you hear me? I made a rather unfortunate choice of phrase."

"I don't understand."

"I said I hoped that the passengers kept their heads. There are a lot of fellows in that bush whose only interest in life is collecting human heads. I could have phrased it better."

"Do you really think that the natives could turn nasty?"

"I've no doubt of it. The Kikorians and the Bungians have been picking each other off for years now and things are warming up to a full-scale battle. If the plane has landed up in the middle of them there could be the biggest blood bath since the bad old days."

"You think they would attack the plane?"

"If they're sufficiently blood-happy, yes. None of these johnnies reckons he is a man until he has slain one of his enemies and taken the head back to his tribe. Families even run their own kind of competition to see who the best warrior is."

"With one side winning by a short head, I suppose," I say to a chorus of groans. Despite my flippant remark I am very aware of the danger we are about to be plunged into, and of the plight of the unfortunate passengers who came down with the plane.

Whatever happens we are not going to be able to set off on foot until daybreak because the D.O. scoffs at any thoughts of trying to make progress by night. "Over that terrain it would be suicide," he says.

The rain is sluicing down against the windows of the plane and I do not envy those poor missionaries. God send that there are not too many injuries. I do not like looking out of the window but I tell myself not to be stupid and try and get some idea of the country we will be operating in. From what I can see it is pretty terrifying but not as bad as the mountains we first saw. It had been intended that we would make an aerial search for the downed aircraft but visibility is so bad, and flying conditions so dangerous, that it is agreed that Ken will try and get us down and then take off to make a recce when the weather is better. We have a wireless with us and will, hopefully, be in constant touch with base.

After flying for about an hour I can see a wide river curling its serpentine course below us. The weather lets up a little and Ken drops the plane's nose down so that we can follow the river like a road. The word goes round that we are nearing our destination and I begin to feel really scared. If only I had kept my mouth shut, I might be sipping a whisky sour on the balcony of some comfortable hotel in Port Moresby at this very moment.

Kate catches my eye and on an impulse I wink at exactly the same moment as her. Now that the chips are really down I realise how fond I am of my flat-mate and I wish there were a few words I could string together that did not sound mawkish.

"Good luck," she says as the undercarriage comes down and we prepare to descend. "Do you think I'll look good with a bone through my nose?"

"Georgeous," I assure her.

We make our approach along the line of the river and I crane my neck to see where we will be landing. When I catch a glimpse of what looks like a field of green corn beaten down by the wind and rain, I wish I had not bothered. There are one or two stunted trees about as well and I cannot seriously believe that we are going to fare any better than the people we are supposed to be rescuing. A vicious cross-wind buffets us as we come in and I can feel the tense atmosphere about me stifling conversation. We hang above the water and then, suddenly, there is a rush of green past the windows and the plane's wheels churn into the sodden earth. Bump! My head flies forward to hit the seat in front and the plane lurches from side to side before eventually coming to a halt. It is not the world's greatest landing but at least we are down in one piece.

The moment that we are on the ground the rain comes down like a bead curtain and there is an urgent conference as to whether the plane will be bogged down if it stays where it is overnight. In the end it is decided that it is too risky to keep the plane with us and we have to stumble out into the pouring rain and pace out the distance required for take off. In doing this we realise how lucky it was that we came down where we did, because the area by the river is dissected by numerous inlets which might have presented a serious hazard to landing. Eventually we find a level piece of ground which is just long enough for take-off and hold our collective breath as New Australia's answer to the *Spirit of St. Louis* churns through the mud and lumbers into the air.

"Lucky devil, going back to a nice warm bed," says Kate, and by the end of that horrendous night I have echoed her words a hundred times.

We huddle under some trees but they afford little protection against the rain which does not stop until daybreak. I do not think that I slept a wink and my mood is not improved by being savaged by insects. Mosquitoes, mainly, but I am prepared to believe that a host of rare and exotic creatures are feasting on my flesh. Luckily Kate and I have received nearly every jab known to medical science – Kate is conceited enough to believe that doctors like looking at her bottom – but they do not afford protection against a plethora of itches.

It has been agreed with Ken that he will radio us as soon as he has been able to take off and locate the crashed aircraft. In the meantime we will strike out for the general area that the last radio message came from so that no time is lost. With a bit of luck Ken will be able to talk us on to our target.

Our first problem is to cross the river. This is normally knee deep to a grasshopper, but because of the recent rains it presents a far more serious problem. It is running fast and deep and the waters are brown and muddy.

"At least it will keep the alligators away," says one of the party cheerfully, while I wish I had packed my vanishing cream.

We have to form a human chain to get across and this means that we are all soaking wet before we have even begun the day's exertions.

"How on earth are we going to be able to get people back across that?" I ask.

"I hope we won't have to try," says the D.O. "If the plane came down where I think it did, there is a stretch of land not so far away which has been used as a landing strip before. We may be able to clear it sufficiently to get a plane down."

Any further conversation is soon denied us by the rigours imposed by the weather and terrain. Never have I studied my knees in such detail as when they rise up to meet my bowed head on the side of seemingly precipitous cliff faces. It is either up, up, up or down, down, down. There is no level going. The rain sluices down and I am soon soaked to the skin and experiencing agonies from my chafed skin and insect-bitten body. What is most depressing is to see what a small distance one has covered in so great a time. Looking across a valley it only seems a couple of hundred yards, yet it could have taken half a morning to get from one side to another.

My overriding fear is that I may be holding the party up and I know that Kate feels the same. We always keep in the forefront of the single file that wends its way through the jungle and try to exhibit no sign of the fatigue we are both feeling.

Thank God we have the D.O. with us. Without him we wouldn't get anywhere. To the inexperienced eye it is virtually impossible to spot the trails, and without a guide one would be lost in no time. I find my surroundings terribly depressing, not only because of the continuous rain but because of the dense foliage that seems to be waging war with itself as well as us. All vegetation fights to reach the sky and vines and brambles strangle each other as they claw their way to survival.

We all wait hopefully for word from Ken but our only radio message is from Port Moresby and infinitely depressing. Apparently the plane has developed engine trouble and not taken off! Now we are strictly on our own and as I look about me at the steaming jungle, with visibility of about a few yards, I wonder again what chance we have of finding the fallen plane.

Despite all we have been told about the war-like inhabitants of the interior, I do not see one of them. There is no sign of human life and it is easy to believe that any individual with a shaft of intelligence would be tucked up in a dry place on a day such as this. I am not at all sorry because I do not relish the thought of a brush with any of the headhunters I have seen pictures of.

We trudge on with a short break for food at mid-day and the D.O. reports that we are about half-way from the region in which he thinks the plane may have come down. Only half-way!? I had imagined that, despite the slowness of our progress, we must have covered ten miles. At last the rain stops and as the mist rises we can catch glimpses of the country through which we are trekking. We seem to be following the line of a long valley and below us I can see a wide basin of thick jungle.

"We keep climbing and at the head of the valley there is a small plateau of grassland where the bush gives out," explains the D.O. "I hope they might have got down there."

"Why haven't we seen any natives?" asks Kate.

"I don't know. Maybe they're out on a war party. They'll have seen us, don't you worry."

"I'm not worried, I'm terrified," jokes Kate.

"Don't get too agitated. Normally, they're not as bad as they're painted." The D.O. shakes his head and acknowledges that he has made another quaint choice of phrase. "The war-paint can be pretty terrifying, though."

"The missionaries have done a good job on them," says another member of the party. "They hardly ever eat people these days."

"Just cut their heads off," says the D.O.

"That's much more refined," Kate laughs and I ask her what is so funny. "I was thinking about the cannibal who ate somebody who disagreed with him." I must say that when it comes to a ghoulish sense of humour Kate has few equals.

We hit the track again and after about an hour the D.O. points to a small fringe of green that tops a hill in front of us like a badly fitting toupee.

"That's the beginning of it," he says. "You stand a chance of seeing some of your native New Guineans soon. They do a lot of hunting in the grasslands."

"Head hunting?" askes Kate nervously.

"All kinds."

"I notice you keep your weapons concealed," says

Michael. "That's so they don't alarm people, is it?"

The D.O. looks shocked. "We don't have any arms. We never have any. The police might carry them on occasions, but we're not policemen. We'd never get anyone's permanent co-operation if they thought we needed a gun to do it."

Kate swallowed hard and tries to wink at me but I know what she is feeling and I share her fears. The presence of a few rifles would make me feel much happier.

"The police will be carrying guns when they come up here to arrest the men who ate us," mutters Kate bitterly. "Boy! when I became a stewardess to see the world I never knew I was going to do it in the pit of a cannibal's stomach!"

Fortunately, perhaps, further discussion is interrupted by a signal coming in on the wireless.

"What is it? Port Moresby? Has Ken taken off? We're going to miss another day unless those jokers get a move on."

"It's not Moresby. I think I'm getting a signal from the crash."

"What!?" The D.O. snatches the headphones and listens intently before nodding his head. "Yeah. That's them. Damn faint. Their batteries must have nearly gone. Can you get through to them?"

The wireless operator speaks urgently and fiddles with the knobs on his set but eventually he shakes his head as we listen to the splutter of the static. "I can't raise them. I think they've probably closed down to conserve their batteries."

"But you've got a fix on their position?"

"Yep. We know where they are now."

There is much poring over the map and the D.O. curses softly. "We're not going to get to them tonight," he says. "If they are where they say they are, it's at the far edge of the strip of grassland. It's going to take us another five hours and we've only got three before nightfall at the most."

"Is there any chance of radioing Moresby with their position and getting a plane in to pick them up?" asks Ross. "You were talking about a landing strip not so far away."

"It depends on the state of the strip and whether they can get anything small enough into the air at Moresby. The strip is about as big as a kid's handkerchief. It might serve to take out the badly wounded one by one. But we don't have any small aircraft operational at the moment. That's why you're here."

As if to underline the feeling of depression that accompanies the news that we have another half day's trek before us, the rain starts to fall again.

"Get on to Moresby and get some food and supplies out to them," says the D.O. "We must make as much ground as we can before nightfall."

I am so tired and depressed that I can hardly drag one foot in front of the other and, though I start off by refusing Ross's offers of assistance, I am very grateful for his arm by the time we make camp. For a man of his age Ross is extraordinarily strong and seems to be able to eat up the miles without disturbing the pattern of his breathing. I know that Australians are an outdoor people but the elder Honey is remarkable by any standards.

"Are you going to be all right?" he asks tenderly, as I sink down under the shelter of some jagged rocks that push their way out of the hillside.

"Nothing that a hot bath and a change of clothes couldn't sort out."

"I know how you feel. I'm feeling about as hygienic as a kangaroo's armpit. You're doing great. I take my hat off to you."

"You're not doing so bad yourself."

"I'm tuckered out. I'm too old for this kind of caper. You should have young Peter to look after you."

Perhaps it is strange but I have not thought about Peter until his father mentioned him. When Honey Senior is about he does seem to hog all one's attention. Maybe I have a father fixation or something but I always feel very much at ease with Ross – even in this miserable situation. Peter is more highly strung and after a while this begins to communicate itself to me.

"Why are you looking at me like that?" I ask.

"I was suddenly reminded of my wife. I think I've told you before how much you look like her sometimes. Not so much look like. You have a number of the same mannerisms. Sometimes, I can be with you and feel I'm with

200

her. I hope that doesn't sound too insulting? I don't mean that I'm fond of you only because you're like my wife."

"You've never said you were fond of me."

Ross shrugs his shoulders. "Not in so many words, maybe. But you must have got some inkling of how I felt. How I feel."

"I thought you liked me. How much because I reminded you of your wife, I don't know."

"I was very influenced by my wife. My attitude to the qualities which a woman must have is still governed by those I found in her. With you I started off by seeing my wife and, as time went by, your own personality came through and became the thing I responded to. You helped me to find that I could still have feelings for a woman that were not just physical." He shakes his head. "I don't know why we're suddenly having a conversation like this in the middle of the bush."

"It's because it is so unlike the places we usually meet in that it makes it easier to communicate. Everything is slightly unreal so one can feel that one's words are not being taken too seriously. It's like a conversation in a dream."

"What I'm saying is quite serious." Ross looks me deep in the eyes and I turn away quickly because I am frightened of what I am feeling.

"Penny, I've found somewhere for us to sleep." Kate saves an awkward situation by her intervention and I excuse myself from Ross and go with her. "Is everything O.K.? You look as if you are about to pass out."

"I'm fine," I say. "Tired like everyone else. That's all."

"You're not sick?"

"Only of people asking me if I'm all right." The moment I have spoken I realise how unfair I have been and apologise immediately.

"That's O.K.," she says. She looks at me closely and then speaks again. "Is there anything between you and Ross?"

I am so surprised by her words that it takes me a couple of minutes to reply. "I don't know. There may be. Perhaps I'll never find out."

"He's a good man," says Kate.

"Very." We stand in silence for a moment and I sense

that she wants me to ask about Michael. Somehow I do not want to feel myself in the position of trading confidences and so I change the subject. "Show me the accommodation. I'm freezing to death. We can talk later."

But we do not talk. When I have shovelled down a plateful of hot tinned stew and struggled into a sleeping bag beneath an overhanging slab of rock, it is all I can do to keep my eyes open long enough to find the zip and pull it up. I am fast asleep before Kate has left the camp fire.

When I wake up it is to feel a cold wind on my face and for a second I wonder where I am. A pattern of moonlight is breaking through to the clearing across which I am staring and I can see other figures stretched out in sleep. The remains of the fire are hidden from my sight but they throw out a glow which flickers across the ground before me. Beside me, Kate emits a noise that coming from anyone other than a lady would be called a snore.

As my eye stays in the middle of the pool of light it is to see a giant shadow suddenly stretch across it. The image is so large that I realise it must be distorted by the perspective. Nevertheless it is eerie. I wonder who can still be up. The shadow appears to be carrying a long rod across its shoulder and I wonder what this is. I am soon to find out.

As I pull up the flap of the sleeping bag to protect myself from the wind, the owner of the shadow appears from behind a rock. He is tall and very, very thin, with hair that it matted and shoulder length. He wears a loin-cloth and I can see that his face and body have been daubed with paint and mud. The long rod is in fact a spear.

My heart turns to a block of ice and I have to stifle the cry of terror that instinctively leaps to my lips. The stranger is peering about him carefully as if taking stock of the number of people in our party and, to my horror, he looks towards me and begins to glide to my side.

I close my eyes tight shut and clench my teeth. Seconds pass and I can feel nothing. I begin to get an itch and the desire to scratch is overwhelming. I half-open one of my eyes and can see nothing. I open both eyes and turn my head slightly. The warrior is kneeling beside Kate and I can see that he is wearing a necklace of teeth. Kate always wears a charm bracelet and it is this that our visitor is examining. She stirs in her sleep and immediately the man starts back and raises his spear. At that moment Kate's life hangs in the balance. I do not know whether to cry out or hold my peace. Luckily, sheer slowness of reaction makes me favour the latter course. Kate relapses into deep sleep and the danger is over. As quickly as he materialised the warrior has disappeared and the clearing is empty again, save for our sleeping party. For a second I wonder if what I thought I saw really took place and then I realise that there can be no doubt of it. We have definitely arrived in headhunter country and will have to look out for trouble.

It may seem strange but I do not stir from my sleeping bag until daybreak. Mainly because I am scared stiff of bumping into a head hunter, but also because I am able to persuade myself that our visitor meant no harm and was only being inquisitive. Another important reason is that while I am considering what to do I fall asleep!

When we stumble out into the cold, grey dawn I tell the D.O. what I saw and he agrees that our visitor was probably an inquisitive member of a local tribe. "I would like to have spoken to him, though," he says. "These fellows probably know exactly where the plane has come down."

"You said that they might attack it," says Kate.

"They might. I think they'll be a bit over-awed for a while until they realise that the plane can't move. Once they get the feeling that it's wounded, so to speak, they might have a go at it. It also depends on how their private war is going. Like I said before, if the witch doctor can blame any defeat on 'The Big Silver Bird' then there could be trouble."

"So the sooner we get to the crash the better?" says Ross.

"Exactly. The longer they are just sitting there the greater the chance of them being attacked."

"Have we got any word from Moresby yet?" asks Michael.

"The plane's O.K. It's taking off at any minute," says the D.O.

"I hope it's packed with corn plasters," says Kate. "I could hardly get my shoes on this morning."

An hour after we have started, I am feeling lucky to have any shoes on at all. The rocky outcrops under which we were sheltering become more and more a feature of the landscape and the going is as tough as anything we have met. I had been expecting that things would get easier as we reached the grasslands, but my hopes are dashed on the hard rocks made slippery by the rain which continues to fall relentlessly.

"I'm not surprised that no white man has set foot in some parts of this country," pants Kate. "I can't think of a single white man who would want to."

I don't say anything because I am too busy conserving my energies and keeping a weather-eye open for our visitor of the previous night and his friends. The country through which we are forcing our way would make an ideal setting for an ambush. I have not talked to Kate in detail about my experience of the previous night because I do not think she would relish knowing that our visitor was within an ace of taking her life as well as her bracelet. My mind is full of my conversation with Ross and as he strides along beside me, one hand always ready to give support, I ask myself if he was saying that he loved me. I am so exhausted and confused that I am in no position to analyse my own true feelings but I do know that I feel something with Ross that is missing in my relationship with Peter. The strongest bond that I have with Honey Junior is a sexual one and I do not believe that this is enough to sustain a relationship on a continuous basis. Don't get me wrong, I believe that sex is important but it is just one factor in the union between two people. Overall, I feel I have more in common with Ross although he is old enough to be my father. I feel I can give him something and this is terribly vital to me. I need to give as well as receive. I do not feel sorry for him solely because he lost his wife. I sympathise because I believe that nobody ever really understood how he felt about her. As soon as we get back to Sydney I will have to take stock of my feelings and decide what I am going to do about my relationship with the Honeys.

I say 'as soon as' but in my mind I am thinking 'if'. The jungle and the rain are beginning to sap my spirits to an alarming degree and I do not know how the D.O. can work there permanently without going mad.

Somebody else whose spirits seem to be at a low ebb is

Michael. He struggles along without complaint but his smooth ebullience is definitely a thing of the past and he hardly opens his mouth for hours on end. Kate retains her cheerful, take everything as it comes, personality and though she tries to rally Michael with a word or affectionate gesture he does not respond. I cannot help contrasting his attitude to that of Ross who has not ceased radiating confidence and support for every member of the party — especially me. I think that Kate has noticed this and I wonder if it is having any effect on her feelings for Michael. If our grisly trip succeeds in cooling her passion for the man, then it will have achieved some positive purpose.

At last we begin to shake off the grip of the jungle and at the brow of a hill I snatch a glimpse of uninterrupted grassland stretching ahead of us.

"This is it," says the D.O. "Another two hours and we should be there."

The grass is much higher than it looked from a distance and sometimes rises to almost shoulder height. Fortunately there are well-defined paths and the D.O. leads the way without faltering. I am not thrilled to see a long green snake slither across the path in front of us but the fact that we appear to be on the last stretch of our journey does help me to find a little extra strength from somewhere.

"At least it will be all downhill on the way back," says Kate and I groan.

"Don't start talking about going back yet," I plead with her. "I think you're going to have to carry me out."

As if to cheer me the sun suddenly decides to put in an appearance and ten minutes later I am sweltering. The extremes of temperature are almost unbelievable. Not only does the sun appear but with it a host of voracious insects, all intent on eating me alive. In this merciless country there seems to be no respite from suffering in any weather conditions.

"Well, at least we haven't met any of your headhunter friends," says Kate. "Are you sure you weren't dreaming?"

I have no need to answer her because, as she speaks, we come abreast of a low hill and look down into a long wide valley. What we see makes us suck in our collective breath and gape in amazement.

At first glance there seem to be about a thousand painted warriors milling about below us. They are carrying long spears and are identical to our visitor of the previous night. As we look longer we can see that there are in fact two factions engaged in a battle. There seems to be no pattern to the fighting which is conducted at long range with sudden sorties and abortive spear-throwing. It is difficult to believe that in the third quarter of the twentieth century one is watching men fight as they must have done in the caveman era.

"What are we going to do?" asks Michael, sounding as nervous as I feel.

"Hold our ground and wait for them to make a move," says the D.O. "That's the Bungians and the Kikorians up to their old tricks. They should feel properly ashamed of themselves when they see me." He sounds like a schoolmaster standing unseen at the door of the classroom and watching the lower fourth engaged in some rag.

As he speaks one of the warriors falls with a spear sticking from his thigh and there is a sickening flurry of stabbing which makes me turn away in disgust. When I look back to the conflict a large section of the combatants are withdrawing in disorder and their rivals are grouped about the body of the slain warrior, waving their spears in triumph.

"There is no mass slaughter in this kind of warfare," explains the D.O. "One or two deaths can settle an encounter. That's why their war can go on for years."

"I think it's ridiculous that we don't have any weapons," says a very agitated Michael. "Surrounded by blood-crazed savages who could cut us to pieces and we have nothing to defend ourselves with."

"We'd be inviting trouble if we carried weapons," says the D.O. "I hoped I'd made that clear to you. Being a white man still carries some kudos around here. We'd be undermining our position if those fellows thought we needed guns."

Michael looks as if he would like to continue the argument but he does not get the chance because something happens that to my mind supports his case more eloquently than any words. A group of triumphant warriors breaks

206

away from the body of their victim and races towards us brandishing their spears.

"My God!!" I don't know which one of us says it but it could easily have been me. Ross moves to push me behind him but I am nestling in the small of his back before his hand has made contact with my arm. Michael turns and has taken three steps before the D.O.'s voice stops him in his tracks. "Hold your ground!!" I catch a glimpse of Kate's face and her eyes are tight closed.

"Don't move, any of you. They won't attack."

I am not so certain that I agree with the D.O. The faces of the men running towards us belong to my worst nightmares. Hideously painted to strike terror into the heart of the beholder, they match the intimidating actions of the spear-waving New Guineans who keep drawing back their weapons as if about to hurl them. I am absolutely terrified and expecting to be dead at any second.

Fortunately the D.O. is made of sterner stuff and he steps forward resolutely and holds up his hand. This gesture brings forward one of the group of warriors who are now dancing before us, and words are exchanged in a language which I at first take to be English. In fact it is a tongue called pidgin which employs many English words, but in a most unusual way. I believe that is used as a kind of Esperanto in a number of primitive countries where there are a variety of local dialects.

"What are they saying?" I ask.

"The D.O. is saying that they are very naughty boys and the chief is saying that the man who died was a murderer who had killed many of his tribe. Now that the man has died there will be no more bloodshed. He also says that they are not going to eat him."

"That must make everything O.K.," says Kate. "How can you get angry with anybody who isn't going to eat somebody?"

"What about the plane?" I ask.

"The chief is just coming to that," says Ross. "He says that the plane is very near here and that he will guide us to it."

"Thank God it's near. I can't walk much further."

"You may have to," says the D.O. "These people always

say that everything is near because they don't want to discourage you."

An hour later I know that the D.O. was right. I can see the jungle looming up before us and there is still no sign of the plane.

"Why don't they make some kind of signal?" I ask. An unpleasant thought strikes me at the same time that it does Kate.

"I suppose there are some survivors?" she says, uncomfortably.

"The chief said that there were," says one of the party who is tuned in to our conversation.

"Look!!"

I follow the pointing finger and there is a thin column of smoke rising ahead of us. One of the natives who is guiding us nods his head to a question from the D.O. and I realise that, at last, we have reached our destination.

I feel terrified. It would be awful if, having come all this way we found a plane full of corpses. My imagination paints frightening pictures of what the interior of the aircraft might look like. Is the smoke a signal or – I find myself lingering behind as the other members of the party press forward towards the source of the smoke. There is a clump of trees and through it I suddenly catch a glimpse of the silver tail of a plane. I know I am being cowardly but I do not want to be the first person to reach that plane.

As she has done so many times in the past Kate rallies me to a realisation of my responsibilities. "Come on," she says. "This is what we came for." There is no reproach in her voice. It does not occur to her that I am not eager to leap into action. What can you do with a person like that? She may be foolish and headstrong sometimes but when it comes to the crunch she does not waver.

"I was just getting by second wind," I say, trying to excuse my tardiness.

"Second wind? I'm on my two hundred and second."

Kate strides on and I follow her with a rekindled sense of purpose. I notice, though, that I am not the only person who is none too keen to approach the aircraft. Michael is lagging behind and he makes no move to quicken his pace. Significantly perhaps, Kate does not bother to spur him on.

A cheer goes up ahead of us and as I come level with the trees I see one of our party being embraced by a man of about fifty who is hugging him passionately. The plane is tipped up on its nose but seems to have suffered no serious damage. More figures appear from a collection of ramshackle tents and the surrounding bush, and the first scene of greeting I witnessed is re-enacted a dozen times. The crash victims are overjoyed to see us and it takes a few minutes to piece together a coherent account of their ordeal.

Apparently they were forced down by a storm of near-hurricane proportions and miraculously landed without loss of life. The second officer has a suspected broken skull and there are three broken arms, a dislocated shoulder and a number of passengers with multiple abrasions and bad bruising. Food has run out and attempts to obtain help from the local tribe have been rebuffed. The victims bear out the D.O.'s assessment that the locals could easily turn nasty. None of the missionaries come from this region but they say that it has a reputation as being the home of the toughest tribes in the whole of New Guinea. The D.O. smiles wryly at this.

They also say that, until recently, weather and visibility have been so bad that although they once heard a plane they were unable to make any signal that stood a chance of being seen from the air. As we had surmised their wireless is now defunct.

One of the rescue party is a doctor and, at the D.O.'s request, we take a look at the wounded with a view to seeing if they can be moved. I share the doctor's view that it would be dangerous to move the second officer, and there is one little boy who appears to have a multiple fracture of the right arm which is causing him a good deal of distress even when he is motionless.

We report back to the D.O. who nods his head grimly. "I don't want to have to stay here a minute longer than we have to," he says. "There's only enough food for another day for all of us and I don't put it past the Bungians to do something unfriendly. If we could get going now we could make enough ground by nightfall to give us a chance of getting back to the river sometime tomorrow."

"Fast movement is out of the question with the injured we've got at the moment," says the doctor. "We'll have to get a helicopter in to lift them out."

"And that's going to take time," complains the D.O. He does not get the chance to say any more because there is a loud clattering noise and we see a spear shimmering beside the fuselage of the aircraft it has just struck. It is not the only one. I have my hair parted and the D.O. collapses cursing and gripping his leg. A spear has pierced the soft flesh of his calf and dug into the ground.

"Get in the plane!" The voice is Ross's. He drops to one knee and tries to remove the spear, the blood welling over his wrists.

"Leave me alone!" The D.O. tries to push Ross away.

"Don't be a fool."

"Leave me and get in the plane!" The D.O. continues to struggle and Ross's right arm suddenly flashes out and connects with the side of the man's jaw. His head jolts back and then topples forward so that Ross has to support his body weight with his shoulder as he snaps the spear in two with his strong hands and draws it from the wound.

"In the plane!" I try to help him lift the body but he shrugs me aside and helps me on the way to the aircraft with a boot up my backside. Another missile clatters against the side of the open escape hatch as friendly hands reach down to pull me up and, in a matter of seconds, I have found temporary shelter.

No sooner have I scrambled to my feet than the D.O. is pitched through the opening like a sack of coal and Ross clambers aboard. Again I am amazed at his strength. For a man in his fifties he is in remarkable condition.

"Sorry, sport," he says to the groaning body of the D.O.

"What about the rest of them?" asks Kate. "All those people in the tents."

"Yeah. We'd better sort these jokers out, hadn't we?" Ross looks about him and his eyes light upon a fire extinguisher. Outside, a warrior is approaching the aircraft with a spear in his hand. Ross grabs the fire extinguisher and moves towards the exit.

"What are you going to do?"

"Never you mind."

210

"You're not going out there?"

"Look. Do something about this fellow's leg before he bleeds to death." Ross leaps out of the aircraft and faces up to the warrior who is so surprised that he does not move for a moment. The instant his spear arm goes back Ross steps forward smartly and bashes him on the head with the base of the extinguisher. An imposing torrent of foam is released and this Ross directs into the startled warrior's face. Dazed and half blinded the man turns on his heel and runs for his life, blundering into one of his colleagues who does not wait for an encounter with Honey Senior but runs even faster. The other attackers follow suit and by his action Ross has routed the attack single handed.

"If we had a few more fire extinguishers all our troubles would be over," says Ross advancing towards the tents. "Come on, let's see how your patients are."

He goes into the first hastily conceived structure and, to my embarrassment, we arrive at the moment that Michael Papadoulis is crawling out from underneath a litter. Ross shakes his head. "I don't think I want to do business with you," is all he will say as he turns on his heel. Michael would do better to leave well alone but he tries to fabricate a story about taking up an ambush position which is so transparently unbelievable that it might be funny in less serious circumstances. Fortunately, Kate is not there to share my discomforture.

"I don't know whether it's best to take up a position in the plane because it affords most protection, or to get as far away from the thing as possible because it attracts attack," says Ross.

"Surely we would be very vulnerable out there in the open," I say. "There's not a lot of cover."

Ross looks at the swirling grass and nods thoughtfully. "It's quite dry now, isn't it?"

This, if anything, is an understatement. It is now stiflingly hot.

"What are you getting at?"

Ross ignores my question and licks a finger and holds up his hand. "The wind is blowing away from us, right?"

"Yes, but —"

"Let's talk to the D.O. I've got an idea."

211

I follow in Ross's wake and we find the D.O. feeling his jaw tenderly.

"Thanks for what you did out there," he says. "All of it. I won't give you any argument next time."

Ross pats him on the back good-naturedly. "I'm sorry I had to sock you, but I was getting scared, hanging around out there. Listen, I've got an idea. Those jokers are going to be back and we're nearly out of food and a day and a half's trek away from the river." The D.O. nods. "If we're going to get the injured guys out fast we need a plane right here on our own doorstep."

"Yes, but —"

Ross holds up his hand. He is not used to being interrupted. "I think we might be able to get a plane down here. If you get rid of the grass the ground is flat as a witch's tit." He holds up another hand in self-admonition. "I've just been testing the direction of the wind with Penny, here. If we could set fire to the grass, it would burn away from the plane, frighten off your headhunter friends and mark our position from the air. Most important, it might clear us a landing strip. What do you say?"

There is a pause while the D.O. considers. "Supposing the wind changes direction?"

"That's a chance we have to take. At least it will get rid of the source of all the trouble. We've got nothing to lose." He reflects for a moment. "Nothing that we don't stand a chance of losing anyway."

"Do you think that stuff is going to burn?" asks one of the crash victims.

The D.O. nods. "If we used some of the fuel from the plane."

"Exactly!" Ross can see that he has just sold an idea.

At that moment the wireless operator appears at the doorway. "I'm in contact with the plane," he says. "They should be above us in about ten minutes."

"That's great," says Ross. "Tell them what we're doing and to keep circling."

"If they're carrying supplies it might be a good idea to drop some of them away from the ditched aircraft. It might distract the Bungians."

"Good idea." Ross nods approvingly and, turning to the

wireless operator, repeats our plan of action.

Ten minutes later he and three volunteers are fanning out into the grass carrying containers of aircraft fuel.

"For Heaven's sake, don't set yourself alight," I call after him. My fear for his safety is as intense as anything I have ever felt and even succeeds in stopping me thinking about myself. He waves his hand cheerfully and disappears from my sight as I go to sit with the wounded. We are now prepared for another attack, and rescue party and crash victims ring the camp with a variety of makeshift weapons.

"Are we going to be all right, miss?" asks a little boy, nervously.

"Oh, yes," I say, trying to sound convincing. "We could be out of here much sooner than you think."

At that instant there is a wild shriek from outside the shelter and I realise that we are under attack again. The child's mother is with us and, as she throws her arms round her son, the tent flap bursts open and we are faced by a ferociously painted warrior. For a moment we stare at each other and I will always remember the markings on the man's face. I could sit down and draw them at this moment.

The man looks from me to the woman and finally to the little boy. His nostrils dilate and an expression almost like a smile appears on his face.

"Get out!" screams the woman. "Get out! Get out! Get out!" The man nods and then suddenly jerks up his arm.

"No!" My scream coincides with a noise from outside the shelter reminiscent of a gas leak being found with a lighted match. A column of flames leaps into the sky and the warrior takes a step backwards. Neither the mother nor myself are slow to capitalise on his uncertainty and we practically push him out into the open. A wall of flame stretches the length of one side of the camp, and on seeing it the man turns on his heel and starts running in the opposite direction. For a moment I am tempted to follow him. The flames appear to be wavering and a cloud of smuts blows into my face.

"Is it going to be all right?" asks the woman, echoing my doubts. Everybody had been told about the plan, but seeing is believing.

"At least we've got rid of that character." I leave the woman to comfort her little boy and go over to the wireless operator as Ross emerges from the brush.

"Hey. Steady on!" Ross parries my attempt to hug him and asks the wireless operator what the situation is.

"He's got us in his sights. In fact – look." Up above us we can just make out the shape of New Australia's most ancient aircraft flying its most important mission.

"Is this going to work?" I ask Ross.

"I think so. You can see that the grass is really beginning to burn now."

There is indeed a broadening swathe of blackened earth opening up and the roar of the flames fills our ears. It is surprising how flat the ground is once the foliage has been burned away.

"He'll have to come in through the smoke, won't he?"

"Yes. It's going to be tricky unless we've got a lot of ground to play with."

We watch in silence and check with Ken in the aircraft what he can see.

"He needs another hundred yards to be on the safe side," says Ross, after the fire has been going for about ten minutes and appears to be racing away from us. There is some more confused chatter from the wireless and Ross curses. "Ken says that there's a ravine bisecting the landing area."

"Does that men he won't be able to come down?"

"It means he'll be cutting it fine. Look."

As we watch the flames ahead dip down, I realise that this must indicate that they are feeding on the side of the ravine.

"At least we seem to have seen off the Bungians."

"Don't be so sure. We've only narrowed down their field of attack."

"He's going to try to land," interrupts the wireless operator.

"O.K. Let's have everyone standing by. You supervise the wounded, Kate."

Despite our situation I have to smile at the way Ross has stepped into the D.O.'s shoes. I almost feel that he was glad of the opportunity afforded by that stray spear.

The wounded are carried to a position under one of the wings of the stricken plane and we wait anxiously for deliverance to appear through the pall of smoke.

"How's he going to see?" asks someone.

"Don't worry," says Ross, exhibiting a confidence I am sure he does not feel. "That man has landed in dust storms, heavy fog, just about every weather condition you care to mention."

As he speaks Ken Goodall materialises through the smoke at a height of about twenty feet from the ground and then soars into the sky.

"A good job he wasn't twenty feet too low," says Kate cheerfully.

"I hope he doesn't try bracketing," mutters the D.O.

On an impulse I turn round and see to my horror that there are now flames behind us!

"The bastards must have taken a leaf out of our book," says Ross bitterly. "They're trying to burn us out."

"Hurry up, Ken," says Kate.

In no time at all smoke is beginning to invade our nostrils and the second officer is in a very bad way. Kate and I try to attend to the wounded but soon everyone is coughing and has streaming eyes. A spear clatters against the fuselage and this suggests that the Bungians are advancing behind the flames.

"If he doesn't get that crate down soon – " begins Ross. And then, through the smoke and ash, we see Ken making what would be an outstandingly good landing in any circumstances. He taxis towards us and the door hatch opens while the plane is still moving. The ash thrown up by the propellors adds to the general discomfiture but at least there is now a smokescreen to shield us from the headhunters. I have to hand it to everyone because the discipline is impeccable. Definitely women-and-children-first kind of stuff. In fact the missionaries are almost leaning over backwards to usher each other on first and Ross has to make with the stentorian bellows to speed them up.

The flames are nearly up to the fallen plane by the time the door is closing on the last of the rescued, and I catch a glimpse of our attackers as we turn to taxi down the strip of blackened earth. I feel so strange saying "fasten your

215

seat belts" in the circumstances, but one of the missionaries' wives tells me later that it was the moment when she really believed that we were going to be saved.

I see that those who can be strapped in are secured to their seats and, leaving Kate to look after the second officer, make my way to the sharp end. Ken is looking decidedly nervous.

"Great landing, Ken," I say, trying to cheer him up.

"Landings I don't mind. It's taking off I'm worried about. I reckon I'm going to end up shunted into the back of that other crate. One of those fuzzy wuzzies is going to run out of the bush and pour a bucket of water over us."

Ross laughs. "That's very funny."

"I'm not joking. We're pushed for space. I wouldn't walk my dog out here and expect to keep my boots dry."

I have to admit that Ken has a point when I see the ravine looming up in front of us. Ken turns the plane round so that we are facing into the wind and our tail is virtually hanging over the drop. The grounded aircraft seems disturbingly near and is now surrounded by our attackers.

"O.K. Hang on to your hats."

The engines roar and we lurch forward over the bumpy ground. Smoke and ash from the scorched earth serve to obscure my vision but I can see that we are heading straight for the crash. The plane is poised between two clumps of trees so it is the lowest of the objects that have to be cleared.

"They're coming for us."

"Cheeky bastards."

A group of spear-waving Bungians is advancing towards us but they stop in their tracks when they see the aircraft bearing down on them. I see one, braver than the rest, hurl his weapon but the rest scatter or disappear under the wheels. I feel a jolt as if we have hit someone but I must confess that the possibility of having claimed a victim does not disturb me too much.

"Come on, my beauty." Ken is talking to the plane as if it is a horse he is trying to coax over a jump and the analogy is far from inappropriate. As I hold my breath we hurtle towards the stricken aircraft and I feel that we are being drawn to it as if towards a silver magnet. For a ghastly moment it seems as if Ken's prediction is going to

216

come true and my body tenses in terror. Then Ken pulls back the stick and the plane rises into the air. There is a flash of silver beneath us, a hanging cloud of black smoke and then – blue sky, the jungle falling away beneath us and the aircraft climbing steadily. We are safe!

I am the first person to kiss an embarrassed Ken but not the only one who feels like doing it, I am certain.

"Don't tell me you've left your cigarette lighter behind because I'm not going back," says Ken.

I laugh to stop myself from crying and go back to the passengers. Their eyes read my face like a news bulletin. The little boy with the badly broken arm is held tightly but uncomfortably in his mother's arms. His lower lip is tucked between his teeth as he bravely bites back the pain.

I look at all the faces which have been through so much pain, fear and uncertainty and make the announcement which brings me more pleasure than any other I have made in the whole of my flying career.

"Don't bother to unfasten your seat belts unless you intend to leave your seats. We will be landing in approximately ninety minutes. Everything is going to be all right."

CHAPTER FIFTEEN

When we get back to Port Moresby another tropical storm is lashing the airport and our arrival is something of an anti-climax. I had been expecting crowds and bunting but we have to be content with a fleet of ambulances. If there is a shortage of planes on the island they need only start fitting wings to ambulances!

As so often happens, I only begin to feel the full weight of our ordeal when the pressure is off. As the last ambulance speeds away and I stand wet and bedraggled outside the reception area I am poised to shout "wait for me!" after its receding rear lights. I can hardly keep my eyes open and once again I am grateful to find Ross's comforting arm around my shoulders.

"You should have a check-up," he says.

"I don't want a check-up. I want twenty-four hours' sleep – at least."

Ross smiles sympathetically. "You're probably right." He looks at his watch. "Are you prepared to put yourself in my hands?"

"After what you did out there I'd be a fool not to."

"We've got a place up the coast. It's just what you need. What we both need. We can rest up there for a few days. I think we deserve a break."

"And Kate?"

"Of course. If she wants to come."

"Mr Honey, will you talk to the reporters now?" A trim blond member of the airport ground staff has appeared at our side.

"Do you fancy being interviewed by the world press?" asks Ross.

I shake my head firmly. "Not tonight. I can't think straight."

"I can," says Ross. "When there's all that free publicity available for New Australia I'd be a fool not to grab some of it. Your boyfriend would never forgive me if I didn't. You hang on here and I'll be back in a few minutes."

'Your boyfriend.' I think of Ross's words as he strides away from me. It is strange but I feel a sense of physical deprivation as I watch him go. After our days together, I have become dependent on having him near. I was surprised that Peter was not at the airport but not disappointed. If anything, pleased. My current feelings for Ross would make his presence almost an embarrassment. I am surprised to find myself feeling like this. It seems so cold-blooded. Perhaps it is because I am tired, and I will feel different in the morning.

Kate appears from the powder room and I tell her about Ross's proposition. She looks as bad as I feel and I do not think that it is only as a result of her physical ordeal.

"At the moment I don't feel that I want to go anywhere," she says. "I'm in a complete state of anti-climax. While we were out there, while we had those people to worry about, it was all right. Now I've just got my own problems to occupy my mind."

"What about Michael Papadoulis?" Once again I throw the name at her like a challenge and this time she responds.

"What about him, indeed. What did you think of him out there?" Her tone is bitter. "Do you know? I thought I was in love with that man." She searches my face for sign of an emotion. "Of course you knew. I couldn't bring myself to talk to you about it. I knew you wouldn't approve. That you'd point out all the reasons why it wasn't a good idea. And I knew they'd all be right. Despite all that I was crazy about him. I lived for the moments when we could be together. The physical side of our relationship was unbelievable. He was on the point of leaving his wife, you know."

"That's what *he* said, Kate."

"He meant it," says Kate, vehemently. "Oh, yes. He meant it all right. His wife was going to be well looked after. Money would be no problem. They'd grown apart, you see. She hadn't kept pace with his interests." Kate laughs bitterly. "Don't you wish you had ten dollars for every time you've heard that remark?"

"So it's all over?"

"Yes. And do you know what makes me sickest about the whole business? The fact that it took a hike through the jungle to make me realise that he didn't have any guts. Real girl guide stuff, and I'd been taken in by all the gloss and superficiality. I could have broken up a home and ended up with a man who would hide under the bed if a car back-fired. I was so easily fooled."

"It can happen so easily, Kate." I try and comfort her. "Look at me and that other Michael. A wife and kids and I didn't even know he was married. At least you worked it out for yourself."

"Yes. We do pick them, don't we?" Now it is Kate's turn to look at me quizzically. "I noticed that Ross Honey was doing all the things that I wished Michael was doing. How are things, there?"

"I don't know. I think I love him." I hear myself saying the words as if I am listening to someone else speaking.

"Oh, Penny!" Kate sounds horrified.

"What's the matter? He's not married."

"I know. But he's so old. He could be your father. I

219

wondered if you were seeing him when you used to go out on those secret dates."

There is an irony in Kate's remark which does not escape me.

"I never think about how old he is. You saw how he was when we were in the bush. He behaved like a man half his age."

"Yes. I know he's remarkably well preserved and all that. I'm certain he's gorgeous in bed."

"I haven't been to bed with him," I say firmly.

Kate looks surprised. "Oh, I thought – "

"That because I said I thought I loved him I must have been to bed with him? No, it's all in the mind." I feel like saying 'you wouldn't understand that' but I check myself. "What are you going to do about Michael?" The question is asked to take the spotlight off myself.

"Nothing. Tell him that it's over, that I don't feel the same. If he's got any sensibility – and I give him credit for that – he must know already."

"The best thing you can do is come with me. That will save you the embarrassment of travelling back on the same flight as Michael. It might help you sort yourself out, as well. Help us both sort ourselves out, perhaps."

I look to Kate for an answer but it is the newly returned Ross Honey who speaks.

"What a fantastic success that was. I must have mentioned New Australia a dozen times. I don't think that anyone will ever fly anything else. Now, are you two lovely things coming to one of our little retreats for jaded businessmen? I must tell you that I intend to milk you for a few exclusive interviews while we're up there. Your promotional potential is unbelievable. If we hold the newshounds off for a few days and say that you are recovering – which of course you will be – and then let them at you, we could make every front page in the world. Your friend Bruce Wilson will know how to handle it."

"Is it us you want, or the publicity?" I ask. Ross looks surprised and immediately I wish that I had not been so sensitive.

"I'd love to come," says Kate and helps to gloss over an awkward moment.

220

Of course, I agree to come too and we are packed into a taxi and whisked away into the night. I have no idea of the kind of place we are going to and it is a fantastic surprise to find that it is an imposing executive-type mansion over-looking the romantically named Coral Sea. Apparently it is always kept fully maintained for the use of any of Ross's senior staff who are visiting the island.

"It can be tough working for me, as you know better than most, and I think the boys who put up with it deserve a little bit extra," says Ross.

"I don't know if you're planning eating anything," says Kate, yawning. "But I'm so tired that I'm going straight to bed."

"Me too," I say, feeling myself beginning to yawn in sympathy with Kate.

"I'll show you where you're sleeping." Ross takes the torch from one of the servants and guides us across a lawn to where I can see a number of chalets sheltering under the trees.

"Tea or coffee?" he says to Kate as he steers her through the door of her sumptuously-appointed little house.

"Morning tea in bed? Yes please." Kate says good-night and I walk on, seeking Ross's arm for support. I must need it too, because I suddenly feel myself slipping and the next thing I am fully aware of is lying on a bed. Ross is bathing my forehead with cold water and making soothing noises but most of my senses have already fallen asleep.

"Darling," he murmurs, "I love you."

"Which darling?" I hear myself whisper.

"You, Penny. Only you."

That must be what I am waiting to hear for, with the ghosts of the past exorcised, I snuggle closer to him and, as I feel him shift his whole weight on to the bed, fall fast asleep.

Have you ever made love to someone in a dream and then awoken to find that the dream was reality? That is my experience with Ross. I will swear that when I felt my clothes being peeled off the action took place only in my mind. The sensations that sped through my body were so marvellous that they could have had no substance in fact. I do not decry my previous physical experiences when I say

221

that. I merely mean that they were not fully harnessed to the ultimate trip; the feeling of love and identification with another human being. I cannot analyse all the things that Ross did to me, I can only say that he was the most sublime lover, using every part of his body to give pleasure to mine, yet always gently and inventively.

So sad that our beautiful night of love has to end as it does. One moment I am ruffling the hairs on Ross's sleeping head as it nestles into my shoulder, the next I am gazing horror-struck at the tall figure filling the open door.

"Peter!!"

The word explodes from my mouth like a bullet and it is one that kills two romances.

Peter looks down on us for a moment and unleashes a cry of pain and betrayal that will stay with me all my life. He starts forward, trembles, and then turns on his heel and runs from the chalet. I can hear his disjointed sobs crashing through the trees. If anyone had ever told me that Peter Honey could cry I would have called them a liar.

After that fateful incident the story of my adventures 'Down Under' comes to a speedy close. I learn that Peter had been on the island when our aircraft came in but had gone to the hospital and so missed me. Learning that we had left for the rest house he had set off to catch us up, with the tragic results you already know.

Ross asks me to marry him but I refuse knowing that the presence of Peter would be more a barrier to the romance than his dead mother had ever been.

In the circumstances there is only one thing to do. Both Kate and I hand in our resignations and bid a sad farewell to New Australia and so many of the friends we have made 'Down Under'. We both know that we are going to miss those hard-living, hard-loving Aussies but when your love life has a habit of getting as complicated as Kate's and mine you don't have a lot of alternative but to pull out sometimes.

Peter drops out of my life just as suddenly as he came into it at that party in Earl's Court. I do not miss him as much as Ross but I know that I will always feel something for both of them. If only they could have been one person!

New Australia was our reason for coming to Oz and since

both Kate and I are fly-girls to the core we know that we will have to find another airline, somewhere.

"Where are we going to go?" I ask Kate.

"I don't know," she says. "But I bet it will be somewhere with men."

All Sphere Books are available at your bookshop or
newsagent, or can be ordered from the following address:

Sphere Books, Cash Sales Department,
P.O. Box 11, Falmouth, Cornwall.

Please send cheque or postal order (no currency), and allow
7p per copy to cover the cost of postage and packing
in U.K. or overseas.